P9-DGM-833

Praise for the novels of Carsten Stroud

"A compelling work that grabs your attention from page one."

—Karin Slaughter

"Terrific dialogue, oddball characters, and a wild story make this a great read."

—Elmore Leonard

"Stroud offers surprises, shocks, moments of lyricism, explosions of humor and unrelenting suspense…. Superior storytelling."

—*The Washington Post*

"An A-ticket thrill-ride…. As enthralling as a tale by the Brothers Grimm."

—*The Wall Street Journal*

"The place where noir, thriller and paranormal fiction intersect."

—*Kirkus Reviews*

"Holds up against anything Hollywood can offer…. Stroud works with the precision of a watchmaker."

—*Richmond Times-Dispatch*

"The last time I was so swiftly taken over by a work of fiction was probably when I read *A Game of Thrones*."

—Peter Straub

"A truly one-of-a-kind tour de force. *Niceville* may be hard to categorize by genre, but it's easy to describe as a reading experience—wildly, insanely entertaining."

—John Lescroart

Also by Carsten Stroud

The Reckoning
The Homecoming
Niceville
Sniper's Moon
Cobraville
Cuba Strait
Black Water Transit
Deadly Force
Iron Bravo
Lizard Skin
Close Pursuit

CARSTEN STROUD

THE
SHIMMER

mira

If you purchased this book without a cover you should be aware
that this book is stolen property. It was reported as "unsold and
destroyed" to the publisher, and neither the author nor the
publisher has received any payment for this "stripped book."

mira

Recycling programs
for this product may
not exist in your area.

ISBN-13: 978-0-7783-0894-2

The Shimmer

Copyright © 2018 by Carsten Stroud

All rights reserved. Except for use in any review, the reproduction or
utilization of this work in whole or in part in any form by any electronic,
mechanical or other means, now known or hereafter invented, including
xerography, photocopying and recording, or in any information storage or
retrieval system, is forbidden without the written permission of the publisher,
MIRA Books, 22 Adelaide St. West, 40th Floor, Toronto, Ontario M5H 4E3,
Canada.

This is a work of fiction. Names, characters, places and incidents are
either the product of the author's imagination or are used fictitiously, and
any resemblance to actual persons, living or dead, business establishments,
events or locales is entirely coincidental.

® and TM are trademarks of Harlequin Enterprises Limited or its corporate
affiliates. Trademarks indicated with ® are registered in the United States Patent
and Trademark Office, the Canadian Intellectual Property Office and in other
countries.

For questions and comments about the quality of this book, please contact us at
CustomerService@Harlequin.com.

www.Harlequin.com

Printed in U.S.A.

For The Love Of My Life

THE
SHIMMER

THE
SHIMMER

An afternoon in late August, a Thursday, four hours and sixteen minutes left on Day watch, cruising down the A1A twenty miles south of St. Augustine in an unmarked shark-gray Crown Vic, Sergeant Jack Redding of the Florida Highway Patrol and his rookie trainee were watching a black Suburban with heavily tinted windows and Missouri plates. They were watching the black Suburban because it was lurching across two lanes of heavy traffic like a wounded rhino.

Far out over the Atlantic a tsunami of storm clouds was filling the horizon. An onshore gale gritty with beach sand was lashing at the rusted flagpoles over the tired old lime-green and pink stucco motels—Crystal Shores, Pelican Beach, Emerald Seas—the gale fluttering their faded awnings. The air smelled of ozone and sea salt and fading magnolias.

Redding looked over at his trainee, a compact sport-model blonde by the name of Julie Karras. Since she was fresh out of the Academy and this

was her first day on the job, she was on fire to pull
the truck over and carpet bomb the driver's ass.

"What do you think, boss? Can I hit the lights?"

Redding went back to the truck. It had eased
up on the lurching. It was now more of a wobble.
Maybe the driver had been fumbling around in the
glove compartment or checking his iPhone and
had finally stopped doing that. Or maybe he was
totally cranked out of his mind and had just now
noticed a cop car riding his ass. Whatever it was,
the guy was slowing down, doing a little less than
the 60 per allowed.

"Grounds, Julie?"

He could see her mentally running the Traffic Infractions List through her mind. She was
too proud to check the sheet on her clipboard. Although he'd only met her at 0800 hours, when Day
watch started, Redding liked her. She had...*something*.

Style was the wrong word.

No. She had *bounce*.

"I Five," she said, after a moment, "Improper
Change of Lanes."

Julie Karras was in Redding's unmarked cruiser
because her regular training officer—who had been
born in Chicago, the frozen attic of the nation—had
confused Canadian ice hockey with a real American sport, such as football, and had gotten all of
his upper front incisors duly redeployed. So the
CO had handed her off to Redding for the week.

"Try not to get her killed on her first shift," said

the CO, whose name was Bart Dixon but every-body called him, inevitably, Mason, often short-ened to Mace. "It's bad for recruitment."

Dixon, a bullet-shaped black guy with a shaved head and bullet scar on his left cheek, had grinned at him around an Old Port cheroot that smelled like burning bats. The part about not getting her killed wasn't entirely irrelevant because Redding's main job wasn't Patrol.

He worked Serious Crimes Liaison with the State Bureau of Investigations. He'd killed five men and one woman while doing that because, while he didn't go looking for gun fights, he didn't do a whole lot to avoid them either. And in a hell-hole city like Jacksonville, gun fights were always on the menu.

Redding didn't mind taking on Julie Karras. She was crazy pretty, it was a fine summer day—or had been up until just now—and late August was slack time for the SBI, with most of them off on vacation. So if you were a career criminal and you desperately wanted to get your ass busted you were going to have to wait until after the end of the month.

Karras was from up North he remembered her saying. Charleston or Savannah so she had that sweet Tidewater lilt in her voice. She had the in-fraction number wrong though.

"I Six, you mean," he said, but gently.

I Five was Improper Backing. Both infrac-tions, but when he'd been in Patrol that's where you started off, with a possible infraction. It hardly ever stayed there, but you had to have probable cause before you could make a stop. Otherwise everything that flowed from the stop—drugs, guns, illegal transportation of underage gerbils across state lines—would get thrown out of court.

"How about you run those plates first? Let's see what we're getting into here."

Karras swiveled the MDT display around on its base, punched in 407 XZT, hit the search tab.

The Suburban had steadied and was now doing the speed limit. *Exactly* the speed limit. Redding's unmarked was several cars back, in heavy traffic. Maybe they'd been seen and maybe not. But something was going *ping* in Redding's cop brain.

He didn't like big black SUVs with dark-tinted windows. Most cops felt exactly the same way. Big Black Boxes packed with Explosive Situations.

A gust of wind blew a cloud of beach sand across all four lanes of A1A and everybody's brake lights flared as the drivers reacted. Grains of sand were peppering the glass at his shoulder and he could feel the car rocking. He looked east past the roofs of the beach houses that lined the coast, and there it was, heading their way, a white squall.

Karras looked up from the computer screen.

"Comes back with a Gerald Jeffrey Walker. DOB November 10, 1971. Address of 1922 Halls Ferry Road, Florissant, Missouri. No Wants No Warrants."

Redding started to back off, letting his *ping* fade. Not every black Suburban was full of—

"Now this," said Karras, giving him a puzzled look. "It just popped up on the screen. A ten-thirty-five? What's a ten-thirty-five?"

Redding kept his eyes on that black Suburban. It had suddenly become much more interesting.

"That's the code for Confidential Information."

"What does it mean?"

"You'll see in a moment," he said, letting the Suburban drift farther ahead, falling back out of the guy's rearview, if he was watching the cruiser at all. Which he sure as hell was because everyone did. A cop car in your rearview was like a scorpion in your martini. People noticed. He heard the MDT chirp, and Karras read off the radio code.

"It says ten-seventy-six?"

Redding was expecting that.

"It means switch radio channels," he said, leaning over to click the channels controller to Tactical and picking up the hand mike.

"Central, this is Jax 180. Come back."

"Jax 180, this is Six Actual."

Six Actual was Mace Dixon.

"On that Suburban you just posted, St. Louis PD is asking for a ten-seventeen on that. Can you give us your twenty?"

Karras was getting a little bug-eyed but Redding didn't have time for that right now. A 10-17 code meant *maintain surveillance but do not stop the vehicle.*

"Roger that, Central. Our twenty right now is southbound on A1A at Cedar Point Road. What's up, Six? Plates come back No Wants No Warrants."

"Roger that, Jax 180, wait one."

Silence on the radio, and outside the windshield the weather was building up fast, the way squalls do along this coast. The traffic had thinned out, people looking at the skies and running for cover. In this part of the North Coast the A1A ran right along the shoreline, the ocean maybe a hundred yards away, booming and roaring.

On the west side, sprawling residential blocks, a few gated but mostly not, and beyond them, scrub forest, swamp and wetlands and then the Intracoastal Waterway, the inland canal that ran all the way from the Chesapeake to the Florida Keys.

The Suburban was speeding up, starting to pull away, which was okay with Redding. There was nowhere for it to go but south on the highway or turn off onto a side road, and they were all dead ends, either into the swamps to the west, or turn east and drive into the ocean.

"What's going on, Sergeant Redding?" Karras asked in a tight voice.

"Call me Jack, okay? Dispatch is asking us to monitor that truck but not to spook them. St. Louis cops are following up for some reason we don't know yet."

Redding could feel Karras's adrenaline rising. She had her hand on her sidearm and her skin was getting a tad pink.

"Are we stopping it later? I mean, what's—"

"Not sure yet, let's—"

"Jax 180, this is Six."

"Six."

"Yeah, look, Jack, what we have here is that the St. Louis PD is listing Gerald Walker and his wife and their three daughters as Whereabouts Unknown. Relatives up in Florissant have been trying to contact them for over ten days now. They were staying in their condo on Amelia Island. Management checked the condo and there's nobody there. Signs that the departure was sudden. Clothes all over, dishes in the sink. Security logged the truck out of the north gate at 2013 hours ten days ago. Guard couldn't confirm the occupants of the vehicle because of the tinted windows. Gate camera's no help either, wrong angle. Family is not answering their cells. Can't GPS them because their phones are turned off."

"Roger that, Mace. Not getting the urgency. So they went for a shore drive, didn't call the relatives. Maybe the relatives are all pains in the ass. I know mine are. Are they using their cards?"

"St. Louis says yes. Gas and motels along the coast. They were in the Monteleone in New Orleans seven nights ago. Then east along Ten… Ruby Tuesday and Holiday Inn and Denny's along the way."

"Any security video at the check-ins?"

"Not yet."

"So we're ten-seventeen on it until when?"

Dixon respected Redding's gut feelings. He thought it over.

"Okay. Take your point, Jack. Just watch the truck for a while, see what develops."

"Well, we maybe had an I Six on him. But he's stopped doing that."

Silence from Dixon. The CO was telling him to use his own judgment. Redding put the mike down, keyed it off. Thought it over. Stop or not.

Decided.

"Okay, Julie. Got an assignment for you."

She came on point.

"Survey that truck. Gimme a plausible reason for making a stop."

They were now in much thinner traffic. In this part of the coast, A1A ran on a kind of elevated levee. The palms and scrub brush along the shore were bending and whipping in the wind. The sky was closing down like a lid.

The Suburban was running straight and steady at 65 per. Staying in the curb lane. They were now about fifty feet back, and holding, with no other cars in the way. Karras was staring hard at the truck's tailgate. She went on staring. Redding felt her pain, because she was about to say…

"I got nothing."

Redding gave her a grin.

"Me neither. Maybe you could shoot out a tail-light. That would give us an E twenty-one."

She gave him back a look and a fake-perky tone.

"I think you should be the one doing that, you being, like, the responsible adult and all."

Redding smiled.

"Hell, I probably couldn't hit it from here," said Redding. "I suck at rolling fire. Why don't—"

And then the Suburban went full jackrabbit, a sudden growling roar from the engine, the rear end dropping, a burst of smoke from the exhaust as the driver just *jammed* it, accelerating, racing away up the highway, going away *fast*.

"Hit the lights," Redding said, checking his side mirrors as he jammed the accelerator down, "and tighten your belt!"

"*Fuck* yes," said Karras, as the roof rack lit up and the siren started to wail. "And on my first day too. Fuck yes! Thank you, Jesus!"

"Call it in."

She snatched up the mike.

"Central, this is Jax 180—we are ten thirty-one in pursuit southbound on A1A at Flagler Beach of a black Suburban, Missouri marker four zero seven x-ray zulu tango. We have just crossed Eighteenth Street—"

She glanced at the speedometer.

"Speed ninety, Central."

"Roger that, Jax 180, we have a unit northbound on A1A at Ocean Palm. Jax 250, come in."

"This is Jax 250. Ten-four lighting up now."

"Jax 180, we have County units available too."

"Tell him no thanks," said Redding.

Karras clicked the button, said, "Negative on County, Central."

"Roger that."

Karras wanted to know why they didn't call in some Flagler County Sheriff cars on this pursuit.

"Because so far this is containable, and highway pursuit is *our* thing, not County's. They're good folks, but in a car chase they go all squirrelly because they don't train for it. We do."

"Got it," she said.

What little traffic there was veered right and left out of the way as Redding closed in on the Suburban, which was whipsawing as the heavy truck lurched in and around other vehicles.

A pickup truck popped out of a side road, almost T-boning the Suburban before the driver wrangled his ride into a ditch, the guy getting out to shout something at Redding as the cruiser flashed by. Karras stayed on the mike, calling the cross streets—Nineteen, Twenty-One, Twenty-Three— as the Crown Vic's Interceptor motor rapidly overtook the Suburban, the siren howling.

Gusts of wind were lashing the highway, and now the white squall hit, sideways rain and clouds of sand, shredded palm fronds and scrub branches tumbling across the highway, flying through the air.

Redding put the wipers on full but they could hardly see the truck through the rain. The truck was not slowing down, although visibility had dropped down to twenty yards. Karras strained

to read a street sign as they powered past it, keyed
the mike again.

"Central, this is Jax 180. We are southbound
A1A at Twenty-Seventh still in pursuit—"

The Suburban's brake lights flared on, bright
red smears in the driving rain, the truck tilting
wildly to the left as the driver bulled it into a right-
hand turn. The right side wheels of the truck actually lifted off the road for a second, and Redding
tapped the brakes, falling back, waiting for it to
roll, but it didn't.

The wheels came back down with a thudding
impact, the truck wobbled and weaved as the driver
fought for control, got it back, and now the Suburban was accelerating down a residential street
lined with ranch-style summer homes and palm-
shaded yards.

"Central, vehicle made a right turn onto Twenty-
Eight."

"Roger that. Copy that, Jax 250?"

"Jax 250. Ten-four copy we are a half mile out."

The Suburban almost took out three kids in wet-
suits walking in the street, carrying surfboards,
shoulders hunched, heading home to beat the
storm. They dropped the boards and dodged as the
Suburban blew by them. It struck one of the boards,
smashing it into shards, and one of the larger pieces
flew up and smacked into their windshield, making them both flinch away. The truck reached an
intersection—South Dayton—veered hard right
again, accelerated away, now headed back north.

"Shit," said Karras. "He's going to kill somebody. Should we back off?"

Redding flashed a sideways look at her.

"You wanna?" he said. "Remember we have a dash cam. This goes south we might be in the barrel."

"We? Or just you?"

Made him smile.

"Me. I'm the one in charge."

"Then fuck no," she said, looking back at the truck, her right hand braced on the dashboard.

She keyed the mike again.

"Central, target is now northbound on South Dayton—we have just crossed Twenty-Seven."

"Copy that."

South Dayton was a long residential street that ran along the edge of a shallow slope covered with trees, a few large summer homes on the east side, no one on the streets now that the storm had hit and hit hard, the branches on the trees thrashing in the gale, the undersides of their leaves showing silvery white. A palm frond struck their windshield, got jammed into their wipers.

Redding swore, jammed the car to a stop, jumped out and tore the frond away, leaped back into the vehicle before it stopped rocking, accelerated hard, the tail end sliding on the slick tarmac.

"Ask Jax 250 where they are," said Redding, fighting the wheel as they hit a pothole in the road and the Crown Vic slammed through it, bouncing crazily, the rear end coming loose.

Karras keyed the mike again.

"Jax 250."

"Roger, Jax 180."

"What's your twenty?"

"A1A northbound crossing Twenty-Eight."

In this section South Dayton was a straight run, and the truck pushed it to a flat 100 miles an hour. *Jesus*, thought Redding, *this is not good*.

"Ask Jax 250 to go to afterburners, get north of us and turn left. If they really punch it, they might be able to block the guy off there."

"Roger, Jax 250, can you shoot up to block at Nineteen and South Dayton?"

"Ten-four, Jax 180."

"Roger that."

The truck blew through stop signs, almost nailed a van pulling out of a driveway, braked crazily and spooled it right back up to 60…70…

The Suburban's brake lights flared up and beyond it they could see the flicker of red and blue lights and the glare of headlights as Jax 250 squealed to a skidding halt that blocked the intersection. The truck slid to a stop, sat there for a brief moment, wavering.

They were almost on it.

The brake lights flicked off, the truck swung a hard left and punched it, racing west toward the swamplands and the Intracoastal.

"There's nothing down there but South Palmetto," said Redding. "It's a crescent, no way out. Nothing west of that but swamplands. Guy's trapped."

"Unless he breaks into a house along here, takes a whole bunch of hostages."

Redding shot her a look. She was having the time of her life. Hell, so was he. Who didn't love a totally batshit car chase? Was this a great country or what?

"Jeez, Julie. Don't even *say* that."

"But wouldn't it be, like, a teachable moment?"

In the middle of all this vehicular insanity the kid still had her bounce. He was still grinning when the truck powered away down a short block, wheeled crazily right around the curve onto South Palmetto, big ranch homes, maybe a dozen of them, spread out on the east side, and on the left, dense forest, broken ground down a slight slope—the only kind of slope Florida had—and then the driver hit the brakes.

Hard, the truck slewing around crazily, correcting and then skidding to a stop in the middle of the road. The driver's door popped open and a woman—not young, but lean and solid-looking in tight jeans and hiking boots and a black leather jacket—hopped out, nothing in her hands, which were the first thing you looked at.

She sent them one quick glance. They got a glimpse of a tight hard face, no fear at all, even a fleeting defiance, strong cheekbones and wide eyes, maybe green, black hair flying in the wind as she ran. Something in Redding's memory flickered like a goldfish in a pond. *He knew that face.* Then she was gone, racing across the street, running like a wolf. She vanished into the trees, a flash of blue, and then the forest folded her in.

Redding slammed the brakes hard as Karras got onto the radio, telling Jax 250 what had just happened. Then they were both out of the cruiser, doors still open, running toward the truck, which was idling in the street, engine rocking the frame, windshield wipers still ticking, rain steaming off the overheated engine hood.

As they reached it, Jax 250 came rushing up and stopped on the far side of the truck. Two troopers got out with their guns drawn, LaQuan Marsh and Jim Halliday.

"A runner, LQ," Redding shouted to them. "White female, black hair, black jacket, blue jeans, no visible weapons. She went into the trees."

Marsh and Halliday broke right like a pair of pulling guards and went flying into the forest after her. People were popping out of their houses, standing on porches, on lawns. Redding shouted at them, warning them off, gave a go sign to Karras, and she moved in, her gun up and trained on the passenger-side doors of the Suburban. The windows were closed, dark as black ice.

The truck engine was running hot and loud, the rain hammering on its roof. Water was running down Julie's face and she blinked it away, wishing she had put on her Stetson.

Redding was going left, and he came to a stop

about ten feet off the left rear wheel, his gun up. Karras had taken the same position on the right rear side. They could smell scorched rubber and overheated metal steaming in the rain.

The driver's door hung wide-open, the seat belt dangling. From the interior of the truck, someone crying, a woman's voice.

"In the truck," said Redding in a voice of brass, "show me your hands. Do it now!"

Faint, from deep inside the truck, a shaky female voice, young. "Don't shoot us. Please."

Karras moved up a yard, reached for the rear door. Redding told her to stop. He stepped up to the left-side rear door, leveled his gun and jerked the rear door open.

Two teenage girls were lying on the rear bench seat. They were cord cuffed to the front-seat floor struts. They were crying, beyond hysterical.

"Help us," said one of them, dark haired, possibly the older one.

"Please. She's crazy. She kidnapped us."

Karras popped the other rear door, put her gun on them, wary, tense, her finger almost inside the trigger guard. Both girls were in jeans and boots, T-shirts, hair every which way, eyes red from crying, faces flushed and frightened.

In shock, scared to death.

"Who are you?" he asked, in a softer tone.

"I'm Rebecca Walker. This is my sister Karen. Help us please? That woman kidnapped us!"

Redding looked at Karras. She looked back, and

they both did a quick check of the interior. Luggage scattered around. Remnants of a Happy Meal, candy wrappers, water bottles. No one else. Just the girls, cuffed to the floor.

Redding lowered his weapon and after a moment Karras did the same.

"I'm gonna go after the runner. Can you take care of these two?"

Karras said she would, lips so tight they were blue.

"You go, Sergeant. I'll get EMT in here."

"Search them first, Julie. *Before* you cut them loose. You never know."

"I will. Go get her."

Redding took one last look at the girls, showed them his teeth, a quick smile that was supposed to be comforting and wasn't even close.

Redding turned away and raced down into the trees, a big lean rangy guy who could move like a linebacker when he had to. He pulled out his portable.

"LQ, I'm coming in."

"Roger that, Jack."

Redding jogged into the trees, ducking under the dripping branches, feeling the mossy ground squelch under his boots. He had his Glock out, down by his side, and every nerve on redline.

The stand of scrub trees was dense, maybe a hundred feet deep. When he came out from under them after a paranoid two-minute jog-trot during which he checked out every treetop he passed under, he could see Marsh walking the shoreline, gun out but down at his side, his back to Redding. He was facing out across the swamps and reed beds toward the Intracoastal, head turning back and forth. Halliday was down the shore about fifty yards.

Marsh heard Redding sloshing through the seagrass, even with this rain lashing down and the wind ripping through the trees.

"Jack."

"LQ. Got anything?"

"She left a trail all the way down," he said, his face slick as patent leather in the rain, a puzzled expression in his eyes.

"You can see it over there, that silver streak in the grass. Comes right down to the shore here, stops dead."

Redding looked out over the swamp, sort of a mini Everglades, clumps and islands of sawgrass and reeds and cattails, all of it bending down under the rain. The sky was shredding, wisps of lighter gray showing through the cover. The wind was backing off but it was still raining hard.

Halliday walked up the shoreline toward them, staring down into the shallow murky water that ran in curving channels under and around a thousand little islands of seagrass. He was a big blond Panhandle kid who had played two years as a starting DB for the Gators. He did a 180 to check the tree line one more time, and then came back to them, his face as blank and confused as Marsh's.

"Sure she's not back in the woods?" Redding asked. Halliday and Marsh shook their heads in unison.

"Not back there, Jack," said Marsh. "We were close, we could see her going through the forest—"

"She ran like a fucking gazelle," said Halliday.

"Yeah, she could move real good," said Marsh. "Faster than us. We lost her in the rain here, and the branches were in our faces like whips. By the time we cleared the trees all we could see was that."

He tilted his head toward the silver track in the tall grass.

"Ending at the water," Halliday finished. "Broad just flat-out *vanished*. Fucking weird, Jack. Like into thin air. Too fucking weird. We walked the shore up and down, looking for a ripple where she coulda gone in. Mud bottom kicked up. Nothing."

"That's right, Jack. Vanished."

All three of them turned back to the swamp.

It was about two hundred yards wide at this point, running for about a mile along the shore. On the far side of the marsh was the Intracoastal. The Intracoastal was like a marine version of I-95. In the summer it was as crowded as an interstate, although the squall had driven everyone except a few crazies into the marinas.

"How deep do you figure this is?" Redding asked, meaning the swamp.

Marsh, who was a bass boater, shook his head.

"No more'n two maybe three feet. But the bottom is thick muck, just like quicksand. You think she had a boat waiting? Why she came down this way?"

"You see one?" Redding asked.

They both shook their heads, water running off the brims of their Stetsons. Redding looked back at the muddy water and the reeds bending in the rain.

"What do you figure lives in there?" he asked of no one in particular.

Marsh laughed.

"Nothing you'd want to take home to the wife."

Marsh immediately regretted that comment, considering what had happened to Redding's wife and their little girl last Christmas Eve, but it couldn't be unsaid, and Redding didn't react. So Marsh went on.

"Snakes. River rats. Leeches. Every kind of biting, stinging, itching bug you can think of. I've seen gators around here, but not real big ones."

Redding smiled at him.

"Define 'not real big.'"

Marsh just grinned back at him.

"Could even be monitor lizards," said Halliday, trying to be helpful. "They been finding huge ones—two, three feet long—down in West Palm. People had them as pets till they got too damn big. Let them go into the rivers. Monitors. Smart as dogs too. They got these monster mouths full of huge backward-curved fangs, sharp as needles. But huge."

"And don't forget the giant anacondas," added Marsh, just to complete the picture.

Neither man had any intention of letting Sergeant Redding order either of them into the swamp to start searching. If Redding did, Marsh had already decided he was going to push Halliday into the water instead and say he stumbled into him. Which Halliday was already braced for, because he knew Marsh only too well, and he wasn't going in there either.

Redding, aware of all this, and thankful that they hadn't thrown in mutant vampire unicorns, looked up at the sky. The storm was starting to break up. The rain was coming down hard.

"Can the dogs follow a trail in this weather?" Halliday was asking, mainly to distract Redding from the whole "into the swamp, boys" idea. Redding had run a K-9 car for a couple of years.

"A light rain will freshen up a scent, but heavy rain and wind, that's a lot more difficult."

"Been done," said Marsh. "Remember that case last year, prisoner goes into the Glades, in a hurricane, but the dogs found him anyway?"

"Because he was half eaten by a gator," said Halliday, "and he'd started to stink. My mom coulda found him."

"Doesn't matter," said Redding. "Worth a shot. Let's get the dog cars down here. And I want some Marine units out there. And let the Flagler County deputies know what's going on too. I want a tight perimeter—lady could sure as hell motor—"

"Damn straight," said Halliday. "She was going away so fast I thought I had stopped to pee."

"So where the *hell* is she?" Redding said, a rhetorical question.

"Gotta be here somewhere," said Marsh.

"LQ's right, she's still around. Have Flagler County set up a cordon around these blocks."

"All this for an F thirty-seven?" said Marsh.

"I know. A lot of overtime. I just…"

"Got a feeling she's worth chasing?"

"Yeah. I do," he said, thinking about the expression on her face, cool, defiant, not frightened at all. And he knew her from…*somewhere*. "She got my attention."

Marsh was reaching for his portable to make the calls when they heard two sharp flat cracks close together, a brief pause and then one more.

"Gunfire," said Halliday, but Redding and Marsh were already running back toward the trees.

By the time Gerald Jeffrey Walker and his family arrived at their vacation condo at Amelia Island on Florida's Atlantic coast—after thirteen hours on the road from St. Louis—the feeling inside the family's GMC Suburban was sharply split on the issue of the Harwoods.

The Harwoods—Marietta, pronounced *Mayretta*, and her husband, Ellison—were Christian Evangelicals and they ran a very large and very rewarding ministry—*financially* rewarding at any rate—called the New Covenant Celestial Ministry, and one of their many income streams came from the sale of their Evangelical Christian audiobooks.

Walker—sometimes known as "Jerry Jeff" after the blues guy—was a forensic archaeologist working for a unit of the US Army Corps of Engineers based in St. Louis. His team was called in whenever artifacts or bones were unearthed at a construction site, sometimes in remote corners of the world.

He considered this calling a sacred duty, since it involved an effort to determine exactly where these artifacts or bones came from, and what sort of spiritual beliefs had once been attached to them. This information was hard to come by.

It required bone and DNA analysis, the assessment of causes of death, including weapons that might have been used if there were indications of murder or human sacrifice, as well as a grip on local cultural history and a great deal of spiritual imagination.

Perhaps because of his work and the moral challenges it presented—bringing peace to the spirits of the dead—in his off-hours Walker served as a Worship Leader at the Glad Day Assembly, an Evangelical Christian megachurch in their hometown of Florissant, Missouri.

Walker and his wife, Marilyn, who ran the child-care center at the Glad Day Assembly, tried very hard to believe that they had a Personal Relationship with Jesus Christ, a difficult exercise in faith that met with varying degrees of success, particularly for a man with a PhD in forensic archaeology and a woman with a master's degree in education.

In an effort to bridge this gap they had invested in the Marietta and Ellison Harwood Collection of inspirational Christian audiobooks.

They did this because Walker's work had brought him face-to-face with mass graves, with human sacrifices, with the residue of every kind of violent evil, and the only protection from the fallen world, both ancient and modern, seemed to be found in the teachings of Jesus Christ.

So they decided to take advantage of the drive down from Florissant to share the Harwood Ministry's latest releases—Ellison's *The Power of Love* and his wife Marietta's *My Celestial Heart Sings*—with their three daughters, admittedly a captive audience.

The Suburban seated seven, but divisive forces relating to the Harwood Ministry had affected the family dynamic on the way down Interstate 75.

This had resulted in the front bucket seats being occupied by Walker and his wife, Marilyn, of course, since they shared the driving, and the bench seat immediately behind them had become the private domain of the youngest Walker daughter, six-year-old Alyssa.

Alyssa had set up housekeeping across the entire bench seat, surrounded by her Hello Kitty and Littlest Pet Shop collections.

Jerry and Marilyn and Alyssa composed what had become the pro-Harwood faction. Since the trip from St. Louis covered just under a thousand miles their time on the road lasted several hours, which is a long time to be in a car listening to inspirational evangelical audiotapes; it was longer for some than for others.

Which brings us to the anti-Harwood faction, the two older Walker daughters: Rebecca, seventeen, and Karen, sixteen, both very beautiful in that Midwestern corn-fed style, and both of them in many ways typical American teenage girls. And, as it turned out, in other ways, not at all typical.

Rebecca and Karen were sitting at the very back of the truck, in the two fold-down seats, pressed up tight against the luggage stacks that crowded the rear deck, isolating themselves as much as they could from the pro-Harwood faction up front, because, after a few hundred miles, they were both totally sick unto eye-rolling, please-kill-me-now *death* of Ellison and Marietta Harwood.

So it won't come as a surprise to hear that, upon finally reaching their condo, a four-bedroom Italian-themed palazzo with a terrace overlooking the Atlantic Ocean, Rebecca and Karen had thrown their luggage onto the king-size bed in their shared bedroom, torn off their clothes, slipped into their strictly forbidden Tommy Bahama bikinis, censored by Ralph Lauren hoodies and baggy shorts, and bolted for the beach at a dead run.

Where, around sunset, strolling north through the crystalline water toward Fernandina Beach, the surf rolling and booming and sparkling all around them, the echoes of Ellison Harwood's well-oiled baritone gradually fading from memory, they saw a woman walking south toward them.

She was alone. She was barefoot and tanned and wearing a one-piece suit in creamy white under a gauzy tourmaline beach wrap. She moved as if she were *inside* music, something rhythmic and Caribbean.

Her face was partially hidden by a broad-brimmed white straw hat, secured around her neck with a scarlet ribbon. Her eyes were cast down, as if she were lost in thought. She was less than twenty feet away before she seemed to *sense* rather than *see* them, and then she stopped and lifted her face up and considered them, as if she knew them, as if she had been *looking* for them.

Which, of course, she had.

They stopped to talk, then walked and talked and found themselves gradually…enchanted. How old she was—thirty, forty, even fifty—it was impossible to tell, and, after a short while in her effervescent company, it didn't seem to matter.

Later, sitting by the palm-tree-shaded pool, sharing sips of her margarita with the girls when the waiter wasn't looking, she told them her name was Diana Bowman, that she was a dealer in antique jewelry based in Palm Beach, that she was here on a much-needed vacation from her wealthy and demanding clientele, and that she loved meeting young people like Rebecca and Karen.

They each felt that galvanic spark of instant rapport that is not an uncommon event when people go on vacation, and by the second round of margarita sharing they decided that they should be newfound friends together and have *such* great fun while they were all here at this beautiful resort.

By now, thanks to the margarita factor, the girls had relaxed enough around their new friend that they had begun to open up to her about their trip down from St. Louis, and the Harwood-inflicted grinding hell it had managed to become.

Diana Bowman was cautiously sympathetic.

"Well, yes, I confess I do find certain types of religious practice to be, how to put it, so spiritually *confining*...but I sometimes feel that it is as much a sin to *ignore* the sensual pleasures that God has given us as it is to, what to say, *overindulge* in them?"

Rebecca and Karen agreed, or thought they did, although her reference to *sensual pleasures* definitely touched them on a more primal than theoretical level. But Diana seemed to feel she had said too much.

"You know, I have no doubt that your parents—they are here with you, yes?—oh, how nice—Jerry and Marilyn? And Alyssa, the youngest? That they are doing this out of love. I'm sure they just want you to be...happy and safe."

"Too safe," said Karen, with some heat. "They never want us to have any fun—"

"You'd think we were in jail," Rebecca finished, caught up with the injustice of it all.

Diana listened with every sign of sympathetic understanding as the girls raved on for a while about the unbearable oppression of patriarchal fascism disguised as parental kindness.

Eventually they ran the subject down, realizing from Diana's sleepy-eyed attention that perhaps they were boring their new friend. But what she said next surprised them.

"I'm a Roman Catholic myself, on my mother's side, and I do feel that the effect Jesus had on the world was, on the whole, a good one. You need only to look at the world these days to see how important His teachings were to Western Civilization."

Rebecca, the historian, brought up the Crusades and Diana, sipping at her margarita, agreed that the Crusades were simply awful, but that they had happened nine hundred years ago, and what Jesus had brought into the world, long before the Crusades, could be seen in the artifacts connected to Him.

"Oh God," said Karen, "don't tell us about *artifacts*."

"Really?" said Diana.

It turned out that Rebecca and Karen knew all about artifacts and relics, since Daddy never shut up about them—he had even brought a lockbox full of them along to *classify* or *decipher* or something—but by now their heads were dizzy with the surging sea and the margarita sipping so they missed the sudden sharpening of Diana Bowman's attention.

"So your father works with these artifacts?"

"*God* yes. He brought them along, these…"

"Artifacts," Rebecca repeated with careful precision, feeling the tequila. "He lays them out on the dining room table and studies them for, like, *hours*. He has a microscope and all kinds of tools."

Diana was intrigued.

"Truly? He sounds very dedicated. What sort of *artifacts* are they?"

Rebecca made a hand-waving gesture of dismissal.

"Creepy old dead stuff. From wherever Daddy has to work. All over the world. From New Orleans, this bunch anyway. They were moving graves after that stupid storm?"

"Katrina?"

"Yeah. That. It was like years ago, but now they're doing something about flood protection, so the graveyards have to be built up. You know the way they bury people in New Orleans? In those concrete churchy-looking little stone houses?"

"Crypts," said Diana. "They have to be aboveground because the water table is so high."

"Daddy says they just stuff new bodies into the crypt and shove the old ones to the back of the… whatever…the…?"

"The vault."

"Yeah, the vault, so that whoever was buried there a hundred years ago gets all crammed up with the new people and it's all mixed up in a jumble."

"So your father is trying to sort out who was who, now that the bodies have to be moved?"

"Yeah, although it's only temporary, 'cause they're putting them back when the work is through, but he has to figure out which bits belong where, and then there's all the jewelry."

"You mean, like gold bracelets and rings and that kind of thing?"

"And lockets and brooches and stuff," said Karen, not really interested in whatever her daddy was up to. They both felt a spreading warmth moving through their bodies as the tensions of the trip receded and Diana's silky voice seemed to pull them into a conspiratorial circle. They were too young to notice the voltage that the word *locket* had sent pulsing through the woman's body.

"Well, it sounds as if your father is doing the Lord's work," Diana said, changing the subject. "You should be proud of him."

"Oh, we are," said Rebecca, feeling that they were sounding disloyal. "I mean they're good people and all that. It's just this whole Christ thing. *Christ* this and *Jesus* that, all the way down from Florissant. It was all, like, so...*lame.*"

Diana gently disagreed.

"But there's a true *power* there, girls. In Jesus. Do you know about the Shroud of Turin?"

This was something important to Diana. They could both feel her...chemistry...change. In spite of their reflexive dislike of the subject, what she was saying—or rather *how* she was saying it—got their attention.

She was talking about the Shroud of Turin, the moment of Christ's Resurrection, when His Spirit had flashed out, shimmering so brightly inside that darkened sepulchre...

"A *shimmer* so powerful that it actually burned itself into the burial cloth he was wrapped up in," said Diana, leaning in close and placing a soft warm hand on Rebecca's knee.

"Can you imagine what that must have been like? And Jesus teaches us that that very same

Shimmer is inside each of us. That divine spark shines inside us all, waiting to be...*released.* How *beautiful.*"

Rebecca found she liked the feel of Diana's hand on her knee, but the subject of Jesus Christ's Light Bulb Moment was not nearly as interesting to her, at this twilight hour, as the particular hazel-and-gold colors in Diana Bowman's eyes and the spicy scent that was coming off her body. From the look on her sister's face, she was feeling the same sort of sensual pull.

Rebecca felt a warmth rising on the skin of her belly and flooding up to her breasts, her throat, her cheeks. *She's gay,* Rebecca was thinking. *And she likes us. Both of us.*

Diana drew back, smiled at them.

"But it's getting dark, and you two need to be going back to your room, don't you? Your parents will be worried, no?"

Rebecca looked at her cell phone.

There were three text messages, all in the last few minutes. She had felt the phone buzzing but ignored it, knowing what they were about but feeling that, where Mommy and Daddy were concerned, it was easier to get forgiveness than permission.

Mommy: We're going out to get something to eat. Coming?

Mommy: Leaving in five?

Daddy: Girls?

After a moment's thought, as Diana watched her with some amusement, Rebecca texted back.

> **Becca:** We're at the Chapel for Eventide. So pretty here. Can we stay?

A pause. The resort was fenced and gated, studded with security cameras and patrolled by armed guards. And it did have a little chapel beside the tennis courts.

> **Daddy:** Okay. But home by midnight. Pinky swear.
> **Becca:** Pinky swear. Hugs.
> **Daddy:** Karen got her puffer with her?

Rebecca tipped the phone to Karen, who read the message, fumbled in her pocket and came up with a small silver canister with a little plastic mask attached—her rechargeable puffer. Karen had asthma, usually caused by stress.

> **Becca:** Yes, Daddy, we just checked.
> **Daddy:** Okay be good love you both.

Rebecca put the phone away, looking up to catch a strange, almost *hungry* expression on Diana's face, a kind of pale yellow light in her green eyes.

But then Diana smiled and it was gone.

"Was that your parents, Rebecca?"

"Yes. They're going out to dinner."

"So late? Without you?"

"Yes," she said. "They like to eat late. Alyssa

won't go to sleep unless she has something later on in the evening—"

"She's so *spoiled*," said Karen.

Rebecca ignored that. "We can stay for now, but we have to be home by midnight."

Diana looked at her watch.

"That's a while away. Perhaps we can have a quick dinner? Room service? In my suite?"

The words were innocent, but both Karen and Rebecca understood what wasn't being said.

"We'd love to," they said in one voice.

"How *perfect* you both are," said Diana, taking them in. "How simply…delicious."

the lady in the lake

As soon as the three cops disappeared back into the tree line, she surfaced. She was two hundred feet away, in the heart of the swamp, neck deep in the stinking water, hidden behind an island of seagrass, her face coated in lagoon muck.

She slowly lifted her head up, her black hair matted to her skull. She had a pretty good idea of what had happened back there at the Walkers' truck, what the gunshots really meant, why the cops had bolted, and it warmed her through and through.

The girls had done what she had asked them to do. Well, they had done what Diana Bowman had asked them to do, but she was no longer the woman called Diana Bowman. She was Selena.

———

She had never actually been Diana Bowman, but she had met the original at a resort in the Keys last year, a lonely older woman without family or close friends, looking for affection, or at least kindness, which Selena had freely given her with all of her loving heart.

And they lived happily ever after, until late one shining afternoon while they were out cruising in Diana's boat, when Selena had shoved her over the side into shark water.

Four minutes later, while Selena fended the terrified woman off with a boat hook, a big whitetip, attracted by her thrashing struggle, flashed in, hit her hard and took her under in an explosion of bloody foam.

Other sharks arrived, and things got nasty, the way they do when sharks disagree. For a brief moment Diana's horrified face reappeared in the middle of a churning vortex of pink water, staring wide-eyed at Selena, her open mouth filled with blood. Then she was jerked back under, the sharks shredded what was left of her and it was over.

Selena had watched the whole thing, fascinated, wishing she had thought to film it for YouTube. But it was too late for that now, and anyway it would have been a risky thing to do.

Amusing, certainly, but risky.

Since Diana, being newly dead, didn't need her life anymore, Selena took it over, maxing out all of her credit cards and discreetly liquidating her assets—which were considerable, since she was a very successful dealer in estate jewelry and antiques—over a few months.

She banked the results in one of her accounts in the Caymans. Selena was good at that sort of thing because she had been doing it for years and had pretty much perfected it. Bowman's banker was troublesome, but nothing Selena couldn't finesse. You could say it was her profession, what she did for a living, but it wasn't her *purpose*.

That was something else entirely. And it had to do with finding something she had lost somewhere in time, something perfect and round and made of gold, a locket, and inside the locket was peace and her last childhood memory of loving kindness.

———

Selena thought about the cops, the way they had run back up the slope and into the trees, three big heavy men, slow and clumsy and stupid. They had been easy to outrun.

She felt a smile coming but suppressed it. Her teeth were very white and they would show. Some kind of crawling sucking things were up under her clothes and digging into the flesh of her back and her lower belly. She could feel them starting to feed on her. Leeches.

A tiny carp-like fish was nipping at the side of her neck but she didn't try to drive it away. A large red centipede was moving slowly across the exposed skin of her left wrist. She could feel the feathery tickle of its feet. Mosquitoes and midge flies hovered in a cloud around her face and neck, biting and stinging whatever they could get at through the mud she had smeared all over herself.

She had a long filleting knife in a sheath at the nape of her neck, so if there was a big snake or a gator in this water, she could probably kill it. But killing it would require movement and movement would show the police where she was.

Her long and complicated time in this world had taught her many things, and one of them was that the secret of the hunt was not to run. It was to be *still*. Humans were born predators. Some of them, anyway, the ones who weren't born prey. But, like dogs, they were attracted to motion. They would chase anything running. They never saw the thing that was perfectly still.

Cats were different. Cats could be still far longer than their prey. Fear made the prey run to meet its death when it could have been still and lived a little while longer. This was why cats were better hunters than dogs. This was why cats could hunt alone. It was in their nature to hunt alone.

But she had learned that all police officers were like wolves. They hunted in packs. That was *their* nature. Like those three cops. They heard the gunshots; they all ran off together. In a wolf pack. But they would come back.

The rain was drumming on her skull and she could feel her body heat draining away into the swamp all around her. In a while she'd be shivering badly. She considered the sky. The clouds were breaking up. The white squall would end soon and then the sun would come out.

Full dark was hours away.

They would bring boats to search the swamp but that would take a while. They might call in police dogs but Selena had learned that police dogs were no threat to her. They would set up a perimeter with their cars, a few blocks out, and then wait for her to move. If they caught her, they would put her in a concrete box for the rest of her life.

No. Not right. This was the South.

They would *kill* her.

She suppressed a sudden flaring of rage, and the fear that shivered underneath it. She couldn't just *die*, she couldn't just be *ended*. Not before she had accomplished her *mission*, her reason for being alive. It wouldn't be fair.

It wouldn't be *right*.

So...be still.

She lowered her face into the reeds, made herself go limp, sinking deeper into the little island, becoming a part of it. She visualized herself as a shapeless patch of black mud in a cluster of reeds. And soon that was what she was. It was one of her particular gifts, to blend into the background, to seem to disappear. To vanish.

She ignored the clouds of mosquitoes and the leeches that were crawling on her flesh and feeding on her, and all the tiny fish that had come to nip at her, and the fat white snake that was staring at her from his nest in the clump of marsh grass. She ignored the miasmic reek of the swamp itself. She went inward and shut down. She waited.

———

Halliday was right beside Redding and Marsh as they broke through the trees and came out onto the roadway. Julie Karras was sitting on the ground beside the Suburban, leaning back against it, blood running down the side of her face. She had her Glock out and was holding it on one of the teenage girls who had been cuffed in the back of the truck.

The girl was lying on her belly on the ground, her hands cuffed behind her. She was swearing and screaming, spitting rage into the slick hot pavement under her chin.

The left rear door of the Suburban was wide-open and the other sister was sprawled in the open doorway, half in the truck and spilling out onto the ground, down on her knees, facing out, upper body thrown backward into the truck, head hanging sideways, painted lips slack. She had a bullet hole in her left cheek and another one in her neck just under her chin and a third one in her belly. You could see it on the exposed skin, where her T-shirt had ridden up as she slid down to the roadway. A little black hole, and blood oozing from it onto her jeans. The T-shirt had bright red cartoon words on it: I'm a Belieber!

Blood and brains and hair and bone shards were splattered over the side of the truck. Her eyes were wide-open, sightless, staring at whatever comes next after this life ends. Lying on the road below her right hand was a collapsible steel baton called an ASP. It was extended, and there was blond hair and blood stuck to the tip.

People, gawkers, were standing around in the dwindling rain, mouths slack, gaping at this scene, but no one had come in closer to help or shelter or comfort Julie Karras. She tried to sit up as Redding came to her, her eyes unfocused, shock setting in.

"She…she *hit* me. Pulled my baton out while I was helping the other kid out of the truck and… she hit me."

Redding was saying something soothing as he gently lifted the Glock out of her right hand. He ejected the mag, checked it, put it back in, but he didn't chamber a round. He slipped the pistol into the back of his belt. He lifted her face up by the chin, gently, assessed her eyes, his manner calm but his heart was hammering in his chest.

She looked back at him, both eyes the same— fear. Shock, anger—but no sign of brain injury, pupils the same size, reactive. Her lips moved in a whisper and then in a stronger voice.

"Is she alive?"

Marsh had been checking the girl out while Halliday was kneeling beside the other sister, on the ground, looking for injuries. And weapons.

Marsh glanced over at Redding, shook his head.

"No. She's gone, honey," Redding told her.

Karras started to cry, choked it back.

"Can you stand, Julie?"

"I…I think so."

Redding did a quick inventory, decided she was not hurt in some way that he couldn't see and she couldn't feel, put his hands under her arms and got her to her feet, put her back up against the driver's window of the Suburban, turned her head to the side and studied the damage.

It was a nasty wound.

The ASP was an impact weapon, two feet of solid steel when extended, with a little balled tip. It was meant to be used on muscle mass—thighs, calves, biceps. Never against bone. Bone shattered. Used like that the ASP was a killing tool.

Blood was still pulsing out of a three-inch rip in the flesh just above Karras's right ear. Her ear had actually cushioned some of the impact. The upper part was crushed and flattened and ripped open. An inch higher and the blow could have punched through her temple. She'd be dead, or brain damaged. The girl had meant to kill her and had come damn close.

Halliday jerked the other girl to her feet and had her up against the hood of the squad car, spread out on it, facedown.

He was searching her pockets, putting whatever he found onto the hood of the unit—a wallet; an iPhone; a roll of candy; a small silver can with a breathing mask attached, presumably an asthma puffer; a small notepad with a unicorn on the cover. She was ferociously *angry*, her voice a birdlike screech, steel on slate.

"She *killed* her. That bitch killed Rebecca. You're dead, you *cunt*, you're so *fucking* dead."

Halliday finished searching her, told her to shut the fuck up in a low growl and frog-walked her around to the rear door of his cruiser, not gently. He popped the door and shoved her in, ran her cuffs through a ringbolt and chain welded to the floor of the cruiser and slammed the door on her string of obscenities. He walked back, his face white, scalded by her anger.

He collected the items off the hood.

"Got ID there?" asked Redding.

Halliday flipped open the wallet, found a Florissant High School ID in the name of Karen Anne Walker, age sixteen, a couple of credit cards and a membership card for something called the Glad Day Assembly, with an address in Florissant, Missouri. Florissant was a suburb of St. Louis, Redding recalled.

"Check the other one, see if she's got any ID on her, but don't move her body if you can help it, okay?" Halliday stepped away, went over to the dead girl and carefully went through her pockets, looked back at Redding.

"Nothing."

"See if there's a purse or something in the truck."

Halliday checked the truck, came back with a small lime-green leather wallet, flipped through it, found a Missouri driver's license.

"Got a Rebecca Walker, seventeen, same address, picture matches."

"Run the names, Jim. Let's see what we get."

Halliday went off to his cruiser to do that.

Redding turned to Marsh.

"Let's get an EMT for Julie and bring some County units in here. We need to control this scene."

"Still want the dogs?" Marsh wanted to know.

"Hell yes. Two units."

Marsh stepped away to make the calls and then went back to his cruiser for a roll of crime scene tape, started to string it all around, from signpost to telephone pole, herding the people back as he did this, the rapidly growing crowd babbling and staring, their smartphones and iPads out, taking video, chattering into their phones, snapping shots.

Whatever they were doing, Redding could feel the electrons radiating out into the cyberworld, flashing around the town, the city, the state, the globe. Redding asked Karras if she could walk.

She said yes, and he walked her back to their unit, sat her gently inside on the shotgun seat, tugging a first-aid kit out of his glove compartment.

He put a sterile pad up against the wound and then wrapped it in place with a roll of gauze, making those pointless little comforting sounds parents make when their kids are hurt.

It reminded him of when he'd been a husband and a dad. That hurt to think about so he stopped thinking it and concentrated on what he was doing.

Karras was staring through the window at the Suburban, where Marsh was draping an aluminum foil thermal blanket over the dead girl's body.

"She's really dead, isn't she?" she asked in a hoarse whisper.

"She is. You okay to tell me how it happened, before all the official machinery starts up?"

She managed to look at him, one eye half-covered with the gauze strip.

"I did what you said. I checked them both for weapons, knives… They were crazy, panicked. I got them calm, but I searched them first, I really did, Sergeant Redding… They were both in shock. At least, that's what I thought. I wanted to get them into the back of the cruiser, away from the truck, because it was now a crime scene, get them out of the rain…"

She went away for a moment and Redding let her. She'd have to tell this story over and over again. Let her remember it as it came to her.

He was thinking about the dash cam. It would all be on the dash cam. Not just on the dash cam either. It was likely that half the people in the crowd gathered around had already been taking cell phone shots when the shooting happened.

It was entirely possible that somebody was loading it onto YouTube right at this second. Or selling it to one of the cable networks.

He hoped to God it was a righteous shooting because if it wasn't, they were both in the barrel, but especially her.

Although, now that we're on the topic, he was the dickhead who left a rookie in charge of two kidnapping victims while he raced off like some dumb-ass greyhound chasing a mechanical rabbit. No, whatever happened, this one was on *him*, not her.

"I was helping the younger one—Karen. I think she said Karen was her name. I was helping her out of the truck, she had trouble walking and I remember holding her up and walking along with her—she was holding on to me like she was drowning, I was half carrying her…and then she looked back over my shoulder, like behind me, back at the truck, where Rebecca was, and I saw her eyes get big, and she—"

Karras went quiet, remembering it.

"She *smiled*, a big happy grin, and I turned to look and I felt a tug at my belt—Karen was holding my arms down, wrapping me up tighter, like she was *holding* me? I threw her off, I was turning—and my head exploded—I went down—I was trying to get my weapon out… Rebecca was right over me with that baton and Karen was screaming, 'Kill her kill her smash her skull,' and Rebecca started to swing it down at my head and I had the Glock in my hands and I shot her. Saw the rounds hit her. I don't know how many I got out—"

"Three rounds."

She thought about that.

"Three? Okay. I don't know."

Redding had already checked her mag. She had fifteen rounds left in the seventeen-round mag. And she'd had one already chambered, as she'd been trained to do. Which was good because, if she'd had to take the time to rack the slide and chamber a round and then aim and fire, she'd probably be dead now. So three rounds out, and all of them hits.

"Three is pretty damn good, Julie. Most cops would have emptied the mag into her. Or tried to."

"I…was thinking about the backstop. About ricochets. About all the people standing around."

"Good. Good for you. That's trigger control. All three shots were right on target, center of the visible mass. That's textbook fire discipline. Remember that, when they ask later. The shooting board."

Karras took a moment to absorb that idea—the shooting board—and then shook it off.

"Anyway…she was going back and down, back into the rear door. I pivoted on my hip and Karen was coming right back at me—I could hear her coming, her shoes scraping—and I figured she was after my weapon because that was what she was focused on. I put the gun on her and I said… I have no idea what I said. She lay down on her face, I went over and cuffed her…and next thing I knew my legs gave out and my ass was on the ground and my back was up against the side of the truck and there was blood in my eyes."

She looked down at her hands.

"My first day," she said, mostly to herself. "I can't fucking believe it. I'm on the job *five hours* and I've fucking killed someone."

Tears close but not there yet, her blue eyes wide, blood in the right eye and on her cheekbone, a little blood on her teeth as she tried to find the words. Redding put his hand on her right shoulder, feeling the warm wet blood on her uniform shirt, the red stains on her gold braid.

"If the dash cam shows the same thing—"

She hardened up.

"It will."

"Then it was a good shooting. Take a deep breath. You did just fine. Better than fine. I'm proud of you, Julie. Remember that."

The EMT bus had arrived, complete with sirens and lights, and now there were County cars rolling in from both ends of the street, along with two K-9 units of the Highway Patrol. And right behind them, Mace Dixon in his Supervisor truck.

Redding leaned in close to her, speaking low but urgently, making the point.

"It's going to get real intense real fast, Julie. You're not to talk, got that? Not to *anyone*. You can answer health questions for the EMT people. Everybody else, you have nothing to say. Got that? Nothing. Not even to the CO. You're just confused. Your head is killing you—"

"It *really* is," she said, trying for a smile.

"You're too shook up to talk right now. Mace will understand. You don't talk until you're discharged from the hospital and you've had a good night's sleep, and we're back at Depot, and your Patrol Advocate is sitting beside you. And I'll be right there too. It'll take a couple of days before that happens. They'll be taking you to Immaculate Heart to look at that head wound. Our guys will be around everywhere and they'll keep you safe. They won't ask you about the shooting. They all know better. But you don't talk about the shooting to Flagler County. Or any city cops. Or to the medics. Basically, not even to Jesus Christ Himself if

He appears in your room with a six-pack of Coronas and a box of Krispy Kremes. Not to *anyone*."

She managed to laugh at that, and then the tears finally came, and she was looking at her hands, at the blood on them.

"I killed a living person," she said. "That girl was alive just a few minutes ago, and now she's dead, and she will be dead…forever."

Redding put a hand under her chin, lifted her head and turned her to face him.

"Yes, you did. It was your sworn duty to do that, and you did it. You put the aggressor down and you stayed alive and no civilians got hurt. It was your job to protect the public, and you did that. You killed a crazy bitch who was trying to kill you. And when you were dead she'd have taken your gun and then what could have happened? She could have started firing into the crowd and killed a lot of innocent people. But you stopped her. Stopped her dead. And you know what you need to think about, every time you think about this?"

"What?"

"*Fuck* her. Better her than you."

She looked up at him, trying to take that in.

"Really?"

He put a hand on her shoulder, a thin smile.

"Yeah. Really. Welcome to Cop World, Julie."

———

A few minutes later Redding and Marsh and Halliday watched the EMT wagon roll away with Julie Karras, lights but no siren, as Mace Dixon, who'd been speaking to a Flagler County staff sergeant, came across to talk. To listen, actually.

They laid it out for him in the most basic terms, and he took it all in without a comment, other than one or two clarifying questions.

Dixon made sure he got it all straight, and then he lit up an Old Port, using the brim of his Stetson to shelter the match from what was left of the rain.

"Okay. We'll look at the dash cam. If it holds up, I think we're gonna be okay on this. Media is gonna make a BFD out of it being a kid killed. A female. And all of these people around here, the civilians, every one of them has probably got sound and video on the whole thing. Look at them, they're *still* shooting cell phone video. They're like goddamn zombies with little metal rectangles attached to their foreheads. What happened here, it's going all over social media. They probably know about it in fucking Oslo by now. Nothing we can do about that. It is what it is."

The Officer Involved Shooting Unit was on the scene, dropping tiny yellow cones all over the place and taking video. Two satellite trucks from the Jacksonville stations, Fox and CNN, were being held off a block away. So far no Eye in the Sky news choppers had arrived to screw up the crime scene with rotor wash. Redding could see the hard white lights as the reporters did Eyewitness to the Shooting interviews with everyone who wanted to be on television, which was close to a hundred people by now.

Dixon blew out the smoke, turned to the three of them. "You figure she's still out here somewhere?"

"Has to be," said Redding. "Flagler County guys have sealed off the entire neighborhood."

"Might have broken into any one of these houses along here," said Dixon. "We'll have to get foot patrols out, go from door to door."

"Might be out there in the reeds," said Dixon.

"I think she is," said Redding. "That's where we last saw her. We'll get the flatboats out looking for her. If she went in there, Mace, we'll flush her out."

They turned as a burst of angry barking came from the direction of the Suburban. Two K-9 Unit officers were dragging their dogs away from the driver's side of the truck.

Redding watched the dogs, both big German shepherds. They were both fighting to get free of their leads, barking furiously. The handlers were pulling them away from the truck, the dogs resisting as hard as they could, straining against their harnesses. Both handlers were looking confused, angry, fighting the dogs.

"What the..." said Redding, walking across to talk to one of the K-9 handlers, a serious heart-attack blonde named Jennifer St. Denis. St. Denis had the dog under a tight grip as Redding reached her.

"What's with the dogs, Jen?" Redding asked.

St. Denis shook her head, looking exasperated and puzzled. "I have no idea."

Now her dog, a big muscled-up German shepherd, was staring up at Redding, panting heavily, gazing up at him as if he knew him, which he did.

He'd once spent nine months with this fine dog before he'd handed him off to another K-9 officer, the one before Jennifer, a guy who was KILO now, killed in the line of duty, after which this same dog, Killington, had mauled the shooter so badly he lost his left ear, most of his left cheek, all of his left eye and over two quarts of blood from his ripped-out carotid. Killington's DNA made him nothing less than an apex predator.

Guy later sued the Highway Patrol and the State of Florida for Excessive Use of Force. He was on Death Row at the time. He lost. A while later they spiked him dead and buried him in unconsecrated ground.

The dead K-9 officer's friends took Killington out to the convict's grave every now and then and they'd stand around drinking beers until they were all charged up, at which point everybody would unzip and piss on the grave, including Killington.

Redding bent down and offered a hand to the dog, which took some nerve, even if they were old friends.

"Hey, Killington. What's up? What's the problem?"

Killington twitched his ears and then whimpered, showing the whites of his eyes. He ducked his head and then licked Redding's hand.

"What's with Killington?" he asked.

"You ask me," said St. Denis, in a low voice,

"I'd say he doesn't like whatever he can smell in that vehicle. I've never seen him do this. Never."

Across the road the other K-9 guy was putting his shepherd into the back of his cruiser. He glanced across at St. Denis and Redding, shaking his head, lifted his hands in a WTF gesture.

"Got a feeling we're not gonna get a lot of help from the dogs today," said St. Denis.

One of the forensic guys walked across to Dixon and got into a close conversation with him, Marsh and Halliday listening in.

Redding said goodbye to Jennifer, ruffled Killington's neck again and walked across to hear what the techie had to say.

"I don't get it," Dixon was saying.

The tech, Redding didn't know his name, a skinny kid with glasses and large ears, shook his head, staring down at something in his hands, a small digital camera. On the screen, a picture of a steering wheel with black smudges all over it.

"No prints, but it hasn't been wiped."

"You saw the woman, Jack, when she hopped out of the truck, didn't you? Was she wearing gloves?"

Redding thought about it. He had a good memory for things like that. And you always looked at the hands first. He went back for the image, concentrating on the brief glimpse he had gotten.

"No, Mace. Hands were empty. If she had gloves, they were pink. Skin colored."

He glanced at Marsh, who grinned back at him.

"Okay, *white* skin colored," said Redding.

"So maybe latex?" Dixon asked.

"Not latex," said the tech. "We'd have residue. Anyway, there was fresh sweat on the wheel, which you wouldn't get if the driver had been wearing any kind of gloves."

"*Human* sweat?" Marsh asked. Of course everyone stared at him like he was totally bats.

He sent the vibe right back.

"Hey, she fucking *disappeared*, into thin air, like she was a fucking ghost. Didn't she, Jim?"

Halliday wasn't backing away from it either.

"Well, we were right on her ass, Cap, and she broke outta the trees and… LQ's right. It was like she just…*vanished*. I'm just sayin'."

"Lousy visibility with this rain," said Dixon, and then there was an uneasy silence.

"Ghosts I don't know about," said the tech, after a moment, and mostly to himself, as if the idea was a new one to him. He smiled.

"Tell you what," he said. "We'll run it for ghost DNA."

"You do that," said Marsh, not amused.

"And while you're doing that," said Jack, "run it for real DNA too, see if she comes up on any database. Tell the lab we want this done right away, not a week from next Tuesday."

The tech promised to push it to the top of the list, and then Dixon's duty cell phone beeped at him. He glanced down at the screen, gave everybody the "sorry, gotta take this" look, stepped away a couple of yards.

The three of them, Marsh and Halliday and Redding, watched the accelerating activity that was buzzing all around them, and the people on their porches and under their garage roofs, staring out, watching. Getting it all on cell phone cameras.

The block was swarming with uniforms, the tan and black of the County guys, the charcoal gray of the Highway Patrol, the OIS people in their white pajamas. The rain was tapering away and far off in the west the sun was threatening to show up for a brief appearance at the tail end of the afternoon.

"What do you want us to do?" asked Marsh.

Redding considered the girl in the backseat of Halliday's squad car. She was staring back at them, gunning them, a fixed and angry scowl on her pretty young face.

"Jim, you drive that…creature…to see the docs, but don't Mirandize her yet. You follow? No Miranda. It'll just get her attention. Get her to Immaculate Heart ER, have her checked over, and then get her admitted into one of those secured rooms on the fifth floor. Put a PW into the room with her. Tell her she's in Protective Custody until we can figure what's going on. Tell her it's because her kidnapper is still on the loose. She's in our *care*, right? Not under arrest. Here's why. She'll likely end up being charged with Resisting Arrest with Violence, Battery on a Police Officer and Attempting to Elude. Accessory to Attempt Murder of a Police Officer, if I have anything to say about it.

But she's a kid, a *yoot* like they say in the Bronx, and I don't want her skating on some fucking juvie technicality."

"I ran her ID," said Halliday. "No hits other than a misdemeanor shoplifting beef last year. Nothing on the dead kid either."

"Okay. Look, LQ, you go up and see to Julie. They took her to Immaculate Heart too. Stay with her. Stay close. Don't let anybody from Depot or HQ lean on her. You are hereby authorized to shoot any media folks who get within ten feet of her. If they keep her overnight, can you stay with her?"

"I can," said Marsh.

"Good. Thank you. Call her people, if she has any. Call whoever you need to. Take good care of her, LQ. She's a keeper."

"What about you?"

"I gotta see that this Suburban is sealed up and towed to the Depot. I want Forensics to take it apart in the motor pool. There's luggage in the back, backpacks, a couple of boxes too. And it's stuffed full of fast-food junk, candy wrappers, soda cans, like there was some kind of rolling party going on. Like serious fun was being had. I should have picked that up."

"Lot of shit going on at the time," said Marsh.

"Should have seen it anyway. Make sure Forensics goes through all that stuff. Get receipts for everything. Truck has OnStar so get our IT people to contact them for any route info they might have. I want every parking ticket and restaurant receipt and candy wrapper bagged and tagged. We've got their iPhones so lean on the carrier to unlock them and get location data and a list of calls. Also get our people to look at all the security film they can get from gas stations and restaurants they went to. That stuff will be on their credit card records, so jump on VISA and AMEX and those guys."

"They always give us grief, Jack."

"Give them more. Scare the fuck out of them. Tell them there's a killer loose, and if she kills again because they fucked us over, we'll put it on Fox and CNN and make them look worse than United Airlines did last year."

"Yow. Okay."

"Yeah. Look, mainly I want to know why a kidnapped girl would try to kill the cop who freed her, and why her sister was helping. I want to know where the rest of the Walker family is, the dad and the mom and the other sister. I want to know where those three broads have been the last few days and nights, why were they in New Orleans and what they were doing there and who they were doing it to."

"If she'll talk," said Halliday. "She could lawyer up, the PD would start up with all that Juvenile Offender bullshit—"

Redding glared at him, a cold steel look.

"We're not gonna make it look like that. Like I said, we're just gonna be these Officer Friendly cops, we're just *worried* about her—is she traumatized, can she tell us what happened? That's why no Miranda. If she does lawyer up, we make sure she gets the right PD—"

"Hobie Pruitt is the PD on duty tonight," said Marsh. Redding took that in.

"Good. That helps. He's not a complete idiot, and his father was a city detective in Savannah."

Marsh and Halliday said nothing.

They knew he wasn't finished.

"One last thing, guys. I think that runner is still around. If she is, I'm gonna try to have her in the back of my squad before the night's over."

He paused, smiled at them.

"So. We're good to go?"

"We are," said Halliday.

———

Dixon finished his call, stepped back to Redding, a troubled look on his face.

"That was Rod Culhane from HQ. Fernandina Beach PD called a while ago. They were doing a search around the island."

"Yeah? And?"

Dixon's expression was grim.

"They located the rest of the Walker family."

"That doesn't sound good."

Dixon shook his head.

"It isn't. Couple of their harness guys found them in a storage unit that belonged to the Walkers' condo. Down in the second-level basement, off in a corner. Padlocked, pretty much airtight to keep out the bugs and rats. But it had one of those roll-down gates. Stuff was leaking out from under it."

"Oh jeez."

"Yeah. They were inside, all three of them—mom, dad and the little sister. If it was done by the runner, she must have had a gun on them. Not easy to control two adults without one."

"Didn't find one in the truck."

"So she's still got it, I figure. They'd been tied up with plastic cable binders, had their mouths duct-taped, left there on the floor. Ten days."

"Cord cuffs and duct tape sounds like she came prepared. The runner, I mean."

"Not really. The storage unit was full of that kind of thing. The dad is some sort of collector, had boxes full of bones and shit."

"All dead?"

"Two of them. The wife and the little girl. Heat stroke and dehydration. But the father, Gerald Walker, he was still alive—"

"After ten days?"

"Yeah. Guy must be half-lizard. He's in the ICU at Baptist. Got a pulse like a moth in a bottle. Might make it. Might be a vegetable. No way to tell. Who the fuck could do something like that?"

It was a rhetorical question. They'd both been cops long enough to know that the world was packed with people who could do that and much worse.

Dixon shook his head, threw his Old Port into a ditch. He sighed heavily.

"Fuck this. I'm gonna go up to the ER, see how Karras is doing. Then I'm gonna go up to that kid's room and turn her inside out. You wanna come for that? If your runner is still here, which I doubt, Flagler County will find her."

Redding thought it over.

"No, I'm gonna stay here, Mace. Whatever the hell happened up at Amelia Island, this runner is at the heart of it. I'm not leaving until we get her."

Dixon considered him for a while.

"Is this *personal* with you?"

Redding thought about it.

"I don't know… Maybe… I sort of felt like… like I had *seen* her somewhere."

"Like on a Wanted sheet?"

"No. Something else. Don't know what. Anyway, now that we got a rookie hurt, that makes it personal."

"Yes, it does. See you later."

"Mace, you be careful when you talk to the kid. Now that what we have is two, potentially three dead victims. That kid is sixteen going on sixty. She knows what the hell happened. Don't Mirandize her. We don't want her to ask for a lawyer—"

"If she *does* ask?"

"Try not to *make* her ask. I told the guys, we're Officer Friendly. Be *nice*. Be *caring*. Get one of the PW's to bring her milk and cookies. Get her a fucking blankie. She's not under arrest, she's a *victim* in Protective Custody."

"And if she asks for a lawyer anyway?"

"If you work it right she won't. If she insists, the duty PD is Hobie Pruitt. He's a good man. If you *have* to get her a PD, make sure you get *him*, and not that stainless-steel bitch—"

"Marylynne Kostic."

"Yeah. Her. *Anybody* but *her*. We can slow-walk that issue for twenty-four hours. Mace, this is too fucking serious now. This is Attempted Murder of a cop. One of ours. I know you're pissed—"

"I'm pissed, yeah, of course, but this isn't my first rodeo, Jack."

"I know that. I just…"

You're a great cop, Mace, but you have already fucked up two good beefs when you lost your temper.

Redding didn't say that.

He didn't have to.

"I know," said Mace, aware of what was not being said. "We don't wanna lose her on a…technicality."

"Yeah."

A technicality.

Like throwing a handcuffed suspect down a flight of stairs. On camera.

"Well, neither do I," said Dixon, hardening up. "And I won't. Any OT you need, I'm authorizing it. Good hunting. See you back at Depot. You bring that woman in, Jack."

"I will."

Redding stepped back, watched Dixon pull away, put his Stetson on, squared it up, took a couple of deep breaths and headed back into the trees.

———

A squad of Flagler County Deputies was moving through the forest, slowly, working their way down to the shoreline. Night was coming on, the short sharp twilight you got in these latitudes, the sun a dying flame in the far west, low enough to light up the underside of the clouds.

He got to the shoreline and watched as two flatboats marked FHP Marine Unit were slowly paddling their way through the reeds.

Redding pulled out his portable.

"Jax 180 to Marine."

He saw one of the cops tug out his radio, put it to his lips.

"Roger, Jax 180."

"That you, Leo?"

"It's me, Jack."

"How you doing?"

"Bugs are murder out here. Driving us all nuts. Must be a billion of them."

They were buzzing around Redding as he stood on the shoreline, but not as bad as it must have been out there.

"Getting anything at all?"

"Other than my nose and ears bit off? No."

"Well, do your best, Leo. They found the rest of the Walker family."

Leo didn't come back for a second.

Then he keyed his mike.

"All three?"

"Yeah. The mother and the kid were dead."

"But not the dad?"

"He's still with us. So far."

"In the ICU?"

"Baptist Hospital in Fernandina Beach. Listed as Grave."

"How'd it happen?"

"Someone left them tied up in a storage locker. Ten days. The wife and the kid died of dehydration."

"Eventually."

"Yeah. Eventually."

Silence.

Then, "Shit."

"Yeah," said Redding. "That's about it. So look real hard, Leo. We want this woman."

"If she's in here, Jack, we'll find her."

But they didn't.

———

They came close.

Close enough for Selena to hear what the boat cop was saying into his radio. They had found the mother and the father and the little girl. The father was still alive. She regretted that. He must have had a very strong life force to survive that long. When Rebecca helped to force them into the storage unit, helped to bind and gag them, the mother had begged her daughter not to do it, with tears and pleas.

But Selena had the pistol, and Rebecca really wanted to go to New Orleans, and the sex was pulling her along, so the thing was done.

She wondered if, in the airless dark of that place,

the father had seen the Shimmer when his wife and child passed. It would have been better to kill them all—and perhaps to have taken the Shimmer for herself when she did it—but the girls weren't up to that. Not yet. They were too young.

But they had done very well, Rebecca and Karen, right up to the end here in this place. Selena was proud of them. They had been strong and brave. They had made it possible for her to escape and continue her work.

The three gunshots might have been for them, because they had tried to do what she had asked of them. If that was true and they were safely dead, it was all for the best. Selena would always remember them with fondness. And they *had* been delicious.

The hull of the boat actually brushed against the back of her jacket as it drifted by and she could smell the cigarette one of the cops was smoking in a vain attempt to ward off the mosquitoes.

In a way, what saved her were those mosquitoes, because they went for the eyes and the faces and straining to see clearly through a swarm of biting flies was a difficult thing to do properly. And she was being still, even as she felt the hull of the boat sliding across her shoulder blades and little icy jabs of panic were flickering up and down her belly. That was the hardest part, not moving with the boat so close, not giving in to the urge to burst up out of the water, knife them deep, kill them both before they could do anything but die.

But then the men in the other boat would shoot

her and she'd be dead. And that was unthinkable. So she did not move. And after a long while, the boats went away, rowing back out into the waterway, rowing back to the big motor launch that had brought the flatboats in two hours ago.

Another half hour and the dark was now almost complete. She lifted her head…slowly…slowly… and there was one lone figure at the edge of the marsh, facing out into the dark.

That big cop, standing there in the dying light, was one of the three who had chased her until they heard the gunfire back on the road. This was also the same cop who had spotted them first, back there on the coast highway.

She had seen his face in her side mirror as he followed the truck, a craggy cowboy face, a big man with heavy hands on the steering wheel of his cruiser, his pale blue eyes, sharp and steady, fixed on her. He had the look of a raptor. She'd known then that she was going to have to run. She'd told the girls to prepare to do what they had talked about if something like this happened.

The same cop was now standing on the shore, stone still. She could see gold chevrons against the dark gray of his uniform, a sergeant. His right hand was resting on the butt of his service piece, and he was staring out at the swamp. Selena could *feel* his mind reaching out for her, feel the force in his animal spirit. He was *burning* for her.

He stayed there for an unknowable time, watching as the police launch slowly churned away to the main canal and the night came down. She got a vibration off him that wasn't like the feelings she got from other officers, that wolf pack feeling.

This one was different from the others. She had encountered his type once before, but not in a very long time. She couldn't quite catch that distant memory. But this cop was strangely *familiar*. As if they had known each other in another life.

She put these thoughts away. Eventually he would tire and leave and she could come back to shore. She knew what to do once she got back to the shore. She had done it often. So she waited.

Time passed slowly and still it was just the two of them, the police sergeant standing motionless by the shore, and Selena two hundred feet out, shivering violently in the water, aware that something large and slithery was close by her, only a few yards away, resting on the floor of the swamp, lidless eyes considering her.

She could feel its reptilian mind working, thinking dim slow thoughts about catching and ripping and swallowing, maybe mixed up with a bit of doubt, getting strange signals off her, its hunger and its fear fighting with each other. There was nothing to be done about that.

She was very cold and very hungry and starting to be just a little afraid, her skin on fire with bites and wounds and stings.

Beyond the trees the streetlights came on, and over her head the stars were shining through shreds of cloud. She could hear the cop's radio crackling with chatter and out on the roadway blue and red and white lights were slicing up the sky and spearing through the treetops.

And still he stood and still he stared.

And now he was beginning to *worry* her.

She idly wondered if she should slip a hundred feet down the shoreline, try to get behind him and kill him. If he didn't go soon, she might try it, even though moving—not being still—would be acting like prey instead of predator.

But a few minutes later he walked away up the slope until he reached the tree line. He stopped there and turned back to the swamp. And called out, a deep rolling voice, a strong Southern accent, Georgia or the Carolinas.

"Lady, if you're still out there, I have something to tell you. I *know* you. I've seen your face somewhere. So I'm gonna look everywhere I can until I find you. Every police record. Every newspaper story. Every official site in the US. I'm gonna *hunt* you. And when I have your file, I will come for you. My name is Sergeant Jack Redding of the Florida Highway Patrol. Enjoy your evening."

Then he turned and disappeared into the trees and Selena was alone in the swamp and she had a lot to think about. *Redding.* She *knew* that name, but she couldn't quite remember from where, or why.

She was still thinking about it when she reached the shoreline a while later and moved silently, invisibly, a darker shadow in the night, gliding up the grassy slope and slipping through the trees toward the backs of the houses, where most of the people would be out on their front porches, watching the police cars, talking to their neighbors, having a lovely time savoring all the excitement, enjoying the delicious idea that something dangerous, something *fatal*, had happened right in front of them.

But it hadn't happened to *them*.

———

Two Flagler County Deputies, Danika Shugrue and Luke Cotton, knocked on the front door of a trim little white bungalow two hours later. The porch lights were on and old-timey music was coming through the door, what used to be called big band music. While they waited for an answer, Deputy Shugrue checked her clipboard, a list of local residents.

"We've got a Willard Coleman, eighty-seven, a widower. Lives alone. He's in a wheelchair—"

"Hence the ramp we're standing on," said Cotton.

"Stop saying *hence*, will you? Next it'll be *hither* and *forsooth*."

Cotton, who was hunting a promotion, was taking a college-level English Lit course online and Shugrue felt it was having a bad effect on him.

The door opened. A pretty woman was standing in the doorway, in a ratty powder blue terrycloth bathrobe, obviously naked underneath, since the robe was not quite pulled in tight enough for modesty, her hair wrapped up in a big white towel and her face covered in some kind of lime-green cream. She smiled at them.

She had a *great* smile.

"Evening, miss," said Deputy Shugrue, the senior deputy in this pair. "Can we talk to Mr. Willard Coleman?"

The woman made a pursed-lip expression, thinking about it, but then she brightened.

"Well, I think he's asleep, but of course, come on in. Is this about the shooting thing earlier?"

"Yes it is, Miss…?"

"How *terrible*. I've been watching it on Fox. They have all sorts of video on it, I guess from people and their cell phone cameras and stuff. That poor lady police officer. The whole thing is on film. They're playing it over and over. Is the lady officer okay?"

"She's in the hospital," said Shugrue, stepping inside and scuffing her boots on the doormat to clean off the mud. "But we think she's going to be okay. Thank you for asking."

"And the little girl who was shot? They're not saying whether she was okay too?"

Shugrue exchanged a look with Cotton.

"She, ah, she died, I'm afraid, Miss…?"

"Oh, I'm so sorry. I'm Catherine Marcus. Call me Cathy. I'm with Helping Hands? We're the assisted-living people?"

Marcus backed away from the door, inviting them into a neat little front room with a green leather sofa and two chairs, antique lamps, a fireplace with family pictures, a flat-screen TV with the sound off—Fox News—an oxygen tank in one corner.

"I'm the resident nurse for the night," she was explaining. "Will… Mister Coleman…has some mobility issues, and he suffers from sleep apnea. So we try to have someone here through the night."

"Can we talk to Mister Coleman?"

Marcus seemed worried, distracted, as she wiped some of the night cream off her face.

"He's finally gotten to sleep… He has a terrible time…insomnia. But, of course, you need to check on him… Let me take you to him. His room is just down the hall here."

She led the deputies down a narrow wooden-floored hall past a bright galley kitchen, dishes piled neatly in a rack, the counter gleaming in the glow of halogen downlights.

She reached a door, half-closed, tapped gently on it. "Will…are you awake?" she asked in a whisper. No answer, but the sound of some sort of breathing machine came from the darkened interior.

"Like I said, Will has sleep apnea," Marcus explained. "That's where your breathing just sort of stops, while you're sleeping. It can be fatal. He has to wear a mask at night, to keep him breathing. Poor dear, he *hates* it. Says it's too hot. But he needs it."

"Can we just look in?" asked Cotton.

"Of course," said Marcus, in a whisper.

Shugrue pushed the door open softly. The room had been stripped down to the basics, a dresser, a small flat-screen TV on top of it. Wooden floors. It was spare and neat. There was a single bed in the center of the room. In the dim light from a night table lamp they could see an elderly man lying on his back in the bed, covered by a fluffy pale blue comforter.

His eyes were closed and sunken but his bony chest was rising and falling in a steady rhythm. A rubber mask with a flexible tube attached to it covered his nose and mouth. The hose ran down to a machine that was puffing and venting in the same rhythm. The room smelled vaguely of antiseptic and some kind of lemon-scented air freshener, and under that just a teeny tiny hint of old-guy pee.

The cops stood in the doorway for a while, listening to Willard Coleman breathe. Then they backed out quietly.

"Okay with you if we do a walkabout?" asked Deputy Shugrue. "Make sure there's nobody in the house who shouldn't be here?"

Marcus gave her a broad smile.

"You go right ahead. It's a pretty small house, just one floor. There's no basement because of the water table around here being so high."

Shugrue and Cotton went off down the hall, poked around in the bathroom, a tiny second bedroom, stepped out into the lanai-covered backyard, looked at the locks, flicked on the backyard lights for a moment and then they came back down the hall, where Marcus had stayed to wait for them.

"Everything looks good," said Shugrue, and they all headed back down the hall, two large deputies carrying heavy gear, looming over a curvy barefoot woman in an increasingly scandalous bathrobe—in all the distraction, Marcus seemed to be unaware that her robe was not quite doing all it could to keep her decent.

They went out into the living room and across to the front door, where Shugrue stopped, as if she had just remembered it, and asked Catherine Marcus if she had some ID.

"Of course," Marcus said. "Hold on, I think I left it in the kitchen."

She fluttered off, leaving a soapy scent in the air, came back in a moment with a laminated ID card, the Helping Hands logo, and a photo with a security hologram over it and the name printed under the photo, which read Catherine Marcus, RN.

Shugrue studied the ID, made a note on her clipboard, tipped her Stetson to the nurse.

"Thank you, Miss Marcus. We'd like to advise you to keep everything locked up tight tonight. We've got a dangerous fugitive in the area, so don't be answering any knocks on the door, okay?"

"Well, I had to answer *yours*, didn't I?" she said, with a bright smile and a touch of tease.

"Yes, you did," said Shugrue. "But no one else. Okay? Be careful. Have a good night."

"You too, Officers," said Marcus, holding the door open as they left. "And you both be sure to get home safe tonight, okay?"

"Thanks, miss," said Shugrue, and they walked back down the wheelchair ramp and out to the street.

"Pretty lady," said Cotton, who had enjoyed the half-open bathrobe more than was quite right for a happily married guy with two kids.

"Yeah she was," said Shugrue, writing something on her clipboard. "Except for the acne. Her cheeks looked like she'd been bitten to death by ducks."

"Didn't notice her cheeks," said Cotton.

"Yeah," said Shugrue. "Because her cheeks were all up here and her boobs were all down there. I thought you were gonna trip over your tongue."

"More likely my dick," said Cotton.

"You wish," said Shugrue.

———

Back in the bungalow Selena watched through the blinds as the two deputies walked away into the darkness between two streetlights. Then she slipped back down the hall and into the bedroom where Willard Coleman lay on his back in the hospital bed. She pulled off the sleep apnea mask and contemplated the old man for a while.

The mask was still breathing in and out for him, but Willard Coleman had drawn his last voluntary breath an hour and fifty minutes ago, when Selena had pinched his mouth and nostrils shut and then held them that way for six and a half minutes, because there was no point in doing something if you didn't do it right, and it had been her experience that six and a half minutes did the trick for pretty much everyone.

She'd watched his eyes as he fought for life, his bony fingers scrabbling at her wrists. She had hoped for the Shimmer, but it didn't come, which happened most of the time, the Shimmer being as elusive as St. Elmo's fire. She had rarely seen the Shimmer come when old people died. Maybe their life forces were already at a low ebb.

She had better luck with younger subjects, but so far only a few of them had been able to bring the Shimmer in a way she could use.

———

Once she was sure the old man was dead, she had found an old bathrobe in the bedroom closet, gone down the hall and taken a long hot shower, which she really needed.

While she was showering she thought about the cops who would be around soon, making sure all the residents were safe and not taken hostage by that horrible evil fugitive person. She had a plan for that. She always carried a variety of IDs and credit cards and cash in a waterproof belt.

So she was safe for now, once the cops had come and gone, and afterward there was work to do— yes, a lot of work. The old man had a big iMac computer in the second bedroom. She would need that.

Redding. Jack Redding. *Sergeant* Jack Redding.

She was going to have to think about him, be-cause he showed every sign of turning into a big problem. But that was for the morning.

———

After her shower she had watched the cell phone video on all the news reports, showing the police shooting out on the street. That female cop had shot Rebecca dead, but Karen was still alive.

She had already planned for that. There was a better than even chance that it would take care of itself, possibly sooner rather than later. Not a cer-tainty, but in this life, what was? All you could do was your level best.

Planning. Foresight. Take pride in your work. Selena was meticulous. That was her gift.

And then the cops arrived, much later than she thought, but she was ready for them, and it had gone just the way she expected, as things usually did if you planned ahead. So what she wanted right now was a bottle of cold white wine and something hot and spicy to eat. The old man's fridge was full of food. He even had a wine closet.

And Selena had never been hungrier.

Redding drove to Immaculate Heart Hospital with his mind mainly on the woman in the marsh. He was almost certain that she was still there, but the flatboats had been all over it, and he couldn't just wait her out. He had to see Julie, and then make sure that Mace Dixon hadn't done something radical to get Karen Walker's full attention. Such as throwing her off the roof of the hospital.

The ER entrance at Immaculate Heart was cluttered with ambulances and police vehicles, County and State—another busy evening in Paradise—Redding found a space next to LQ Marsh's cruiser and shut the car down, feeling a wave of exhaustion settle over him.

He checked his watch. It was going on midnight and he had a feeling it was going to be a while before he got back to his seaside bungalow on Crescent Beach.

Not that going back there was anything he looked forward to, but it was where he had lived for many years with Barbara and Katy and he wasn't ready to pack up all their things. Yet.

He leaned forward until his head was resting on the steering wheel, closed his eyes and let the same old feeling pull him down. He had gotten over the central illusion about grieving, which was that grieving was something you got over.

How he felt now was just the new normal, the way it is for a vet who comes back from the wars with nothing below his knees but stainless-steel sticks. Life was *that* before, and now life was *this*.

———

Anson Freitag.

An eighty-three-year-old retired surgeon with cataracts and a pacemaker. Loved by all, so all the papers said. A pillar of the community, so all the cable news folks said.

A celebrated cardiovascular surgeon credited with saving literally thousands of lives over his decades-long career, most of it spent right here at Immaculate Heart Hospital in downtown Jacksonville.

Anson Freitag, northbound on A1A last Christmas Eve, around 9:30. Driving a tank-sized navy-blue Mercedes-Benz 600. At 80 miles per hour. In a fog bank. Coming up on the Matanzas Inlet Bridge at the north end of Rattlesnake Island.

And southbound on A1A, at the same time, in their black Jeep, Redding's wife, Barbara, at the wheel and Katy in her safety seat in the back, strapped in tight, playing with her iPad Mini. Coming up on the Matanzas Inlet Bridge at the north end of Rattlesnake Island.

Barbara was on the hands-free phone, talking to Redding. Redding was on duty that Christmas Eve, the price for getting Christmas Day off. Otherwise he would have been at the wheel, which might have meant Barbara and Katy would still be alive. Or Redding could have managed to die with them, which would have been better than what actually did happen.

Barbara's voice.

Talking to him about Christmas Dinner.

Through the cell phone he could hear music in the background. "I'll Be Home for Christmas" by Bing Crosby. Barbara was a sucker for all those old Christmas songs. "Have Yourself a Merry Little Christmas" by Judy Garland. And the classic films. *Miracle on 34th Street, Going My Way, Holiday Inn, It's a Wonderful Life, A Christmas Carol,* the one with Alastair Sim.

Then suddenly Barbara's voice changed into a horrified yelp—she said, *Jack there's someone in the middle of the road—*

At precisely the same time, Anson Freitag's Benz 600 swerved violently to the left and crossed the median at the dead center of the Matanzas Bridge. The Benz struck the Jeep on the driver's-side front wing at 80 miles an hour, which created, for both drivers, the same effect as driving into a concrete wall at one hundred and thirty miles an hour. The heavier Benz took both vehicles through the guardrail and fifty feet down into the bay.

Redding heard it all over the Jeep's hands-free phone. The grinding clash of steel on steel. Shattering glass. Barbara's scream of pain and terror as the SUV burst through the rail and tumbled down into Matanzas Inlet. The much higher pitch of Katy's frantic shriek. The huge thumping splash as the Jeep hit the water. The secondary splash farther off, Freitag's Benz smashing into the waves a few yards away. Barbara's gasping struggle for air as the water poured in through the broken windshield. She was trying to keep her head above water. He could hear her doing it. He always would.

Then Redding heard her crying out, *Katy, Katy, are you*, and then her voice was abruptly choked off. The sound of her drowning, which seemed to go on forever, or at least until the car's electrics shorted out. Redding heard it all. He was going to hear it all for the rest of his life. The audio memory went round and round in a loop in his head whenever he was alone in the beach house. At least, when he hadn't whacked himself into a near-fatal coma with Chianti and Ativan.

So, no, going back to the beach house right now wasn't real attractive. He had the newspaper clipping in his wallet, but he didn't have to take it out. He knew it by heart:

ANSON FREITAG, 83.

Highly Respected Retired Chief of Surgery at Immaculate Heart Hospital Killed on Christmas Eve.
    Head-On Crash on the Matanzas Bridge.
    Search for "Mystery Hiker" Called Off.
    Tragic Loss for the Entire Community.
    Also killed were:
    Barbara Redding, 28, local resident.
    Katy Redding, 4.

Redding told the Accident Reconstruction guys that Barbara said she saw someone standing in the middle of the Matanzas Bridge, a pedestrian who might have seen, maybe even *caused*, the accident.

Flagler County and all the State guys spent hours looking up and down A1A, stopping truckers, checking out the all-night diners. The local TV stations did PSAs asking anyone who had seen a hitchhiker on A1A around that time to call in.

No one called. No one had seen a lone person walking on A1A that night. They checked security cameras at gas stations and traffic lights for ten miles in each direction. They got all sorts of images and not one of them kicked out a workable lead. They even dragged Matanzas Inlet on the theory that the walker might have gone over the side along with the Jeep and the Benz. Nothing. Nowhere. They never got so much as a breath of this elusive walker.

Time passed.

Other bad things drove the story off the evening news. After a while everybody decided that Barbara Redding had simply been tired, that it was a foggy evening and everyone knew that the lights on that bridge cast weird shadows at night.

As for Anson Freitag why had he swerved at exactly the same moment? What made him do that? What had he seen? Like all orphaned questions that don't have an answer, the question gradually went away, and everybody—well the ones who were still living—went on with their lives.

Everybody but Jack Redding.

———

Redding took the side entrance by the ER gates so he wouldn't have to walk past the huge Anson Freitag Tribute Memorial that took up most of a marble wall at the entrance to the Anson Freitag Wing of Immaculate Heart Hospital, where Freitag had worked for thirty-eight years, healing thousands of patients, saving countless lives and winning hundreds of medical awards and citations.

Most of these awards and citations were up on the marble wall, along with pictures of Dr. Freitag with an assortment of wealthy benefactors and famous local celebrities and media people.

In the center of this memorial was a large oil painting of the great doctor himself, seated in a burgundy leather club chair, a leonine old man with a full head of silvery hair, wearing a navy-blue pin-striped suit, holding a stethoscope in his hands, his dark eyes in half shadow but touched by an inner light, smiling down benevolently on everyone who passed through the lobby. Redding had only looked at it once, but that had been more than enough.

———

Julie Karras was in a secure wing you only got into if someone opened the steel doors for you. Redding knew that Karen Walker would be somewhere in the same sealed wing, probably in Pod Three.

The hall was dim, lit only by the glow from the nurses' hub at the head of a T-shaped section. It smelled of bleach and hospital cooking and gave off that late-night hospital hallway vibe, a mix of insomnia and boredom and fear. The duty nurse, April Cotton—her husband, Luke, was a Flagler County Deputy—watched him coming up the hall over the top of her reading glasses. Redding was a good-looking man and he always hit her girl radar with a silvery little *ping*.

"Jack, honey, you look like shit."

"Thank you for that, April. I feel much better now."

"I'm sorry. I just mean you look so tired. Did you get the runner?"

"Not yet. But we will. You've got Karen Walker checked in, right?"

April gave him an eye roll, but all she said was "Yes. The little dear is in Pod Three."

"How is she?"

"A handful. They've sedated her. With a brick, if I'd had my way."

Redding took that in.

"How far down is she?"

"She's okay. It was just an Ativan. You going to talk to her?"

"In a minute. Is Mace around?"

"Not now. He went down to talk to the ME. They're doing the PM on the sister, Rebecca?"

"That was fast."

"The ME was available and Mace wanted all his ducks in a row before they got into it with Karen."

"They doing toxicology?"

"Oh yes. Behavior like that is pretty extreme. They're looking to see if she had anything spiking her up."

"Anybody do that with Karen?"

"Yeah. We did a work up on her. Other than some intermittent asthma, she's perfectly healthy. No sign of drugs. We did all the blood work. She's been drinking a lot lately, but there's nothing in her veins that explains her behavior, if that helps?"

"It clarifies things. She on a watch?"

"Suicide?"

"Occurred to me."

"No. But she's scheduled for a psych eval tomorrow. You think she might?"

Redding gave it a moment.

"No. Murder, maybe."

"Yeah, me too. They've got a camera on her, but no restraints."

"Okay. By the way, I saw Luke down at the site."

"Yes. He and Danika Shugrue and most of Day watch are doing the house-to-house thing. He called me a while ago, asking about Julie, how she was doing."

"And how is Julie doing?"

"Head traumas worry everybody. They've done an MRI and an EEG. Comes up nominal."

"Nominal? That's good, right?"

"Yeah. It is. She had a brutal headache and she was pretty wired up. You can't give a head wound any sedatives, but LQ came out a while ago and said she had finally gotten to sleep."

She hesitated, looking up at him.

"Can I ask…is she in trouble?"

"No. It was a by-the-book shooting. She put three rounds center mass. Stopped at three. Lot of experienced cops wouldn't have done as well. If there's any grief coming, it belongs to me."

"You? Why you?"

"I left a rookie to deal with two kidnap victims while I took off into the woods after the runner."

April leaned back in her chair, shook her head.

"Jeez, you Catholics. Don't hunt guilt. It already knows where you live."

"We'll see. Where's she at?"

"Four oh six. Down the hall to your left. Tippy toes, okay?"

Redding gave her a look. She smiled at him.

"You know what I mean."

———

Redding pushed the heavy door open as quietly as he could. Marsh was in a chair, tapping at his iPhone, looking dead beat. He tensed up, and then relaxed when he saw it was Redding.

Karras was on the bed, covered with a pale yellow blanket, her eyes closed, her head wrapped in a gauze bandage. Her lips were half-open, her face slack in sleep. She was hooked up to a heart-and-vitals monitor, her heartbeat slow and steady.

They spoke in whispers.

"How's she doing?"

Marsh looked tired. He needed a shave and his uniform shirt was rumpled. Redding was surprised to see that his beard was partly gray. He'd come on duty at eight that morning, sixteen hours ago.

"She's finally got to sleep, no more than an hour back. She's pretty wrecked about the shooting."

"Good for her."

"I got my portable shut off. You have any luck with the runner?"

Redding let out a breath, watching the monitor numbers flicker and pulse.

"No. Marine units went back and forth. Nothing."

Marsh shook his head.

"Whole thing has me a little freaked out, Jack. I can't see how that bitch could have lost us so fast. It was…"

"Creepy?"

"Yeah, a little. And the thing with the dogs? What was that all about?"

"No idea."

"Forensics get anything off the truck?"

"I haven't been back at Depot yet. I just left the scene. You want me to bring in one of the night guys? You look pretty tired."

Marsh suppressed a yawn.

"I am, but I promised her I'd stay. I want to be here if she wakes up."

Karras stirred under the blanket and they both turned to look at her. Her eyes were open.

"Sergeant Redding—"

Redding walked over, looked down at her. She looked maybe fourteen right then.

"How you doing, troop?"

She smiled, or tried to.

"Head hurts. And I'm having trouble…remembering details."

"That's shock," said Redding. "Normal reaction to stress."

"Did you get her?"

"No. She's in the wind. But we'll find her."

Karras closed her eyes for a moment.

"What about the sister? Karen?"

"She's in a lockdown unit down the hall."

Julie looked a little surprised.

"Under guard?"

"Yeah. We've got two PWs on her door."

"Good. Keep them there. Got any charges?"

"Pending. Right now we're telling her she's in Protective Custody."

Karras smiled weakly.

"You're trying to get her to talk. Without a PD there."

"That's the plan."

Karras nodded, seemed to drift. Redding and Marsh were easing away when she opened her eyes.

"Have you talked to her yet?"

"No. Just left the Intracoastal."

"That where you're going now? To see her?"

"Yes."

She closed her eyes again.

"Will she be cuffed? In restraints?"

"Restraints? Probably not, if we're trying to sell her on Protective Custody and get her talking."

Karras was almost gone now. In a voice they could hardly hear, she said "I've been lying here awhile. I've been thinking about that girl, Karen. Be careful around her, Sergeant—"

"Hey, after today? Call me Jack."

"Just watch yourself. There's something really wrong in there. Jack."

————

Pod Three was a serious change of state from the rest of the lockdown wing, originally intended as a containment area if ever any of the various extinction-level plagues the CDC was always gleefully predicting actually happened. Until that happy day it was being used as an informal Psych Ward and Observation Unit.

Cameras everywhere and every door had a double-walled glass window reinforced with chicken wire and a pass-through slot to use if the patient inside was in quarantine. As Redding slid his magnetic card through the lock slot on the entry gates he could see a state trooper tilted back in a chair halfway down the dimly lit hall.

As the doors hissed open the trooper got up, hitching her duty belt and arching her back to get the stiffness out. She was a sergeant, just like him, a tall blonde named Pandora Jansson. She smiled at him as he came down the hall. As Raymond Chandler once said, it was a smile Redding could feel in his hip pocket.

One of the Flagler County guys had made the mistake of cracking the obvious joke about her first name while she was close enough to hear him. He only did that once, and no one ever came anywhere near that joke again.

"Hey, Jack," she said as he passed through the light column of an overhead halogen. "Man you look like shit."

"Well, that makes it unanimous," he said, taking her in because he was a guy and couldn't help it. In the Before Barbara years she and Jack had spent six months in a kind of carnal close-quarters combat that had nearly killed them both. The heat was still there, but banked down deep.

"How's the kid?"

Jansson rolled her eyes—Redding was getting the idea that Karen Walker had that effect—

"Ever see that old movie *The Exorcist*?"

"That bad?"

"Well, so far no projectile vomiting. But the night's young. Let's go see."

She used a key card to open the door, shoved it back. "Hey, Karen, sweetie pie, somebody to see you."

The room was dimly lit by a bedside lamp, and decorated in anemic pastels. It smelled of Lysol and floor wax and whatever hormones the kid in the bed was putting out. There was a dresser on one wall, bolted down, and a couple of lime-green plastic lawn chairs, too fragile to use as a weapon. A one-piece stainless-steel sink and toilet set stood in a corner, partly shielded by a curtain.

As they stepped into the light, she sat bolt upright, her face in a red knot. They had gotten her into a set of Hello Kitty pj's. The effect was pretty jarring when she finally got her outrage in gear.

"I want a lawyer," she snarled. "I want one right now! And where are my parents? Why aren't they here already?"

That got Redding's attention.

Was it possible that she didn't know?

Yes. It was.

"We'll get to your folks in a minute—"

"Lawyer. Now. I want a lawyer. And I want my parents. Why aren't they here yet? They have to fix this."

"Honey, you don't need a lawyer," said Pandora. "You're not charged with anything. You're in Protective—"

"Can I leave right now?"

"Well—"

"Then get me my parents and a fucking lawyer. My Dad works for the US Government and he can really fuck you over if you don't—"

"Yeah?" said Jack, interested. "What part?"

"What part of what?" she said, distracted from her rant.

"What part of the government does your daddy work for?"

"He works for the Army Corps of Engineers. He does frantic archaeology stuff—"

"Frantic?"

"She means forensic archaeology," said Jansson, who had read the Fernandina PD report on the family while she was sitting out in the hall.

"Remember Kennewick Man? That skull they found at a dam they were building? If they find bones or historical remains at a construction site or a pipeline route, Walker and his team are called in to analyze and preserve it."

"Yeah," said Karen. "That stuff. He's a big deal in the federal government and you're not. So get me a fucking lawyer!"

"A lawyer to do what?" said Redding, pulling up a chair and sitting down beside the bed. Jansson went back to a wall, leaned up against it, folded her arms.

"To get that thing shut off, for a start," she said, pointing at the camera in the far corner of the ceiling. Redding was watching her and there didn't seem to be any trace of fear in her. And if she kept asking for a lawyer with the camera running, they were going to have to get her one.

"Karen, we can't shut that camera off. You've been through a terrible experience and we need to monitor your—"

"Where's Becca?"

Redding studied the kid for a moment. She gave it right back. Eyes like blue stones.

"She's downstairs."

"I want to see her."

"Time for that later."

"What are they doing for her?"

"Not a lot. She's still dead, so that's a problem right there."

He heard Pandora Jansson shift her feet, her belt leather creaking, a theatrical and disapproving sigh. Pandora could pack a lot of meaning into a sigh and a belt creak.

Karen didn't flinch.

"That fucking bitch cop shot her."

"That's right. Three times."

"She could have just aimed for her knee or something. She didn't have to *kill* her. We were both, like, traumatized and in shock and stuff. Becca didn't know what she was doing, and that fucking bitch cop shot her dead anyway. My parents are gonna sue your whole stupid—"

"Your sister used a steel club on my trooper. Tried to kill her. Getting shot is what happens when you assault a police officer. And there is no such thing as shooting to wound. My trooper could have shot your sister in the shoulder and she still might have died. You ever drop a big rock into a pond, and watch the waves go out? That's what the body does with a bullet. The body is packed with lots of stuff that goes bad when it gets hit by a bullet. If you were kidnapped, why did your sister attack the officer who was rescuing you?"

Long silence here, and Jack let it run.

"It wasn't like that. It was…complicated."

"So she didn't kidnap you?"

"No, well, like in the beginning, no…but then she got all control freaky on us."

"So you weren't free to leave, then?"

"No. She had all the money. The keys. The phones and stuff. We had no choice but to stay."

"Okay. Tell me how it all started."

"Look, I really want to talk to my parents."

"When was the last time you saw your family?"

A flicker, a shadow across her face.

"I don't know. Couple weeks ago. Why?"

"Where was that?"

"At our place. At Amelia Island."

"What were they doing, last time you saw them?"

She sat back, folded her hands in her lap, looked down at them.

"They were… We weren't getting along so good."

"No. Why not?"

"We wanted to take a trip. They didn't want us to go. We had a fight."

"Where were you going?"

"To New Orleans. Diana was paying for the whole trip. Mom and Dad weren't crazy about it, but Diana convinced them it would be, like, educational. A history thing, you know, the Old Quarter and all that Civil War stuff. Diana knew all about history, antiques and jewels and lockets. She was, like, an antiques dealer? Diana is… She was in the truck with us? She's the one who…like, kidnapped us."

"She have a last name?"

"Bowman. Diana Bowman."

Jack didn't have to tell Pandora to run that name. She already had her iPhone out and was logging in to NCIC.

"Okay. We'll get back to Diana Bowman later. So your parents didn't want you to go on a trip with this Diana Bowman person?"

"Yeah, because, like, we had to be back in school in September, but, well, they changed their minds and in the end, they were okay with it."

"So, you weren't fighting? They told you that it was fine with them?"

"Well, not me *personally*. Diana and Becca said they were cool with it. Diana told me to go wait in the truck. She and Becca came down in maybe an hour, said it was cool with them if we went."

"Have you talked with them since then?"

"Diana did. On the phone. Letting them know where we were and that we were okay."

"But not you and not Rebecca?"

"No. We sorta didn't want to, actually. They can be…preachy. It was nice to be out from under them. They're, like, real religious. I mean, totally nuts about Jesus and being saved. Gets old fast."

"I can see that. Tell me about this Diana Bowman. Where did you meet her?"

"On the beach. And then later we all went to a party. In Fernandina Beach. A private house up there."

"What kind of a party?"

The kid got a little sly looking.

"You're gonna have trouble with this, I bet. It was *girls only*. Get it? Or do you need an emoji?"

A deep sigh from Pandora. She looked up from her NCIC connection. Karen looked over at her, and Pandora looked back with intent, but said nothing.

"We're gay, my sister and me. Got a problem with that?"

Jack said nothing, and so did Pandora.

"Anyway, we wanted to go, and Mom and Dad wouldn't let us. So it was a *thing*, okay?"

"Was this Diana Bowman also gay?"

Karen thought it over.

"I think she was, like, flexible."

Jack nodded, let it hang there for a while.

"Okay. Flexible. So this Bowman woman, she got to be a pretty big deal in your life, big enough for you to defy your folks and go to New Orleans with her?"

"Well…we sorta got into three-ways with her, Becca and her and me. She was staying at Amelia too, so we had, like, some time with her. It got real…intense. Got the picture?"

"We get the picture. Is that how it went weird? Because of the sex?"

"No. Not then. But we were all pretty tangled up with each other, and with Mom and Dad and Alyssa being in our faces all the time, it got kinda sticky, you know, trying to get together?"

"I can see that," said Redding, trying to look sympathetic. He wasn't good at sympathetic looks.

"Yeah, well, and after a while Mom and Dad sorta thought we were seeing too much of her."

Pandora suppressed a "no shit, Sherlock" comment, but she failed to suppress the snort.

"But they ended up letting you go to New Orleans with her?"

"I…I think so."

"You *think* so? You were there, weren't you?"

"Like I said, I was in the truck, waiting for them."

"Your parents?"

"No. For Diana and Becca."

"Okay, right, sorry to keep asking the same questions, but I'm trying to get this all straight. You didn't actually *see* your parents when you left? They didn't come down to say goodbye?"

"No. But Becca said they were okay with it."

"Did you believe her?"

Her eyes flicked away, came back.

"Well, when they came down, Becca and Diana were all sorta like OMG and WTF, like maybe there'd been a big fight. But they said no it was all cool…so we left."

"But you had some doubts?"

"Well, yeah…but I really wanted to go to New Orleans, so if my folks were, like, totally pissed I figured we'd get to have the trip anyway and then deal with the hassle when we got back."

"Easier to get forgiveness than permission?"

"Exactly! Sometimes you gotta, you know, assert yourself. Be an adult. Parents have to see that."

Karen's eyes flicked up to Jansson, and then back to Redding. Both cops got the clear impression that she was starting to get the big picture.

"Look, I gotta know, how much trouble am I in?"

"So far you're not in any legal trouble. You haven't been charged with anything. You're in Protective Custody because this Bowman woman is still out there—"

"She is? I thought you were all chasing her—"

"She got away. She's a fleet little thing, give her that."

A brief flicker of something in the girl's eyes.

Unreadable, but there.

Fear? Pleasure?

"So she's still a threat to you. Even if you went willingly in the beginning, you're still a minor, and she's committed an indictable offense by keeping you under her control, and we are right now trying to sort this all out. That's why you're here."

He took a deep breath, changed gears.

"Look, Karen, you're a sixteen-year-old kid. No matter what the hell went on back at Amelia Island, or even what you tried to do to Trooper Karras—"

"I didn't do anything! That was all Becca! On account of her being in shock and shit!"

"Okay, fine. No matter what, there's only so much trouble you can be in, because you're a juvenile—"

"I can still go to jail!"

"Yeah. For juvies, it's like a tennis camp, only with razor wire. Even that's a worst-case scenario, given the circumstances. Any good defense attorney can make a case for your state of mind, fear of death, even Stockholm syndrome. I doubt it will even get to a trial. This will be pled down, or sent over to Psychiatric for evaluation. And when you're eighteen, it's all wiped anyway. So all we've got is this clusterfuck we're looking at, and if you help us uncluster it, you'll be doing yourself a favor—"

The door opened, and Mace Dixon developed into the room. He was wearing his anvil face. But he didn't say anything, just took a piece of wall next to Pandora Jansson.

After a cautionary look at Dixon, Redding went back at Karen, who was staring at Dixon as if he were a cave bear. He clearly scared the hell out of her. Good timing. Exactly what was needed here.

"Look, Karen, the best thing you could do for yourself right now is tell us the truth. We can see you're dancing around it. So quit that. You suck as a liar. Do yourself a favor and just lay it out."

"I told you, she kidnapped us, sorta, and—"

"Honey, that's total bullshit, and everybody here knows it. Including you. The inside of the truck was like a Panama City condo at Spring Break. It was a rolling Mardi Gras float, complete with the beads and the beer cans. Had to have your hands free to pop all those beer cans—"

"It wasn't like that. We were hostages!"

"Hostages for what? Give me a free beer or I'll kill these girls? Look, kid, don't talk. Just listen. Okay?"

She opened her mouth to say something but Jack waved her off.

"You were in New Orleans, stayed at the Monteleone, according to the hotel records, all three of you in the same room. What'd she do, tie you and gag you and sneak you up the freight elevator in a room service cart? There's hotel security video of the three of you playing in the rooftop pool and having party drinks at that Carousel Bar thing off the lobby."

He took a breath, letting what he was saying sink in to the girl's limbic system, where fear and self-preservation lived together in a too-small room.

"So, our IT guys have found security camera video of you pumping gas into the truck at an

Exxon station in Mobile while your sister and this Diana woman went into the store and came out with subs and a six-pack. And more video of you guys having burgers and white wine at a Ruby Tuesday on I-10 outside Tallahassee. Karen, honey, this whole thing was a rolling holiday, which is fine with me, except it ended with your sister trying to kill my trooper and getting her ticket duly punched."

Redding was lying about the security videos—they were still hunting those—but he could see by her expression that she was buying it all the way down to her toes. Silence, while she took that in and they let her.

"Come on, Karen," said Pandora, in a softer voice. "Get this off your chest, whatever it is."

More silence, her head down, looking at her knees, and then she lowered her head to her knees and started to cry. Pandora—no sigh this time—crossed the room, sat beside her on the bed, put an arm across her shoulders. Karen slipped sideways and came into her.

Redding and Dixon said nothing, did nothing.

Finally Karen shook herself free, accepted a tissue from Pandora, took in a shaky breath and looked up at Redding.

"Look. You don't know what she can do. You don't know what she…what she *is*."

"No, we don't," said Pandora, in a soothing purr. "So help us here. What is she?"

"I'm not supposed to talk about it! Diana warned

us. If we talked about it, then bad people would try to *use* it."

"Use what, honey?" said Pandora.

Karen wiped her eyes, let out another ragged breath, shredding the tissue with her fingers.

"The Shimmer. Diana can use the Shimmer."

The cops ping-ponged a WTF look around at each other, and Pandora came back to Karen.

"And what is the Shimmer?" Pandora asked, staying soft.

"It's inside everybody. It's what leaves you when you die. Like with Christ and that Shroud of Toledo thing. When he died he burned his image into it. You can look it up. There are pictures. Diana said what Christ had was the Shimmer, like we all have."

"Like a soul?" asked Pandora.

"Well, maybe…whatever, it's what leaves you when you die. Diana says they've actually weighed bodies that died and they were lighter by this tiny little bit."

"Sounds like a soul to me," said Pandora.

"Or, what do you call it?" said Jack. "Bio…biomechanical…"

"Bioelectric energy," said Dixon, his first words since he entered the room, his voice a bass rumble. "It's what the body runs on."

Karen, startled by his voice, shook her head, eyes into the middle distance, going inward, remembering.

"No not like that," she said. "Mom and Dad believe that the soul belongs to God. But Diana believes that the Shimmer belongs to anybody who can use it."

"Use it?" said Pandora. "How would somebody be able to *use* the body's energy?"

Karen was vibrating in Pandora's arms.

"She can...*travel* on it. She can use it to take her...take her back in..."

"In what?"

"In *time*."

"In time for what?"

"Not that way. She can use the Shimmer to go back and forward. Through time."

They all looked at each other, the message clear: *Okay we are now in the presence of batshit crazy. No sudden moves and avoid eye contact.*

Pandora kept her face straight, rolling with it.

"Okay, honey, are you saying that Diana can travel through time?"

"Yes. She uses the Shimmer."

"And you've *seen* her do this?"

"No...but she's like real old. She *remembers* stuff from a hundred years back. Like when we were in New Orleans. She knew all about the old places—"

"Like what?" asked Jack, intrigued in spite of himself.

"I don't know. She showed us a place where she said she had an apartment back then. The Pontalba?"

Jack knew it.

The Pontalba was on Jackson Square in the French Quarter. It was the oldest apartment house in New Orleans. Perhaps in America. It was famous. Why was that woman spinning this complete horseshit to a couple of gullible teens from Missouri?

"Did she tell you how old she was?"

Everybody was thinking, *Rubber Room, Rubber Room*, but they just listened quietly. All the deeply crazy ones sooner or later end up in a room full of silent and attentive cops.

Karen was breathing quickly, tense and shallow, as she thought about the question.

"No. But, well she knows all about St. Augustine back in the fifties. The 1950s. When we drove through she was saying, 'Well, this used to be where Marty's Restaurant was, and this was where we used to listen to bluegrass at the Driftwood, and this used to be the Monterey Court Motel where she hooked up with some Italian mob boss every afternoon, and that big building used to be the Alka…Alka Seltzer or something—"

"The Alcazar Hotel," said Jack, amazed that the kid could remember all the old names. "It's now the Lightner Museum. And she's saying she used to go to all these places? Back in the fifties? Didn't you think she was sort of bullshitting you, honey?"

"Yes, at first. But she *knew*…she knew so *many* things. Hundreds of different places. She named them all, empty lots, burned-down places, places that were all boarded up. And she sounded…like she *missed* it all. Like she was telling us about happy *memories*. Places she *loved*. It was in her voice, you know?"

"So she talked a lot. Did she say anything you can remember that seemed, I don't know, nuts?"

"Like what she was *already* saying wasn't nuts?"

"Yeah, I get that. I mean, anything about what she was all about, who she was, what she wanted, why she was doing all this crazy stuff?"

Karen went quiet.

"Well, yeah, there was this thing about…what do you call it? A gold thing you put pictures in?"

"A locket?"

"Yeah. A locket. She was always talking about them, these locket things. Like she had a real OMG BFF about them. If we ever went near an antiques store, she was all over that. In New Orleans, that was like almost all we ever did, hunt for some stupid locket."

"Did she collect them?"

"No. It was like she was looking for this one specific locket. Nothing else would do."

"She say why?"

"I don't know. Sort of. You know, like it was a lucky charm or something. If she found the right one, then she'd be happy."

"The right one?"

"Yeah. Like there was this one perfect locket, one she used to own, and she had lost it somewhere, but she couldn't remember where, and if she could just find it, then everything would be okay, like? She was sort of a bore about it, actually."

"I get that. She is looking for this magic locket. She's obsessed with it?"

"Yeah. Yes, like, *totally*."

"Because her…what, her happiness was all tied up in it?"

"Yeah. I think, underneath all the rest, the sex, the money, the thrills, that locket was always on her mind. After a while, me and Becca tried not to remind her about it, she was so, like, *fixed* on finding it."

Jack took that in, filed it.

"Okay. You're on the road, you've all gone down memory lane with her, in New Orleans and St. Augustine. Did she talk about this… What it is? The Shining?"

Karen didn't like the question. Her body stiffened up.

"You mean the Shimmer?"

"Yes. The Shimmer. Did she tell you how the Shimmer works? How does she call it up? How does she use it? How she can ride it back in time?"

This seemed to trigger a serious panic attack. Karen went white, started to tremble, and then got short of breath. Very short.

"She… I'm not supposed to say. If I say it, she'll know. She'll come and she…she…"

Now she was gasping, began to struggle for air.

"My puffer… I need…my puffer…!"

Everyone reacted to that.

Karen's face was getting whiter. Dixon pressed the Emergency button by the door, and Pandora started rubbing Karen's back.

Jack picked her backpack up, but didn't pass it to her. He rooted around in it—it had been gone over by the nurses—and found a pale blue cylinder with a little plastic mask attached. She reached out for it—hesitated—her breath was coming in short sharp wheezes and the intake breath was like a stone sliding down a grate—

"No...mine...mine is *silver*..."

"Was what, honey? Silver what?" said Pandora, just as the door slammed open and the charge nurse was suddenly right there, a lean black woman with serious command presence, who shoved everyone aside and hovered over Karen, who was still shaking her head, trying to speak, and that terrible wheeze—

"Quit fucking around and gimme that," she said, snatching the asthma puffer out of Jack's hand and putting the mask tight against Karen's nose and lips, her right hand on Karen's back.

"Come on. Slow and deep, honey...yes...again..."

Everyone watched Karen as she pulled the mist in, her eyes wide as she fought for air. The charge nurse was strong, steady, confident. Jack was thinking, *Minor case of asthma like hell*—

And then Karen tensed, arched, went into a convulsion, bent into rigid upward bow, began to make a high-pitched keening sound—pure distilled agony—the charge nurse said something along the lines of Holy Fuck and hit the Code Blue button above the bed…a few seconds later a crash cart crew piled into the room and shoved the cops back against the walls and everybody started doing all sorts of very intense and cool and competent professional "stat gimme ten cc's roll her roll her now okay she's not breathing she's in cardiac arrest gimme the paddles everybody clear okay again clear" stuff like you see on *Grey's Anatomy*…

———

…and none of it mattered a rat's ass, because the kid was stone dead in a little less than four minutes. The look on her face would stay with all of them forever.

In the stunned silence, after they had stared at the dead girl for a while, the crash doc shook himself like a wet dog, checked the wall clock, and said, "Okay. Subject female Walker, Karen, declared dead at one seventeen hours this a.m., note the time and log it."

———

After the crash team had slowly shuffled out and things had gone quiet again, Pandora looked down at the kid and said, "Shit."

"No," said Jack. "Not shit."

He bent down and sniffed her lips, came back up.

"Cyanide. It was in the puffer. That bitch set her up, planned this all out, just in case they got caught. It's probably why she set them up to attack

Julie Karras. She figured it would get them shot. She was half-right. This was just a backup plan."

"How do you know?" asked Dixon. "About the cyanide?"

"I've seen it before. Chuco Barbarini. The Vizzini witness?"

"Oh yeah," said Dixon. "I remember."

Another long pause.

Dixon got the Crime Scene guys started on their way. And they were still alone with a dead girl. She had outlived her sister by about twelve hours. She was rigid and arched. Her face was a horror, her eyes wide-open. They stared down at her for what seemed like a long time.

"Well *shit*," said Dixon.

"I already said that," said Pandora.

"Given the circumstances," said Dixon, "it's worth saying again."

Pandora went quiet. They all did. Then she said, in a tentative voice, "Did either of you guys, like, *see* anything? When she died. I mean, right *then*?"

That took a second to register.

"What?" said Jack. "You mean like a flash?"

"The Shimmer," said Dixon, his tone dismissive.

"I don't know," said Pandora. "Just, well…anything?"

"I saw a bunch of crash cart crazies accomplishing dick all," said Jack. "There was no flash of light. No Shimmer. Jeez, Pandora."

"I don't know," she said, not convinced. She was looking at the security camera now. Because she had seen…*something*. A flicker…something like a strobe light…but the crash cart guy had been wearing glasses and maybe it was just a reflection of the overhead hitting one of his lenses…but the security cameras were running…

And maybe it would be…

Forget that, she decided.

That's just nuts.

Or maybe not.

"Anything come out of the postmortem on Rebecca?" asked Jack, talking to Dixon.

"Nothing much. Cause of death we know. Signs of recent sexual activity, consensual."

"Okay," said Jack to Pandora, "and what did you get from NCIC on this Diana Bowman?"

She smiled a kind of "oh, you're gonna love this" smile.

"Well. Pretty common name. Lots of hits. However, one was kind of interesting."

"Yeah?"

She pulled out her phone.

"A Diana Victoria Bowman, DOB October 30, 1963, with an address in Raleigh, North Carolina, was listed as Missing Whereabouts Unknown over two months ago. Missing Report was actually filed by her banker. Apparently she had no other relatives or regular friends. According to the Incident File, the banker noticed that her accounts were being drawn down, not all at once, but regularly. It was out of her pattern. Last known location was a private resort in Key West."

"He try to reach her?"

"Yeah. He contacted her by email, and she got back to him, said everything was fine, that she was going to be doing some buying overseas and she needed cash for that. But he didn't quite believe it. He said the *tone* was different. Like it wasn't her writing the emails. Missed some in-jokes between them. So he tried to call, staff said she was out or the calls went to voice mail every time. She never responded."

"Buying overseas? What sort of buying?"

Pandora smiled at him. "Exactly the right question. Antiques and estate jewelry."

That got their attention. Pandora held up a hand. "Like they say on The Shopping Channel. Wait. There's more."

"Okay. Shoot."

"The resort is restricted."

"You mean like gay?" said Dixon.

"I don't mean cheerful," said Pandora.

"A lesbian resort," said Jack.

"Not that specific. Services catering to the LGBTQ Community."

"What?" said Dixon. "No separate cabanas for the Two-Spirited Gender Fluid folks?"

"Out in the Annex with the Gay Republicans, I guess," said Jack.

"I believe that qualifies as a clue," said Pandora, quite pleased with herself. "I'm still waiting for the compliments."

"Better than a matchbook cover from the Blue

Dahlia Bar with a Lennox phone number written on the inside," said Dixon.

They gave him a look.

"Turner Classic Movies. *The Big Sleep* was on."

Another long silence.

Karen remained dead.

———

"What do you make of all that Time Travel Ride the Shimmer horseshit?" asked Dixon.

Jack shook his head.

"Total lunacy. But the kid sure bought it."

"What about all those old places?" asked Pandora, making a quiet personal decision to look at the security camera footage of Karen Walker's death as soon as she got the chance. "I don't know much about Old Florida."

"Far as I could tell, she was right about pretty much everything," said Jack. "My grandfather used to be a homicide detective in St. Augustine. Back in the fifties."

"Yeah," said Dixon. "Clete Redding. He was a legend. They were still talking about him when I was in the Academy."

"Yeah. Big Clete," said Jack, remembering. "When I was still a kid, he used to tell me all about those old bars and hotels. Meyer Lansky saw the potential. The whole east coast of Florida from St. Augustine to the Keys was Mafia territory. Sam Giancana, Albert Anastasia, the Genoveses, the Vizzini outfit, they were all down here, cutting deals with Batista over in Havana. The Alcazar Hotel was a big mob base in the fifties."

There was more to the story, something darker, but neither Redding nor Dixon wanted to get into that.

"All gone now?" asked Pandora.

"All the Mafia guys are gone," said Dixon, who knew as much about Old Florida as any cop living. "At least as players, although the Vizzinis are still active, supposedly legit, cars and real estate. What we have now, the Crips and Bloods, the Cubans and the Salvatruchas, the Zetas, the Iranians, they're six times meaner and eight times stupider. Sometimes I wish the Mafia was back. At least you could reason with those guys."

Silence, again.

"Well," said Pandora, after a while and with a final sigh, "looking on the bright side."

"What would that be?" said Jack.

"She never had to hear that her mother and her baby sister were dead."

"Yeah," said Jack, "there's that."

selena contemplates the past and the past contemplates selena

Morning, bright and early, and the sun glimmering out there on the Intracoastal, a sinuous file of brown pelicans gliding serenely above the water, inches from the surface… Selena stood at the old man's back door and watched the river through the screening of his backyard lanai, sipping a delicious black coffee and enjoying a quiet moment with nature before she got back to work.

She finished the coffee and walked back down the hall toward Will Coleman's compact little office, where he kept his iMac computer and a printer and a battered old filing cabinet.

She had already gone through his emails and paper files and was pleased to learn from a printed statement that he had $34,962.07 in his savings account with Regions Bank in St. Augustine. That the VA was in charge of his care and they were, as usual, heroically failing to deliver any. That he had no family and apparently no living friends on this side of the continent, and that, according to a long and ragged string of scathing letters and emails, all of his neighbors were niggers and kikes and spics and rag-head goat fuckers and he despised every last one of them.

From which she inferred that the neighbors were unlikely to check up on the old bastard until there were vultures roosting on his rooftop.

And there was a purple Post-it note stuck to the back of his Mac with what looked like a handwritten list of all his passwords for various banking and internet sites.

She checked them all and found out that the second from the bottom worked on his Regions online banking account, and the second from the top gave him "Platinum Access" to Darling Buds of May, which was, according to his internet history, a much-visited European porn site, featuring pigtailed girls in schoolgirl outfits, all of whom were guaranteed to be eighteen years of age or older and all of whom looked about twelve.

How lovely. She couldn't have chosen a more deserving host. It was as if God was watching over her as she continued what was beginning to feel like her lifelong search.

As she passed Will's bedroom she looked in on him. He was still and silent and would stay that way forever, finally at peace, freed from all pain, freed from his bitterness and race hate, freed from his tormented perversions, freed from what looked to Selena to have been a rather tiresome life.

Selena felt pretty good about herself this fine

morning. She had done him a real kindness, and the happy thought warmed her heart as she stood there for a moment in the doorway, considering what she should do with the corpse, which was going to become a problem soon, even with the air-conditioning in his room set on high.

Perhaps naked and into the swamp late this evening, with a heavy weight to keep him down while the local fauna bit and nibbled and gnawed him into something safely unrecognizable? But remember to take a pair of pliers to his teeth, what few were left, dental records, in her experience, being an important forensic detail. Messy work, but hadn't she seen some gardening gloves and an old apron out in the lanai? Anyway, first things first.

She turned the computer on, waited for it to open, humming a melody from the hit musical *Hamilton*, which she adored, both for its music and its important message, and which she intended to see in New York as soon as she could find the time.

The screen brightened—a picture of a much younger Will on the stern of a big sports fisher, surrounded by a smiling crew and two other guys his age, grinning like a fool and holding up a massive barracuda-like fish she recognized as a wahoo…

…and she was in.

She went straight to Google and typed in Jack Redding Florida Highway Patrol.

She got multiple hits. The top twenty were taken from local TV and newspaper accounts of a fatal car crash that had occurred on Highway A1A at the Matanzas Inlet Bridge on Christmas Eve of the previous year.

She read all the accounts twice, noted all the names—Barbara and Katy and the doctor, Anson Freitag. Pictures of Freitag's widow, Helga, in full-mourning black, standing by the graveside, being held up by a tight group of what had to be family members, daughters, sons, grandkids and hundreds of other mourners, gathered to say goodbye to a much-loved and celebrated pillar of the community.

No sign of any Highway Patrol Honor Guard, no cops of any type and certainly no Jack Redding in the background. There were a few shots of the funerals for Barbara and Katy, buried side by side in a grove of royal palms, Jack in dress blues, backed up by a full FHP Honor Guard, and hundreds of police officers, deputy sheriffs and the men and women of the Florida Highway Patrol. A lovely sunny day but filled with a cold January light.

An interesting contrast, and something to think about—a breach, a rift, between the Freitag set and most of local law enforcement, with Jack Redding at the center of it, the pivot and focus.

Pictures of Barbara and Katy and Jack Redding all together in a picture taken by the pool in the Casa Monica Hotel in St. Augustine—she knew the place well—Redding was a big muscular man with a careful smile, Barbara a lovely brunette with a full rounded sensual figure, and Katy a wide-eyed pink-skinned shapeless human-larva thing in a straw hat and water wings.

Another one of them taken on the fantail of a huge five-masted sailboat off the coast of what looked to her like the Cayman Islands, another port she had visited often, usually to check on her accounts and to top off the various bribery funds that kept her bankers loyal.

Past joy guarantees Future grief.

Anything that makes you deeply happy will one day become your most bitter loss. After her first encounter with the Shimmer, before she even knew what it was and that it was possible to exert some limited control over it, the Shimmer had taken away everything she had ever loved.

She closed her eyes.

For a brief moment she was back at the Pontalba and a jasmine-scented breeze off the flowers in Jackson Square was sighing through the gauzy curtains around her open window and she was happy and safe with her mother's gold locket in her little hand, half-asleep, drowsing…and then it was…all gone.

Taken away by a black gibbering demon thing rushing into her room…a knife blade glittering in the sunlight, slick with new blood—and the sadness came flowing back, as it always did, a black tide of grief and loss.

And then the Shimmer took her away.

Selena had never again allowed herself to become attached to anything or anyone.

———

She sighed, shook herself free of that dark memory, went back to Google and looked for other references, and she got multiple hits. Court transcripts, television coverage, newspaper articles, going back for several years.

Jack Redding wasn't a simple patrol cop.

He was part of a statewide task force called Serious Crimes Liaison, a multiagency operation that investigated organized crime and gang operations all over northwestern Florida.

He had been involved in several violent collisions with gang members and professional armed robbers in Jacksonville and the surrounding counties. He had shot and killed five men and one woman in what you could only call Old West–style gunfights in the violent streets of Jacksonville. Multiple citations for bravery, wounded twice, Florida State Law Enforcement Officer of the Year three years ago.

Selena dumped the stories and pictures into a file and hit Print. While the little Canon chugged out the pages, she sat back in the chair and thought about the implications.

A hard man, his whole family suddenly gone, now a wounded animal, almost feral, with no other passion in his life but hunting criminals. And now he was hunting *her*. A dangerous man, a gunfighter, a killer just like her, a man to be taken seriously.

She switched into a database that gave her tax

rolls and property titles, drilled down to Flagler
County as the most likely place to look, and after a
few false starts and a lot of furious clicking found
herself looking at an aerial shot of a ranch-style
house at 32 Avenue A in Crescent Beach, registered to one Jack C. and Barbara Louise Redding
and assessed for taxation purposes at $956,000.
She zoomed in on it and found herself looking at
a very nice not-so-little oceanfront property.

Not at all new—it had the look of a place put
up in the fifties—it even seemed familiar to her,
someplace she had seen before—but it was a common enough style in Florida, so perhaps not. It was
beautifully maintained and even had an in-ground
pool inside a large Florida-style screened lanai.

Looking at the price and the location and the
condition of the house, she found herself idly wondering what sort of money a sergeant in the FHP
would usually make, and how he had managed to
acquire such a prime piece of coastal real estate
in the first place.

The assessment roll information wasn't helpful
since it was confined to the property taxes and
the various utilities bills generated by the house,
and she didn't have access to the IRS's records,
although she knew people who did.

But contacting those people was a risk she only
took when she had a pressing need, and she wasn't
seeing that here. Not yet anyway.

What she needed was an angle on him, a way

to distract or derail him without the unacceptable risk of a personal confrontation.

While she had a great deal of confidence in her ability to overcome ordinary civilians—lonely middle-aged women, unsuspecting suburbanites, gullible teenage girls—she had no illusions about taking on a hardcore killer, and it was blindingly clear to her that Jack Redding was hardcore.

And underneath everything else, like a dark shadow in a lake, was this very faint trace-memory of his name, Redding. It pinged in the deepest recesses of her past, but she could not quite bring the memory up into the light.

Redding.

But perhaps not *Jack* Redding.

———

She went back into the web, hunting for another Redding, someone who could conceivably have had some remote connection with her at some point in the past. She quickly discovered that when you simply type the word *Redding* into Google, you get a whole lot of information about the town in California, about how beautiful Mount Shasta is in the sunset, how Shasta Lake is slowly regaining its water levels now that the snowmass in the Sierras is melting, and lots more about a company called Redding Tool and Die…hit after pointless hit.

The World Wide Web was an idiot savant and perfectly willing to serve up page after page of meaningless data for as long as she was willing to sit there and take it. When she got thirteen pages in and was informed that bus fare from Milwaukee to Redding was $215 one way, she shut the machine down and walked away.

She poured herself another coffee and went back to stare out at the Intracoastal, where the marine traffic was starting to look like I-95 on the Memorial Day weekend.

She watched as an FHP police boat churned past a floating barge packed with teenagers and putting out a rumbling bass beat she could feel in her chest from two hundred yards away.

Bass beat.

Distant thunder.

A storm coming in off the Atlantic, a black disc of cloud slowly turning as it came, the cell wall clearly marking off the last of the twilight as it wheeled ponderously in, its interior filled with crackling blue fire.

Distant thunder, lightning flaring inside the cell wall, a beach house, twilight.

Redding.

When the trace memory came flashing up out of the pool and filled her mind, her chest went tight and her breathing stopped and the skin on her back rippled with a slithering chill.

Redding.

But not Jack Redding.

Clete Redding.

———

Her lungs encased in ice, her heart hammering against her ribs, locked in denial, she went back to the computer and typed in that name. The answer came back in the form of an obituary column in the *Florida Times-Union*, dated September 23, 2008.

LEGENDARY JACKSONVILLE HOMICIDE COP DEAD AT 87

Cletus "Clete" Redding, the controversial homicide detective who was credited with single-handedly bringing down the Vizzini Crime Family in 1957, is dead of an apparent heart attack.

Redding was famous for a violent confrontation that took place on Saturday, August 31, 1957, in the Vizzini family compound outside St. Augustine, during what was later described as an investigative visit that was met with an unprovoked assault by several members of the Vizzini family. Redding had arrived there unaccompanied by any other officers, which was contrary to departmental policy.

By the end of the gun battle, several senior members of the family were dead and the family never regained its previous status in the criminal underworld of northern Florida.

Redding's wife, Mary Alice (née Kearney), died in an unexplained single-car crash on old Highway One (now A1A) at Matanzas Inlet on Friday, August 30, 1957, a day before Redding's confrontation with the Vizzini syndicate, an event which some have speculated may have been a factor in what was called at the time "The Saturday Night Massacre."

Redding's only child, Declan, was seven at the

time and for safety reasons was sent to live with relatives for several years afterward.

Redding's body was found by a family friend on his antique cruiser, the *Siren*, last Saturday evening. A decorated Korean War Veteran who served with the United States Marine Corps and fought at Inchon and the Chosin Reservoir, Redding was a Detective First Grade with the Jacksonville PD Robbery Homicide Division from 1954 to his resignation, under something of a cloud, in 1963, when details of his alleged connections to Organized Crime and the Batista regime in Cuba came out during a Florida State Legislature Inquiry into Mafia-related activities in Florida during the 1950s. While Clete Redding denied the charges, and fought to clear his name for decades, the shadow of corruption never quite departed.

The Commission accused him of provoking the gun battle at the compound to remove witnesses to his criminal association with the Vizzini syndicate.

This was never proven and was vigorously denied by Redding himself.

In spite of this cloud, Redding then transferred to the Florida State Highway Patrol, where he served with distinction as a staff sergeant in the FHP until his mandatory retirement in 1993 at the age of 65.

Cletus Redding is greatly mourned by son, Declan, 58, daughter-in-law, Rose, 56, and his grandson, Jack, 23. A private family service will be held at the Cathedral Basilica of St. Augustine at a date to be determined, with commission of his ashes

at sea to follow. Donations to the Florida Highway
Patrol Fallen Officers Fund in lieu of flowers would
be greatly appreciated by the Redding family.

———

"His grandson, Jack" didn't have to mean what
she was afraid it meant. If it were true… Well,
it *couldn't* be true. It would change…everything.

But the police connection was troubling. Police
work was often an inherited calling.

She went to Florida Vital Records and started
digging. It took her another hour, and when she
confirmed it, she sat there for a very long time,
staring at the birth certificate.

**Born to Declan Michael Redding
and Rose Redding (née Carmody) at 3:56 a.m.
on Thursday, June 6, 1985, son Jack Christian,
seven pounds nine ounces.**

So Jack *was* Clete's grandson. Which meant that
Jack Redding's wife and child were killed on a
bridge over Matanzas Inlet, and his grandmother
died at almost the same spot back in 1957.

She spent some time trying to work out how
this could just be a strange coincidence, but something about it pinged again in that deep dark part
of her memory.

She had eventually come to understand that los-
ing pieces of the past the way she did was a side
effect of the Shimmer; the memories would often
come back, but only in a fragmentary way and

only when something—some scent, some trick of the light—in this case the memory of a long-ago storm—triggered the return, the way thunder or the rolling boom of a cannon fired over a lake will often bring up the bodies of drowned men. Once again, she took this in: Jack Redding was Clete Redding's grandson.

The birth notice sat there on her screen, quietly pulsing with threatening implications. She went away. She was still looking at it an hour later, but her mind was far away in the past, in the twilight on a deserted Atlantic beach, watching a giant disc of black cloud filled with lightning come wheeling in to the shore, eating up the stars, trailed by black night, the wild waves seething and the air filled with rumbling thunder.

When she came back, still deeply shaken, she knew what had to be done. But it was full dark by the time she knew how she was going to do it.

At midday, after they had both managed to get some sleep—not together—Jack and Pandora met at the Serious Crimes offices on the sixth floor of the Depot. The IT guys—actually three women and one guy—handed Jack a fat envelope filled with printed reports detailing where the trio had been, including the Hotel Monteleone in New Orleans—there were digital copies of the hotel security camera footage that showed the Walker girls and "Diana Bowman" drinking at the Carousel Bar and swimming in the rooftop pool.

Jack liked that detail; the bluff he had run on Karen Walker turned out to be reasonably accurate.

One of the techs had worked on a screenshot of the three of them at the bar, isolating and enhancing a shot of the woman calling herself Diana Bowman. She had printed a full-color shot and included it in the packet.

Jack slipped it out and studied it for a while, then handed it to Pandora. She was looking at an attractive full-bodied, black-haired, green-eyed woman of no particular age—not young however—with high cheekbones, full red lips, her face caught in a sideways smile as she brought a glass of wine to her lips.

She was striking rather than beautiful, and the little black dress she was wearing looked to be made of raw silk. Studying her, Pandora thought, *cold and sexy and sharp as shattered glass.*

"This gone out yet? As a BOLO?"

Jack shook his head.

"No. Not yet. I think we should sit on it for a while."

"You don't want her to know we have a face shot."

"No. I think she's still close. I don't want her to run, or change her look too much."

She handed the shot back to Jack.

"If she's been doing this for a while, she'll change her look as a matter of tradecraft."

"Maybe. But seeing her picture all over the media will sure as hell drive her deeper," he said, looking at the photo, feeling again that sensation that he had seen her, or a picture of her, somewhere in the past.

"What I don't get," said Pandora, "is where the hell is she right now? I mean, it's like she just stepped off the planet."

"Yeah. My guess, she's gone into somebody's house, maybe a deserted one, maybe she's got hostages… Look, how about this?"

"I'm listening."

"Thank you, Frasier Crane. She went dark just a few minutes after we chased her into the Intracoastal. Right there in that neighborhood—"

"Flagler County guys went door-to-door all over those streets. Everybody checked out."

"I know. But…somebody missed *something*. There has to be a ripple someplace, where she dove deep. Know what I think? In one of those houses around there, something's not right. Mace is doing a press thing today."

"One o'clock. If he shows up for it. He hates the media more than steamed broccoli."

"Yeah, so, what if we get Mace to ask all the people in that neighborhood to get out there, phone, go knock on everybody else's door, check up on each other? See if somebody doesn't answer, somebody looks scared when they come to the door—"

"Sounds like a great way to get a civilian shot if they actually do turn this woman up. She does guns. She's a psychopath. A neighbor stumbles on her, she'll stick a gun between his eyes, walk him inside, close the door and kill everyone in the house. Then go back where the guy came from and kill everyone there too."

"Then do phone checks. Text. Emails. All that social media stuff. Anybody who ought to answer and doesn't. Anybody who sounds weird."

"Long shot."

"Worth taking. I'll ask Mace to get it out there."

Pandora, distracted, was looking at her iPhone.

"Okay. Got a message from Mullvahill."

"The autopsy on Karen?"

"Yeah," she said, reading it. "You were right. It was cyanide, in an aerosol form."

"That doesn't sound like an easy thing to do."

"Not that hard. Mix it with water, or even a light olive oil, so the droplets will stick better. Add some CO_2 from a cartridge. The puffer is already an atomizer. Aerosol just means a bunch of tiny droplets. Would get the job done."

"And it did. You know a lot about this. Ever killed anyone? I mean, other than in the line of duty?" Pandora had shot two men dead during a mall robbery. She gave him a sideways smile.

"Not *that* way. I do remember almost killing you one night in the Casa Monica."

"I was fine. I just faked the heart attack to get you to stop."

"Bullshit. It was pure rodeo and you were never going to buck *me* off. Anything from the Feebs?"

The IT team had submitted the enhanced screenshot to the FBI's NGI-IPS facial recognition database, which scanned over 500 million photos taken from criminal, military and driver's license shots in all fifty states, plus, it was rumored, the NSA's massive database of passport and security camera surveillance shots taken at airports and travel hubs over most of the civilized world, and a lot of the uncivilized parts, as well.

The Feds liked to say—privately—that if your face wasn't in their database, you didn't exist and should probably stop paying your taxes.

"So far nothing," said Jack. "But they're still scanning other databases, so we'll see."

"Millions and millions of faces on the FBI database—most of them not criminals—and she *isn't* one of them? Seems to push the odds a little, no? How the hell do you stay off the grid that long?"

"I don't know," said Jack, putting the shot back in the file. "We'll have to ask her, when we run her down."

"Literally?"

"If she gives me an excuse. Let's go see Mollie."

———

Mollie Zeigler, the head of the Forensics team, a big-shouldered red-haired woman with an amiable nature and an eye for critical details, met them at the gates of the Motor Pool Forensics lab in the basement of the FHP Depot building. After asking about Julie Karras and hearing that she was doing okay and would be released the next day, Mollie walked them back into the garage area, which looked exactly the way you'd think it would. Big red metal toolboxes everywhere, three hoists and the comforting smell of spilled gasoline, motor oil and ozone.

Only thing missing was a lanky bald-headed guy in stained blue coveralls with a white oval name tag with *Dwayne* on it in black script. And maybe the Playboy calendar stuck on Miss May 1977.

The big black Suburban looked like it had been hit by an RPG. It was scattered all across the floor and over several tables along the garage wall and a crew of technicians had spent the night going over seat cushions, floor mats, visors, windows, wheels, and slip pockets looking for... Well, they had no idea. Anything that looked like a clue, basically.

Jack was primarily interested in the backpacks and duffel bag that had been in the rear of the truck when he and Julie Karras finally ran it down.

The Forensic unit people had laid the three backpacks and the tan canvas duffel bag down on a long table, with whatever had been inside spread them out neatly in front of each one.

Mollie Zeigler walked Jack and Pandora along the table, pointing out what she found to be interesting.

"Most of this is just girl crap," she said, indicating the array of items—makeup and mirrors, various bits and pieces of clothing, tampons, rings, an iPad Mini with a cracked screen, candy wrappers, gas and hotel receipts. "The Suburban might as well have been a Dumpster. These were not tidy people. Nothing but beer cans and candy wrappers and cigarette butts. Got DNA for the Walker girls off the butts, but nothing on the runner. Now, the duffel bag here, this was more interesting."

They had reached the end of the long table. The duffel lay flat, emptied out, but in front of it was a collection of very old jewelry—rings and cameos and bracelets, beaded handbags, antique watches, brooches, framed pictures, hatpins and scissors and various kinds of hand mirrors, and what looked like a collection of dark brown sticks and stones. Everything was coated in a fine gray powder. Zeigler pointed to the dark brown sticks and stones.

"These are mostly phalanges, and the lumpy bits are metacarpals—"

Pandora, who had been a corpsman in Iraq, said, "You mean *bones*? Human bones?"

Zeigler gave a her a wry smile.

"Hand bones, to be particular. These look to have belonged to an elderly woman, suffered from arthritis, Caucasian descent, light drinker, mainly white wine from the Alsace region, a good dancer—"

"Okay," said Pandora, tumbling to it. "You're heating me up."

"Maybe a bit," said Zeigler, winking at Jack.

"But why bones?"

"See this white ash stuff? It's dried river mud, silt and sand and granular vegetable matter. Coats everything, all to the same extent. So my call?"

They waited. Mollie liked her dramatics.

"A grave that has at one time been underwater. Probably a flood that receded, leaving the silt. And so long ago that everything dried up. The mud tastes a bit salty."

"Jeez," said Jack. "You didn't lick the damn bones, did you?"

"'Course not, you moron. I look like a zombie?"

"Then how do you—"

"I touched one of the lockets and tasted my fingertip—"

"Mollie! For Chrissakes it coulda been fucking poison!"

"Don't go getting the vapors, okay? I had one of the guys try it first. When he didn't keel over and go into convulsions, I gave it a go."

"Which one?" said Pandora, looking around at the techs, all of them involved in things mechanical, none of them paying any attention.

"Yugo, over there in the corner. Not the swiftest starling in the murmuration, if you know what I mean. And he's crazy for me. Anyway, since it's salty mud, I'm thinking a grave near the ocean, or a tide pool, something like that."

Jack was looking at the tumbled collection of antique jewelry. It looked like junk to him. Why the hell would anybody want to steal a duffel bag full of junk jewelry?

Mollie was watching them work through it.

"Want to know where I think it all came from?" she said, letting the drama build up again. She had their attention.

"How can you tell?" asked Pandora.

Mollie reached into her apron pocket, pulled out a little gold locket, battered, and if there had been a picture inside it was long gone, but the locket glimmered in the work-light glow, standing out brightly from the rest of the muddy relics.

She held it out in the palm of her calloused hand, used a grease-stained finger to flip it over. The back was deeply engraved, a flowing script, done by a skilled hand. The engraving was still perfectly clear.

Mammaloi Marraine
Ma Cherie Minou
FWC

"It's in French," said Jack, which got him a look from the women.

"Wow," said Mollie. "You should be a cop."

"Yeah, yeah. Can you read it?"

"Yes. It says, '*Mammaloi Marraine*, my darling *Minou*,' which means *cat*. And then the letters *FWC*."

"FWC? The initials of the guy who gave her the locket?" asked Jack.

"Could be, but I don't think so. I think this locket comes from Southern Louisiana. Probably New Orleans. I looked up the word *mammaloi* and it's gris-gris for a witch, a priestess of gris-gris magic. And *marraine* means *godmother* in Creole patois."

Pandora was considering the locket.

"Did you shine this up, Mollie?"

"No. It was like that. Good catch."

"Yeah. It being the only thing shined up means that, out of all this stuff here, this locket was the only one to get some special attention."

"From whom?"

"Can't say," said Mollie. "But my guess would

be from the woman you're looking for. Why? I have no idea. But the locket sure called to her. So maybe that's something to work on?"

"I get the patois words," said Jack. "But why aren't the letters somebody's initials?"

"They could be. But in that part of Louisiana the letters *FWC* usually mean Free Woman of Color. So taking all this in, and the bones, and the rest of the trinketry here, and the signs of flooding, and you get—"

"Katrina," said Jack. "August 25, 2005. All the graveyards got flooded, didn't they?"

Mollie was impressed, and showed it.

"Not all, but a lot. I'll bet if you had the silt analyzed, you'd nail it down solid. But that's my call."

Jack turned to Pandora.

"The Walker guy, the dad? Didn't Karen say he was with the government?"

"Yes. The Army Corps of Engineers."

"Yeah, but what did he do? Specifically?"

Pandora's face changed as she got it.

"Forensic archaeology. Which is—"

"Old bones and relics."

"Told you so," said Mollie.

"No, you didn't," said Jack.

"Well," she said, shrugging, "I was about to."

Jack looked at Pandora. She looked back. They were both thinking about what Karen Walker had told them, just before she died. That Diana Bowman was obsessed with finding a particular gold locket.

"You got anything pending, Pandora?"

"Two weeks vacation, long overdue."

"Yeah, yeah, but work related?"

"No. Nothing I can't free up. Why?"

"Well, unless Mace objects, I'm gonna take this one on. I want to ask this Walker guy if he knows anything about lockets, anything that might have to do with why Bowman got close to him in the first place. You in?"

"Road trip? All expenses?"

"Yeah. Road trip. And maybe I buy you lunch."

———

They threw together some traveling gear, checked an unmarked slate-gray pursuit car out of the motor pool, and headed north to Amelia Island, specifically to the Intensive Care Unit of Baptist General at Fernandina Beach, where Gerald Walker, the last Walker breathing, was, they sincerely hoped, still clinging to life.

———

Back at the Depot Mace Dixon was up to his garrison belt in a toxic spill of print reporters and TV newspeople, all of them wanting to know how a sixteen-year-old kidnap victim had managed to die in Protective Custody, which seemed, to the media pack, to be something of a contradiction in terms when you looked at the outcome, namely a dead girl.

Dixon was dealing with the barrage of questions as well as he could while keeping one nervous eye on the back of the Press Briefing Room, where a grim-looking rake-thin blonde woman named Marylynne Kostic was leaning against the wall, her arms folded, her face in Full Hatchet and her pale blue eyes locked on him the way a mongoose looks at a chicken.

In his heart Dixon wished he was on the road with Jack Redding and Pandora Jansson. He even closed his eyes and tried to make that happen—if he had ruby slippers he would have clicked them—but when he opened them again he was still *here* facing an angry mob of flying monkeys and those two ratbags were still heading safely out *there*, disappearing into the misty blue distance.

Dixon got them all to shut up, for a moment.

"Look, look—we'll get to the questions in just a second. But we—the FHP—want to ask you guys for some help here."

"Looks like you need it," said the carrot-head dork from CNN. Got a big laugh.

"Well, maybe we do. The woman we've been looking for—"

"Got an ID on her yet?" asked one of the bobble-head media chicks from the local affiliate.

"Not yet—"

"Got a photo? Must have from somebody's security camera."

"Not ready to comment on that yet."

This brought on a babble of objections, which, it occurred to Dixon, for only the fiftieth time, made them sound like a room full of geese. He held up a hand.

"When we're ready. But right now, we are working on the idea that the fugitive might have gone to ground right there in the Flagler Beach area. Flagler County did a house-to-house, but we think it might be possible that she slipped the net somehow, that she might still be in that area, in a house, maybe holding hostages. So what we'd like from the people of Flagler Beach is to check on their neighbors."

"And get themselves shot—" said Carrot Head.

"Not in person. Phone, email, text—whatever. And then if anyone comes across anything even remotely suspicious, they call it in to the Bureau of Criminal Investigations—*not* 911—the number is 850-617-2302—and we will investigate."

"You think she's taken hostages?" said Bobble Head Two.

"We have no information that she has. This is just a request for the people of Flagler Beach to do some very careful checking in their area to make sure everyone is safe."

"So release the picture you've got," said Carrot Head, and everyone started gaggling again, and at the back of the room the mongoose was waving her stick-figure arms and making angry mongoose sounds. Pointing at her, he braced himself and said, "Yes, Ms. Kostic, you have a question?"

She had several.

For an old man dying of multiple and competing causes, Tessio "Cocco" Vizzini was giving Death a serious run for her money. He was confined—perhaps *confined* was the wrong word—to a sun-lit and palatial upper bedroom suite in the large Italianate villa that sat inside the heavily fortified Vizzini family compound, which took up four hundred feet of prime Atlantic shoreline a little ways south of St. Augustine.

Now closing in on ninety-three years of age, he was a hunched and saggy hawk-faced man who always wore blue pin-striped suits and polished brogues and radiated the aura of a clinically depressed buzzard.

Tessio spent most of his days sitting in a battered leather wingback chair placed in the center of a graceful bay window, which opened up onto a marble-tiled terrace with a 200-degree view of the Atlantic Ocean.

His very complicated needs, medical, social, sexual and fiscal, were seen to by his extended family, a phalanx of armed retainers and an attentive staff composed mainly of pretty young female Guatemalan and Honduran immigrants, all of them illegally here and therefore at his mercy.

These servants earned every penny of their salaries because Tessio Vizzini was a harsh judge of service standards, and a single frown frequently resulted in the unfortunate recipient being flown back to Tegucigalpa a few hours later and dumped—not gently—out onto the tarmac, in an exercise the handlers liked to call *il rotolando*, which needs no translation.

On the intricately inlaid table set within reach of his arthritic claws were a decanter of grappa, a set of tiny crystal glasses arranged in military ranks and a box of Ghurka Black Dragon cigars. (For those of you who are not keeping abreast of the market for obscenely expensive cigars, the Ghurka Black Dragons retail for $23,000 a box.)

Tessio "Cocco" Vizzini had made his fortune in the 1950s through gambling and gunrunning and prostitution and heroin-and-cocaine selling, up and down the Florida coast and over in Havana. He had been on a "first-name and hearty *abrazo*" basis with Fulgencio Batista, and Meyer Lansky was his financial adviser—but he made his name because he liked to have people who displeased him thrown bound and naked into a lagoon at the edge of his property.

It was full of alligators who had gotten used to dining there on a regular basis. This was done for the entertainment of his family, and also to convey the standards of loyalty he expected from his capos and button men.

The Italian word for *crocodile* is *coccodrillo* but Tessio preferred to be called Cocco because that was so much sweeter on the ear. Today his ear, as furry as a hamster's butt, was tweaked and piqued by a familiar voice out of the far distant past, and he turned, creaking in his wingback, to watch as a woman who looked oddly familiar, was shown in by a slender Guatemalan girl in a tight black sheath dress.

As the woman came fully into the glimmering light that filled the room, Tessio's heart lurched in the brittle bone cage of his sunken chest.

She came to stand beside him, smiling down, her hair a black bell cut short around her oval face, her green eyes as clear as emeralds. He stared up at her, and wondered if he were dying.

"Aurelia," he said, in a harsh squawk, his lips working, his mouth suddenly dry. "It cannot be you, Aurelia. Am I dying? Are you a ghost, come to call me to God?"

"But it is Aurelia, Cocco," said Selena. "It is your Aurelia. I am not a ghost. I am here."

Selena leaned down to kiss him on the cheek, and he put a hand on her arm, to see if she were not a ghost. "But you haven't changed, *cara mia*. How long since I have seen you?"

She waved that away, said something about the surgical arts and good makeup, speaking over and through his puzzled expression, counting on the years to have slowed him down a bit, and his failing eyes would certainly help.

She found a little deck chair out on the terrace, brought it back in and sat down in front of the old man, crossing her legs in her tight little skirt as she did so, because even a ninety-three-year-old man dying of practically everything possible can't resist a pretty woman in a tight little skirt.

"May I pour you some grappa?" she said, leaning forward, taking the bottle up, smiling as she saw the familiar light fire up in his tired eyes. He watched as she poured out two glasses, handed one to him, making sure it was safely in those twisted and veiny hands, remembering how they had looked upon her body so long ago, brown and strong, taking and possessing.

Time is a thief, she thought, *sooner or later she steals everything you ever had.*

———

Selena passed a pleasant hour in polite and occasionally obscene reminiscences with the old man, who seemed to shed his years as they talked about the old times, about how they used to meet at the Monterey Motel on the canal and make love all afternoon, about the button men and *pezzonovantes* and the made men with silly nicknames and the Alcazar Hotel and the parties they had there and the wine that flowed like blood and the blood that

got spilled like wine…good days…golden days…
all gone now…all gone…

He patted her on the knee, let his hand rest there,
looking into her, seeing her. He moved back, creaking in his chair, put his hands back onto his knees
and let the silence come down and they both sat
there, in the westering sun, listening to the surf
and the wind in the lemon trees that lined the window walls.

He took in a long ragged breath, tilted his head
to one side, and said, "I know you have come for a
favor, Aurelia, and if it is in my power I will grant
it, but first I have a question, if you don't mind."

"Not at all."

"Aurelia, my dear *comare*, what are you?"

She sat back, putting on her *surprise* face although the question had been asked of her many
times before, although usually by people who were
about to be dead.

He waved her *surprise* face aside.

"No, no, please, *cara mia*. I am too old for games
now. I see you here before me, exactly as you were
when I was a young man. This is an *impossible*
thing, even with the doctors and the magic makeup.
Do not treat me as a fool. My eyes are not so bad
as you think. If you wish me to grant a favor, I require to know what it is you really are."

"What do *you* think I am, Tessio?"

"I have wondered about you off and on for many
years, after the family fell and you were gone. For a

time I thought you were some kind of *strega o demone o anche una fantasma*…a witch or a demon or even a ghost."

"Do you still think I am *una fantasma*?"

He considered her.

"No. I had my pet policeman look into your background—don't be offended, but a man in my position has responsibilities and hard things must be done…"

Selena knew the answer to her question before she asked it, but to maintain her cover she asked it anyway.

"And who was your pet policeman?"

His mood shifted from reminiscence to white heat. "That traitor, that murdering pig."

"The one who came that terrible night?"

"Yes. That man. Clete Redding."

"And what did he find?"

"This was the strange thing that for a while made me think that you were a demon. You called yourself Aurelia DiSantis. But he found records that said you were born Selena D'Arcy in New Orleans, in Plaquemine Parish, in 1909, five years before the Great War broke out."

He shrugged it away.

"So this is fine with me at the time. You seemed younger than your years. People change their names, they wish to leave behind an inconvenient lover, perhaps a bad experience, perhaps they avoid the law. This is done all the time. But the woman

I see here before me is not a hundred and nine years old, is she? The Selena D'Arcy name is of no importance to me. You will always be Aurelia DiSantis, but this fact is also before me, is it not?"

"And what have you decided?"

"Two things are possible. Either you are not my Aurelia DiSantis but an impostor come to play a cruel game on an old sick man. Or you really are my Aurelia DiSantis, and you really are one hundred and nine years old."

"And what do you believe?"

"I believe you are my Aurelia. Only my Aurelia could know all the things we have talked about this afternoon. What we used to do at the Monterey Court. I have never spoken of those afternoons to anyone, not even after my wife died. That is why I wanted you to talk about the old days, because I needed to be sure. And I am. But again I come back to my original question."

"Which is, *what* am I?"

He inclined his head, lifted his hands, palms up, a very Italian gesture.

Selena's heart had gone icy cold and her chest was clamped tight. She should never have taken the old man for a fool. He had never been a fool, because if he had been, he would have been thrown to his own alligators years ago.

She hesitated and he saw that, but he didn't try to ease the moment. He expected an answer, and if she didn't give him a plausible one, she could expect no help, and he might even have her walked out of the compound. Or worse.

"Tessio, I don't know. Maybe it's a genetic quirk, but I don't age. I don't know why. I mean, I do age, but it's very slow."

He sat for a time, considering her, and she felt a chill rising up from her belly. But in the end, he seemed willing to let her simple acknowledgment of her age stand.

"So you really were born before the Great War, and you are really one hundred and nine years old? Tell me. Why are you not insane?"

"Who says I'm not?"

He laughed, or at least showed his teeth, a row of yellow tombstones in gray gums.

"Yes. And who is to say I am not insane either, because I do believe you. Do you know why this has happened to you?"

Because of the Shimmer, she was thinking, but would never say.

"I don't know, Cocco. I just accept it."

"Do *you* think you are insane, *cara mia*?"

Yes I do, she thought but did not say. *The Shimmer has made me what I am.*

She smiled, touched his hand, kissed his leathery cheek.

"Yes maybe a little, *caro* Cocco. I know you used to drive me mad in our bed at the Monterey."

A silence came down, but it was an easy one. Finally, it was time for business.

"So, *carissima*...what has brought you to me after all this time? Is there something you wish to ask of me? Or of my people?"

She took a sip of grappa, which she loathed, and set the glass down with a silvery *ping*.

"You were talking about that Jacksonville detective. Clete Redding."

Vizzini struggled against his resurgent anger, grew sad in the memory of that night.

"He came like a black angel, killing as he came in the door—he had a...*come se dice in Inglese*—the gun that fires all the time?"

"A machine gun?"

"Yes. Like that. And two more pistols in his belt. He came for a meet, to talk about the death of his Mary Alice. We met down by the lagoon there. For no reason, he began shooting. He killed my Anthony, killed his cousin Sergio, my dear old friend Salvatore Bruni... They all died. Redding was shot many times I was told, but he would not fall down. Like a black wind he was. He never said a word, until the end, when he was standing in front of me, covered in blood, and all he said was 'Mary Alice.' Then he walked away."

He was silent for a while.

"Mary Alice was his wife, you know. She died the night before, in a car accident. Redding blamed us, our family, the Vizzini family."

"Was he right?"

Vizzini flared again.

"We don't make war on the families. If we have an enemy, we kill him. We are not woman killers. Child killers. It was a car accident, but he believed that we had done it. We did not."

Another silence.

"He died ten years ago, you know," he went on, "in his eighties, in his fucking *sleep*, on that boat of his, the *Siren*, the one he bought with money I gave him, like the beach house—also bought with money I gave him—like a brother he was—he should have gone into the lagoon with the rest of those betrayers those fucking snitches…but no, he lives into old age…in one single night he destroyed our family…we lost the respect of the other capos… the five families moved against our interests…the Traficantes, the Bonnanos…even Meyer Lansky turned against us."

He wandered into a raving reverie again and Selena let him go on for a while, pleased that his anger and his thwarted lust for vengeance burned so bright in his ruined body. After he had subsided once more, she leaned forward and touched him again.

"So," he said, after a pause, "why do you bring this man up now, after all these years?"

"He has a grandson, who is also a policeman."

Tessio's eyes narrowed.

"I have read of him. He is also a killer, like his grandfather. A capo in the highway patrol."

"Yes, he is a killer. He is also a problem."

"A *problem*? A problem for who?"

"A problem for *me, caro mio.*"

Gerald Jeffery Walker was still alive when they got to Baptist General. A charge nurse finally agreed to let them into the ICU pod, where they found Walker on the other side of a glass wall, a pale blond guy, big and rangy looking, but skinny as a bundle of sticks. He was lying in the middle of a matrix of tubes and drips and monitors, machines beeping and whirring in the darker shadows of his room.

His eyes were closed, and sunken, as if in death, his skin sallow and dry, his bony chest rising and falling, but he was breathing on his own, according to the nurse, a large black guy with a shaved head and a gold ring in his left ear and a barbed wire tattoo running right around his neck.

"He's lucky to be alive," said the nurse, in a low whispery rumble. "Nobody here can figure out how he made it. How many days and nights, lying there…no water. He shouldn't be alive at all."

"Can he hear?"

The guy nodded, his face solemn.

"He's awake. The shrinks have been at him, but he's wrapped pretty tight. You want to talk to him, I figure."

"If he can handle it," said Jack.

The nurse looked at them both, cynicism flickering across his face.

"You'd talk to him anyway," he said, but there was no malice in it. And it was true. They were cops, not priests. They said nothing.

"Yeah. He can handle it, I think. He looks like a geek but he has to be tough as a hickory stick not to be dead. He's not too far down. Docs have him on Valium, on account of he is seriously fucking blue."

"How much does he know?" asked Pandora.

"He knows his wife and little girl are dead because he was there when it happened. He doesn't know about the other two, the teenagers. But he's a smart guy and he can see that they're not here at his bedside praying for him. Mind if I ask…?"

"If I can answer it I will," said Jack.

"I heard the older kid got shot. But how'd the younger one buy it?"

Jack told him.

"And you were right there?"

"Yeah. We were."

The guy was quiet for a while.

"My name is Darnell Holt. I was a medic in Iraq. I know shit happens. Don't cart it around with you."

"Who were you with?" asked Pandora.

"421st of the 44th."

"Out of Fort Bragg, right? I knew some of your guys."

"You were there?"

"Corpsman."

"Isn't that 'corpse-man' now?"

"That was the *last* president."

"Good point. Let's go see the guy."

———

Walker heard them coming in the door. He opened his eyes but didn't turn to look at them. He kept his eyes on the ceiling. He opened his mouth, closed it, and Darnell Holt took a glass of water and dipped a sponge into it and wet the man's lips. Walker closed his eyes again, kept them closed.

"My guess…you're cops?"

His voice was as thin as spring ice.

"Good morning, Mr. Walker. Yes, we are. My name is Sergeant Jack Redding of the Florida Highway Patrol. With me is Sergeant Pandora Jansson, also of the FHP."

"That you, Darnell?"

Darnell stepped up, came within the man's sight line, put a gentle hand on Walker's bony shoulder.

"I'm here. You up to talking, Jerry Jeff?"

A pause while Walker worked on breathing.

"No. But I'm gonna do it anyway."

He turned to look at Redding and Jansson, took them in.

"What're you two, from the Vikings Unit?"

The tone was brave but his voice trembled.

"We're from the Florida Highway Patrol Bureau of Criminal Investigation."

"Well, you've come to the right place then. The crap Darnell is feeding me qualifies as criminal."

"You're on a saline drip."

"You could put some vodka in it."

Darnell stepped away.

"Mind if I stay in the room?" he asked.

Jack and Pandora looked at each other. Jack shrugged. Pandora said, "You're gonna have to keep it to yourself, Darnell."

He nodded, made the zipper move across his lips. Jack nodded to Pandora—she gave him a brief "why me" glare and then came to stand by Walker's bed.

"Okay, Mr. Walker—"

"You're gonna break my heart, you might as well call me by my first name."

"Okay…Jerry…"

"It's okay. They're both dead, aren't they? Otherwise they'd be here."

Pandora said nothing, but she put her hand on his arm. He closed his eyes for a time. Then opened them again.

"Did that…thing…do it?"

"In effect," said Pandora. "There was a car chase, your Suburban—we had a notice to watch for it since some of your relatives up in Florissant were worried about not hearing from you."

"Aunt Melanie. They told me. She calls every fricking day."

"So there was a watch, a BOLO, and Sergeant Redding—Jack—spotted the truck southbound A1A on the far side of St. Augustine. There was a chase, Jack and his partner ran them down, but the woman escaped. Got into the wetlands near the Intracoastal. Our guys pursued her, and Jack's partner, Julie Karras, stayed to help Rebecca and Karen. They were still in the truck, cuffed to the floor."

"Cuffed? Why?"

"That's still not clear. Trooper Karras got them out of the truck…and things went sideways. Rebecca attacked Karras with a steel baton—"

"Jesus. Why?"

"No idea. But it was pretty aggressive, and Karras had to defend herself… Rebecca was shot three times. I'm sorry to be the one to tell you this, Mr. Walker—Jerry."

"Was it…was it quick?"

"Yes. It was. Instant."

A silence.

"Rebecca…my own child…helped that thing put us in the storeroom. That day. The woman—she was calling herself Diana Bowman—man I shoulda checked her out—was that really her name?"

"No. The real Diana Bowman disappeared while on a boating trip off the Keys. The woman she was with apparently took over her identity, drained her accounts over a few months, and then she disappeared. Turned up at Amelia Island."

"So she…whoever she is…she does this all the time? Like some kind of parasite?"

"Yes, that's what it looks like. How did she manage to overcome you and your wife in the first place?"

"Easy. She had a gun and we didn't, but what kills me was Rebecca was the one who tied us up. Tied Alyssa, tied Marilyn… Marilyn was crying, begging her not to do it…but Rebecca was… ice-cold. As if she had been taken by a demon… it wasn't Rebecca at all… That Bowman woman changed her…changed them both in such a short time… We watched it happening, tried to put an end to it, but we never thought the girls would *turn* that way… The woman said that once they were gone they'd call the condo office and tell them where we were… I didn't believe that…and they never did. The hours, days—I could see Marilyn's watch—it glowed in the dark…for a while anyway… I stared at it…tried to get free…"

He stopped and Darnell gave him some water.

"I must have passed out… I remember waking up and I could still hear them breathing…then I was gone again…and when I woke up…there was this silence…and I could tell… There was a pretty strong smell…you know? And I figured I was in hell."

Here he paused, and closed his eyes.

After a moment, he said, "I prayed, you know? In the beginning. Prayed to Jesus, prayed to Jesus, who is my personal savior, prayed for him to come and save my wife and my little girl who I could hear dying right next to me hour after hour. Do either of you *believe*?"

Jack, who had until last Christmas, said nothing. Pandora, who tried to but couldn't manage it, said so. Walker took it in, closed his eyes.

"Well, *my* new position is the hell with Jesus and all his friends and family. *My* family died in a black hole praying with all they had and in the end there was no help coming from anywhere. What happened to Karen?"

Pandora was going to answer but Jack put a hand on her arm. "She was in Protective Custody, in a secure wing of a hospital in Jacksonville. She had an asthma attack, she asked for her inhaler and the nurse gave it to her. She went into arrest, the crash cart people did everything they could…"

Jack could feel Darnell and Pandora listening to his version of the events. They said nothing. Walker was quiet for so long they thought he might have fallen asleep. And then he spoke.

"Are they…trying to figure out what happened?"

"They are. They think her puffer may have been poisoned, but that's not clear yet. I'm so sorry about all of this, Mr. Walker."

"Don't be sorry. Go find that…woman…and kill her. She's purely evil and she needs to be dead."

"We do have a couple of questions, if you think you are up to it."

"Anything is better than lying here remembering. What do you need?"

"Did you have a lot of contact with her?"

"No. She was all about the girls. We hardly ever saw them, once they ran into her. She was up to our place once or twice before they left."

He seemed to recall something.

"Yeah, there *was* one thing. She was *real* interested in what I did for a living. She asked me a lot of questions about the way we did things, about the relics and jewels, the human remains. How we researched them, sorted them out. She wanted to know if we cataloged all the names in each crypt."

"And did you?"

"We tried…the records are incomplete…and as you know, they just sort of keep pushing the bodies in the front until the remains farthest back fall through a gap between the shelf and the wall. They drop into a *caveau*, like an open pit beneath the tomb. Where they get all jumbled up."

The cops took that in and both of them quietly decided to go for cremation when their time came.

"Anyway, the *caveau*, that's where we look for significant remains, if we're trying to determine race or cultural connections. There are names on some of the shelves. I had a list, but it was incomplete. Bowman looked at it—I thought she was just curious—but she scanned it pretty carefully, now that I think of it. And she asked me if I had come across a crypt with the name *Dorsey* on it."

"Dorsey?"

"Dorsey, I think. Started with a *D* anyway."

Jack made a note of that name—*Dorsey*—and let Pandora handle the talk.

"And had you come across that name? Dorsey?"

"It wasn't on my list, I know that."

"And the relics, the jewelry, you had some of these items with you, on Amelia, right?"

"Yes. We're helping relocate some cemeteries in the New Orleans area, part of a flood control project."

Again, a pause, and he seemed to go inside himself, remembering.

"You know, now that I think of it, *that* was when she got interested in the names, once she heard that the material was from New Orleans. You know, after Katrina. That's when she got real focused. Like it piqued her interest, the New Orleans connection. I had a box full of things taken from a crypt in New Orleans—rings and pendants, some scattered human bones—"

"Lockets?" asked Pandora.

"Yeah, a few of those."

"Were you aware that she took that material with her?"

A pause.

"No. I wasn't. Nobody told me. Jeez, that's not good. Those things are a trust, we have family members depending on us—"

"We've recovered them, Mr. Walker," said Jack. "She left them in your truck when she ran."

"*All* of them?"

"If you have an inventory record, we can check. But there was a lot recovered. A full duffel bag."

That seemed to calm him down.

Pandora took up the questions.

"Did you ever ask her why she was so interested in your work?"

"Yes. I did. She could turn on the charm when she wanted to, and this was early on. We hadn't started to worry about the effect she was having on the girls yet. She told me she dealt in antiquities, estate pieces, that kind of thing. She had a special interest in lockets. But only from a certain time frame."

"She tell you what that was?"

"Not directly. But from her questions, I figured she was talking about the years just before World War I…"

His voice trailed off and Darnell stepped in.

"You okay to go on, Jerry?"

"I'm… I want to help. But my mind isn't… It's all fogged up."

Darnell gave Jack and Pandora a sideways look.

"Yeah, look…we can pick this up later, Mr. Walker," said Jack. "You've been a big help."

Walker lifted a hand, said "Not yet. I got to know, where are the girls now?"

"They're at Immaculate Heart, in Jacksonville. You're thinking about…"

"Funerals," said Walker. "Yeah. I have to recover… I have an entire family to bury."

Pandora put a hand on his shoulder.

"We can't tell you how terrible this thing is. We all feel angry and sick about it. We can only promise that we'll find her."

"I've seen her up close, Sergeant Jansson. You be careful if you get close. She's not…like anyone I've even seen before. There's something strange about her. She knew a lot about the past, New Orleans in the teens and twenties, St. Augustine in the fifties…knew it like she'd actually *been* there."

"We've heard some of that," said Jack, not wanting to say from whom, and when. "She ever talk about her childhood, that kind of thing?"

"No…well, maybe. Only one thing she said, actually something she asked me, and it seemed to be a personal thing, not just about antiques and estate pieces."

"What was that?" asked Pandora.

"She had this thing about lockets, but like I said, only from a certain period. She asked me if I'd ever seen a small gold locket with something engraved on it. She was very specific. About the engraving. She had it memorized. I could tell."

"Do you remember what she said? Exactly?"

Walker went inward for a time, remembering.

"Yeah. I do. She said it was a little gold locket, oval, the kind with two spaces for pictures inside it. There was an inscription, an engraving, on one face, the letters *R* and *B* sort of entwined the way engravers do it. It's called a signet and it usually has three letters, the first initial, the second and, in the middle, the last name letter. And on the other side, also engraved, the words *To Bea from Will Xmas 1909*. She was pretty specific about it. She also said something weird… She said that it would have some dents in it, as if someone might have been teething on it."

In the back of Jack's mind, another ripple in the memory pool, a flash of gold this time. Pandora could feel him pulling back, going away for a moment, and she glanced at him, taking note.

"And had you ever seen that particular locket, Mr. Walker?"

He shook his head.

"No. I mean, in those years, before the Great War, lockets were all the craze. It started during the Civil War, and then Queen Victoria was wearing a locket with Prince Albert's image in it, as a mourning thing, so that made them really popular. Soldiers gave them to wives, or mothers, if they were going off to fight."

"So, there'd be a lot of them around?" said Jack, coming back. Walker nodded, fading.

"Hundreds of thousands."

"But she was after this *specific* one?"

Again a weak smile. His eyes closing.

A pause. They thought he had gone to sleep, and began to step away, but he spoke again.

"She was…the way she talked about it…she was *on fire* to find it. It was…"

"Important," said Jack.

"No. Not important. It was…it was *vital*. She *hungered* for that particular locket. It meant something to her...something personal... It was like she was...hunting it."

He seemed to pause, gather his energy.

"I think, when she told me about that locket, it was the one true thing I ever saw in her, that *need*. It was almost human. Then, I also think that because she told me about it, she knew she had to kill me. She had shown me too much. I had to die."

Walker subsided, went slack, and he was far down in deep sleep a moment later. Darnell checked his monitors, tweaked his saline, put a gentle hand on the man's chest for a moment, and then he walked them out.

"Any of that help?" asked Darnell.

"Yeah," said Jack. "It did. Is he going to be okay?"

"Yeah. I think he is. He's got some liver and kidney damage because of the prolonged dehydration, and of course he's pretty screwed up psychologically. But like I said, tough as hickory."

"Time will help, maybe?" said Pandora. Darnell looked at her, a wry smile.

"Time? Maybe. Maybe not. My opinion, he'll never be the same again. Nobody is. You lose your family, all of them, just like that? You're totally fucked up. Forever. That's just the way it is."

Pandora couldn't help glancing at Jack, but his face was a rock wall. They said goodbye and thanks to Darnell, gave him their cards and asked him to contact them if Walker had something else to give them. He said he would, and they left and all the way down in the elevator Darnell's words were running around in Jack's head.

You lose your family, all of them, just like that? You're totally fucked up. Forever. That's just the way it is.

———

When they reached the parking lot and their slate-gray cruiser, Pandora stopped Jack as he went around to get in behind the wheel.

"Nope. Gimme the keys."

"Why?"

"Because you're not driving."

"Why the hell not?"

"What Darnell said to us, that's been in your head ever since. You're totally fucked up. Maybe not forever. But you're sure as hell fucked up right now, and you shouldn't be driving."

Jack opened his mouth and shut it and tossed her the keys. When she had them rolling, she asked Jack where they were going now.

"Crescent Beach. My house," said Jack.

Pandora glanced over at him, saw he was dead serious. Put it in gear. Didn't ask why.

nostalgia...from the greek
nostos (to return home) and
algos (the pain)

It was roughly seventy miles from Amelia Island to Jack Redding's house at Crescent Beach. On the way down Pandora tried a couple of times to get Jack to tell her what the hell was going on, but he just shook his head and stared out the windshield so after a few miles of this she just gave it up and did the same thing. She did take the time to put on some chick-flick music, the theme from *Eat Pray Love*, which she knew Jack loathed, the film and the music, so there was that to enjoy as the miles unspooled.

They talked a bit about the name *Dorsey*, and Diana Bowman's interest in it. Pandora ran the name on NCIC as they got clear of Amelia Island, cross-referencing it with the name Diana Bowman. Nothing. Insufficient data. But she filed it away.

Dorsey, or something like it. She was going to talk to Jack about it but from the expression on his face, she could tell he was a long way gone.

The road was oceanside, and off her left shoulder the Atlantic Ocean was the occasional patch of cobalt blue seen at the far end of all the little alleys and side roads that led off A1A and down onto the beaches. Far out at sea a hard-edged charcoal-gray front was slowly turning like a galaxy in space, its vast and swollen belly pulsing with green light. Seabirds were wheeling and crying and there was a hot and sultry stillness in the air.

"Something big out there," she said, to try to get some kind of conversation going, but Jack just glanced past her, registered it, and went back inside himself. Sighing, Pandora hit the Weather Advisory on the MDT.

She got a radar image that showed a storm front that stretched from Bermuda to Nassau, that all-too-familiar shape, turning slowly counterclockwise and eating up all the light.

It was still being called a "tropical storm" but more times than not, on hot sultry afternoons such as this one, that was as useful a term as calling a terrorist attack a "man-made disaster."

"Look, Jack, I hate to disturb you while you're having fun being all silent and brooding, but maybe you should take another look at this huge black cloudy thing off there to our left?"

He did, and then he looked at the MDT.

"It's hours away, even if it does hit this part of the coast."

"Yeah, but if it does, do we really want to be doing whatever the hell it is we are going to be doing down at your beach house?"

Silence, then a non sequitur. Sort of.

"Actually it's not my beach house. Doesn't feel like it, anyway. It was my grandfather's place. For me, it still is. We lived over in Gainesville. Used to visit him during the summer. Sometimes I'd go alone. He and my dad didn't get along. Dad was a Democrat, they always fought about politics. Until my folks moved to Phoenix. He asked me if I wanted to stay with him, instead of going out West."

"You don't talk about your folks much."

Jack smiled, looking down at his hands.

"Dad has always been a little…ashamed…of Clete. Yeah it was 'Clete.' Clete hated all that 'Pops' or 'Poppa' stuff. With him it was either 'Clete' or 'Sir.' I went for 'Clete.'"

"Your dad is Declan, right? Why was he ashamed of Clete?"

She had an idea, but if Jack Redding was in a mood to talk—which happened, like, never—she wanted to give him room.

"Well. To start with, Dad was raised by cousins, Frank and Helen Forrest, because of the death threats Clete was getting, after that Vizzini thing. So Dad resented being sent away. Never really got to know Clete at all. And then it was the seventies, Dad was starting up his real estate business, most of his clients were Democrats, against the war in Vietnam, all that radical lefty shit. Clete was this huge fireball of a guy, fought in Korea, could still fit into his Blue Dress uniform when he was eighty. A hard man all the way to the end. Tough strong quiet."

"Gee. Remind you of anyone?"

Jack sighed, reached for the water bottle, offered it to her—she took a drink and handed it back and he drained half of it.

"And of course there was that Corruption Cloud. Hung over all of us, like that storm cloud building up out there. Mom and Dad wanted to keep their distance, because of their business I think, but mostly they were just ashamed of Clete, ashamed to be associated with the name *Redding*. Eventually they bailed out to Phoenix."

"Not you though."

"No. I stayed. I was in my teens by then. I didn't want to leave the coast… Dad didn't like it, but he agreed to let me stay with Clete. I don't know, maybe he was happy to unload me. I was a handful back then."

"And…?"

"And I loved the guy. He was larger than life, loved big hated big. He drank he smoked he got into fights. You either hated him or loved him. Most people loved him. The ones who knew him, I mean."

"I remember you telling me that his house meant a lot to him."

"Yeah. It did. He didn't come from money, his father was a coal miner in Pennsylvania."

"Oh man. An endangered species now."

"Were then too. Mine explosions. The Black

Lung. Cave-ins. Union Busters. So when he came into some money—"

He paused here, expecting a comment, but she had no intention of saying what the general rumor was. Jack looked sideways at her. He knew what she wasn't saying, and he liked her for it.

"Anyway, he had it built in the fifties. Cost him a couple hundred grand, a lot of money in those days."

"Worth a lot more now," she said, wondering where all of this highly unusual talk was going.

Jack turned the music down, but not off. *He may be a big red dog*, she thought, noting the natural grace that was always in him when it came to little gestures, like not turning off the chick-flick music he loathed, *but he's a gentleman.*

"Yeah, I guess it is. It was worth a lot while he was still alive, but he would never even think about selling it. You didn't say anything back there, about 'coming into money'—"

"And I never would."

"I know that. I know you pretty well."

"Now, there's an understatement."

"But I think, for Clete, the house was something he felt he had sold his honor for—"

"You don't believe that?"

"I believe that *something* happened, and that the house was a symbol of it."

"But if the house was a symbol of something he was ashamed of, why wouldn't he get rid of it?"

"Because I think that he did something about it, and after that the house felt…different."

"Something like that night he went after the entire Vizzini family alone?"

"Maybe that. But…there's something more going on. There was something else…"

"Going on, like in the present? Is this why we're going back to the house now?"

"Yeah."

"But what we're working on, finding this woman who killed the Walkers, that has nothing to do with your grandfather. Right? I don't get it. I mean, I'm fine with whatever we're doing, but…"

"If I tell you, you'll think I'm nuts."

She smiled.

"Honey, I already think you're nuts."

She could see he was thinking about telling her. But he didn't.

"I'm not gonna tell you. I'm gonna show you."

———

The storm had filled up most of the eastern horizon by the time they pulled up to Jack's rambling white stucco beach house at Crescent Beach. A hard onshore wind had risen and was ripping the tops off the rollers far out at the horizon line, a sawtooth ridge, churning and grinding. Pandora parked the cruiser under the carport, tucking it up close to Jack's lime-green sparkle-coat Harley Davidson Electra Glide.

They took a minute to wrap it up in a tarp and tie it off. Pandora didn't bother teasing him about the fact that he actually had a lime-green sparkle-coat Electra Glide in the first place.

Jack was somewhere inside his head and screwing around putting all the loose bits in the car port into the storage cupboard at the back so the storm wouldn't blow them all to Tallahassee.

She left him there and walked down to the end of the driveway, folded her arms and thought about that incoming front.

She also paid some attention to a boxy-looking white Mercedes SUV that was parked a hundred feet up the street. It stood out on this wide-open palm-lined avenue of rambling fifties-era homes.

Most of the cars tucked into their driveways were midrange American models—GMCs and Buicks, Fords and Chevys. The Benz just looked… wrong.

The windows were tinted almost black but she could see that there were two shapes in the car, and it looked like the one behind the wheel was on his cell phone right now. She had good eyes and could make out the plate from here: 939 XXZ.

Jack walked up to her just as she was pulling out her radio to call in the plate. At the same time, the Benz fired up, made a slow three-point turn and headed off up the street toward the A1A.

"What's up?" Jack asked, following her look as she tracked the Benz.

"Don't know. Benz just looked…wrong."

"That's the thing about a Benz. They always look sinister. Around here, if it's a white Benz, it's got a real estate agent inside it, and her name will be Tanya Something Russian and she'll be a five-foot-two-inch bundle of dry twigs in her mid-fifties with a lizard-skin neck and duck lips and Nancy Pelosi eyes."

The Benz turned the corner, was gone.

"Remind me not to ask you to describe me in twenty-five words or less."

"Hah. I only need three."

She put her finger on his upper lip.

"And I have three for you. None. Of. That."

———

The outside of the house may have been Old Florida in that fifties style, complete with a huge screened-in lanai out back that contained the swimming pool and a threadbare garden and a couple of barrel palms, but the interior was all Barbara Redding. Cool pastel blues and whites, open plan with a very modern kitchen in the back, soft white walls with really fine seascape oils and watercolors. One wall was covered from midway to the ceiling with framed photos taken by Barbara, who was—had been—a very gifted landscape shooter.

There were no people in any of her shots, and Jack had told Pandora that if she inadvertently took a shot and found out later that there were people hidden in it, she very carefully Photoshopped them into oblivion.

Pandora checked the fireplace mantel, where there had been a small collection of family portraits or photos taken when they were in the Caymans. They were all gone. There was nothing up in their place. Just a blank shelf. It said all there was to be said about Jack's state of mind.

She had been here before, a couple of times, for a pool party or on some police business, and she knew that the master bedroom where Jack and Barbara had slept was shuttered and locked, and had been since before the funerals.

Katy's room was also locked, and probably shuttered, as well. She hadn't looked, and didn't want to. Jack slept in the guest bedroom, at the back of the house, with a view of the pool. Or so he said. From the look of the long pale blue sectional, and the rumpled-up fake-fur throw lying on the back, Pandora was pretty convinced that if Jack slept at all, he slept on that couch. He was living like a guest in his own house. Or a ghost.

Jack walked through to the kitchen, poked around in the massive stainless-steel fridge, turned to ask her what she'd like.

"Are we still on duty?"

She was feeling a little edgy. She'd never been alone in this house with Jack. There had always been other people around. Now it was just the two of them. Their six months of carnal combat was on her mind. Ever since the deaths, Jack had been an emotional zombie. But somewhere deep inside her, Pandora still felt that...*ping*.

"As Robin Williams used to say, *fuck noo*. Ditch your gear. Call us in to Dispatch and tell them we're ten-seven on an investigation. What's the point of being sergeants if you can't pull rank now and then. I've got Red Stripe, Dos Equis or some of that Barefoot Pinot Grigio."

"The stuff you can get at Walmart for $7.97 a gallon?"

"Yeah. Nice big bottles too. You used to love that stuff."

"Way too much. Still do."

"Ice?"

"One."

He clanked and clattered around in the kitchen, came out with a glass of Pinot Grigio for her and a frosted Dos Equis for him. He handed her the wineglass, with the ice cube, stripped off his gun belt and harness, and sat down on one of the pale blue chairs. She maneuvered out of her gear and dropped the belt on the floor beside the couch.

"I remembered. About the cube," said Jack.

"I never doubted it."

"Actually, I remember *everything*."

She sighed, said nothing.

He sighed too, sipped at his beer.

"Feels a little strange, having you here."

"Yeah. Me too."

He looked around the house, and then out at the ocean, where the storm was rapidly eating up the sky. The wind was whipping the palms and eight brown pelicans went past in a perfect fighter jet formation, riding the currents.

He was still watching them sail past in a sinuous line, but he was speaking to her.

"Most of the time, I hate being here now."

"I know. And I don't blame you. You ever think of selling, maybe getting a condo? Easier to maintain? No bad memories?"

He shook his head.

"Not ready. Maybe someday."

"Just not now?"

He was silent for a while.

"It's not just about Barbara and Katy. It's about my grandfather too. He loved this house, and I kind of grew up here myself. That's a lot of history to sell off."

"But you're not happy here, are you?"

He grinned at her, a twisted smile.

"Well, honey, I'm not happy anywhere else either."

Pandora saw the pain right on the surface. Her heart went out and she wanted to get up and come over and sit next to him. She didn't.

She looked at his service piece in its holster.

He picked up on her look right away.

"No. Jeez no. You can relax about that."

"Can I?"

"Yeah. You can."

She believed him. Mostly.

She sat back in the couch, took a sip of her wine, watching him over the rim.

"Okay. So, are you gonna tell me what's going on? It's got something to do with this house?"

"Yeah. Wait here. I have something I need to dig out. It'll take a bit."

A gust of wind, much more powerful this time, and a sudden blast of rain crashed against the window. Jack got up, went over to a control panel by the door, hit a button. There was a muted hum and a fine steel mesh protection screen slowly drew down and covered the seaward windows. You could still see through the mesh, but the storm seemed a little more remote.

"What if the power goes?"

"It usually does," said Jack. "I've got an auxiliary generator. It'll kick on automatically. Don't worry. Under the stucco the house is solid stone. We'll be fine. I'll be right back."

He went off down the hall toward their storage area. She sat back, listened to the wind rising. The front was still miles out, but the forward edge was already ripping up the coast, like a circular saw spinning northward. Her cell phone rang—Dixon. She picked it up.

"Hey, Mace."

"Where are you guys? I'm watching this storm."

"At Jack's house."

A weighted silence.

"Okay. Well, you better stick there. We're pulling a lot of units off the street just in case this thing gets really ugly. No point getting all our rolling stock blown to Tallahassee."

"How'd the conference go?"

"You know the joke about the barrel? It was my turn in the barrel. How did it go up North?"

Pandora laid it out for him. And, after glancing

down the hall, she included the part where Jack had a big reaction to the locket description.

"And right after, he heads down to the house?"

"Yeah. With a bullet."

"And you figure it has something to do with his grandfather? Like how?"

"No idea. But talked about him, on the way down."

"Yeah? He *never* does that."

"Well, he did today. It was like something triggered him."

"Well, he's a hunter. Let him hunt. By the way, his idea about rechecking the houses down in Flagler Beach paid off. We're pretty sure she was in a house right down there, belonged to an old guy named Willard Coleman. Danika Shugrue and Luke…something?"

"Cotton."

"Yeah, Luke Cotton. They checked it out that night, and there was a woman there, name of Catherine Marcus, said she was one of those Helping Hands nurses. Had ID and she didn't fit the suspect description, although Shugrue said she had cream all over her face at the time, and she had just gotten out of the shower. They looked in on Coleman and he was breathing, had on one of those sleep apnea masks. So they bought the story and left. Today— after the press conference—one of the neighbors went to check on the guy, got no response, although his car was there. I sent a couple of units, but she was already gone. Place was thoroughly wiped, and that included the shower drain, so we're looking at a real pro. No sign of Willard Coleman, but somebody wired thirty thousand out of his bank account this morning."

"Couldn't they trace that?"

"They're trying. It's bouncing around between a bunch of European banks and a couple of them are run by some United Emirates consortium that is pretty hard to pressure from here. It's gonna take a while, if it can be done at all."

"Are they looking for Coleman?"

"Sort of. We figure he went into the lagoon. We'll find him. Or what's left of him. But at least we know she's been flushed out. We'd be out looking for her right now if it weren't for this damn storm. So fill him in, okay? What's Jack doing? I take it he's not there, in the room?"

"Not yet. He's back in the storeroom, banging around."

"Okay. Well, I'm gonna go batten down some hatches. You two stay there, okay? This thing will blow over in a few hours. I'll list you as ten-seven, but if I need you I'm gonna call."

"Look, while I have you, can you run a plate for me? May be nothing, but I'd like to know."

"Sure. Give it to me."

"Late-model white Benz SUV, Florida plates, nine three nine x-ray x-ray zebra."

"Where was this?"

"Just outside here, Crescent Beach, about an hour ago. Two people inside. Maybe more. Windows were tinted. It felt like they were watching this house, waiting for us."

"Just because you're a paranoid wacko doesn't mean they aren't trying to kill you."

"Yeah, well I've got my tinfoil hat on. But you'll run it anyway?"

Mace said he would, and then came another loaded silence. "So you'll be staying there?"

"Yeah. We'll be here."

"Yeah, well…well…"

"Relax, Mace. We'll behave."

"None of my business."

"Truer words have never been spoken."

"I just don't want either of you to…"

"Thanks, Dad."

He was gone and she set the phone down just as Jack came back up the hall, lugging a large clear plastic storage box.

"Sorry. This was way in the back."

He set it down on the coffee table.

"What is it?"

"Box of my grandfather's stuff. Collected it off the *Siren*, and some of it was in the pool shed out back. Mostly scrapbooks and stuff from when he was in the Marines, stuff from Korea. Some of his homicide files. But there's also this."

He rooted around in the collection—medals, some small photo albums, a couple of stacks of police notebooks held together with elastic bands, Zippo lighters—it all smelled of smoke and mold and salt water. He came up with a small black leather bag, held shut with a faded scarlet ribbon.

He opened it, tipped what was in it out onto the tabletop. Pandora felt her belly tighten. It was an old, engraved gold locket with small dents.

They both spent some time staring at it, which under the circumstances seemed like the only sensible thing to do. The wind off the ocean was building into a steady howl and columns of wild rain were lashing against the windows. The room grew dark as the cell wall came down on them like a coffin lid. Jack reached over and flicked on the table lamp beside the couch.

"Okay," said Pandora. "This I do not get. This is just nuts. This can't be the same locket that Walker was talking about."

Jack picked it up, put it into her open palm.

"What'd he say? 'To Bea from Will Xmas 1909'? And these little dents? They sure look like teeth marks. If this isn't the same damn locket, I mean, what are the odds?"

"Is there anything inside it?"

"I haven't been able to open it. It is hinged though, and you can see the edges. But the only way to get it open seems to be to break it, and I just…can't do that."

She held it in the palm of her hand. It seemed to pulse against her skin, but she knew it was just her own blood coursing. She shook her head.

"Neither can I."

Pandora set the locket down on the table, carefully, as if it were explosive.

"So. When Walker was talking about it…"

"Yes. I *recognized* it. I remember seeing it when Barbara and I moved in. Clete's stuff was all in boxes. We went through everything."

"And this was…where?"

"In a large storage box with all of his case files and notebooks from when he was with Jacksonville Homicide."

"Was there anything in them that explained this locket?"

"Maybe. I've never really looked. I thought the locket was just a thing he'd picked up along the way. It was in a shoebox along with one of his old casebooks. I've got it here."

Jack went back to the storage box, started rooting around in it again, came up with a Florsheim shoebox, and inside it was a worn-out leather notebook, bound with an elastic cord. The leather was cracked and seamed and may once have been a rich maroon but now it was the color of dried blood.

He laid the book down on the table, slipped the elastic off and gently opened it. Lying on the first page was a very old brown envelope, marked with a Kodak logo, held closed with a circular tab and a piece of red cord.

"Only thing that connects with the locket is that it was in this shoebox along with the casebook."

"So open it."

Jack unwound the cord and tipped the contents

out onto the table beside the locket. They were faded color shots, the old-fashioned kind with the rippled white borders. They were taken from what looked like the inside of a car, through the driver's-side window. Judging from the cars on the street it would have been sometime in the 1950s.

There were fifteen shots in all, and in each one was a black-haired and very pretty woman in a flowered sundress walking arm in arm with a big-shouldered, black-haired man wearing a light-colored double-breasted suit.

The shots tracked them along a broad street with a row of palm trees next to what looked like the bayside section of St. Augustine and ended when they got to a red-and-white motel called the Monterey Court.

The final shot showed them pausing to kiss outside the doors of the motel, the woman facing directly into the camera, smiling, saying something to the man embracing her. It was a good close-up shot, taken with an excellent camera, and the image of the woman was clear and sharp, the afternoon sunlight full on her face. Jack went right on gundog point, and so did Pandora.

They *knew* that woman.

"Have you still got that enhanced shot of Bowman, the one taken at the Carousel Bar in New Orleans?"

Pandora opened her iPhone, found the shot, held it up so Jack could see it.

"It's her," he said. "It's the same woman."

Pandora picked the shot up, looked from one to the other and again. She sighed.

"I'll admit there's a…resemblance—"

"Pandora. Come on. They're identical."

"So…her mother? A relative?"

Jack was shaking his head, as unwilling as Pandora to accept what he was seeing.

"Yeah. Yes. Has to be. Can't be the same woman."

There was a postcard clipped to the stack, on the front, a photo of a motel from the 1950s.

Jack flipped the postcard over.

Monterey Court
16 Bay Street, St. Augustine, Florida
Phone JA9-8854

Facing beautiful Matanzas Bay, in the heart of historical St. Augustine. Located one block from Fort San Marcos. 33 Units. Air-conditioned, hot water, heat, free television, ample parking, Beautyrest and Englander mattresses, tile baths, tub and shower combinations.
Outstanding restaurant adjacent.
Mr. and Mrs. W. H. McLain, Proprietors

Written in pencil on the blank side of the postcard were two names and a time and date.

Tessio Vizzini
Aurelia DiSantis (???)
Saturday, August 24, 1957, 1430 hours

Pandora was quiet for a while.

Then she said, "You know it always kills me when they say things like 'facing beautiful Matanzas Bay' because *matanzas* is a Spanish word for a massacre."

"Yeah, I know. Two hundred years ago, they killed a bunch of French sailors down on the beach."

"One hundred and eleven men. Because they wouldn't switch religions. And now it's a tourist attraction."

"Jeez, honey. You carry a grudge for a long time. You're not even French."

"Yes. Well, I'm a Viking. We specialize in grudges. We're like that."

A silence, while Jack thought about how much he had loved her. Before Barbara. And still loved her.

After Barbara.

Then a sigh.

"Okay. Let's review here. Whoever took these shots—let's assume it was your grandfather—he's obviously doing some surveillance work."

"Yeah. Question is, for whom?"

"I'd assume for the Jacksonville PD. I mean, that guy in the suit is Tessio Vizzini, the head of the same Vizzini family your grandfather took down? Right?"

"Yeah. Tessio was the *capo di tutti capi*."

"And when did Clete Redding go after the

Vizzini family? I mean, that night he went in after them all? When was that?"

"End of August 1957. The thirty-first, I think. It was a Saturday night."

"So about one week after these pictures were taken?"

"Yeah. Looks like it."

"And a couple of nights after your grandmother was killed, if I remember that right?"

"Yes. She was killed on the thirtieth of August."

"Her name was Mary Alice, right?"

"Yes."

Jack's answers were getting short. He did that when she was getting close to the bone.

"And where was she killed, Jack?"

He shook his head.

"That was just…one of God's little mind fucks. He likes doing sadistic shit. It keeps the light-years flying by. You get bored when you're eternal. Good to have an ant farm to fuck around with during those long cosmic nights."

She sat back and stared at him.

"Well, poetry. I would never have expected it."

"You know what I'm saying."

"I know what you're not saying. Mary Alice died in a single-car crash on the Matanzas Inlet Bridge, in almost the exact same spot where Barbara and Katy died last Christmas Eve."

"Yeah. A coincidence."

"Like the locket? Like the woman in the surveillance shots looking exactly like Diana Bowman?"

"What the hell else could it be?"

"I guess that's what we're trying to figure out here. So, the shoot-out at the Vizzini compound, the day after your grandmother—Clete's wife—dies in a mysterious car crash. And you don't think there's a connection?"

"He denied it. I put it to him straight a couple of times, but he'd always shut down, tell me it was nothing I needed to know about."

"But you've thought about it. I know you have. I know how your mind works. You ever figure out what made him do that? That night? Was it a suicide mission? Or revenge for the death of his wife?"

"I asked him about it. He said he was just trying to get some information and the button guys got ugly and…things got out of hand."

"Please. Jack. You really buy that?"

"Hey. He went in alone. Against policy. Would he do that if he was about to start a war?" said Jack.

"Yes of course he would. If he didn't want any witnesses. Or something else happened, something we don't know about, something that triggered him. Do you know what that could have been?" said Pandora.

"No. He was a wall of rock when I pushed it. And about the crash, the Highway Patrol guys were all over it. Looks like she just lost control—maybe fainted—and went through the guardrail… just like…"

She put her hand on Jack's arm, held it there.

"Jack, I'm sorry to push, but something is going on here. You know what the commission said during the hearings in 1963?"

"Yeah. They said he went in to wipe out everybody who knew he'd been taking money from the Vizzini syndicate for a couple of years. That they'd fed him high-profile busts, made his career, and that one night he just decided to go in and take them all down."

"He denied it."

"Oh yeah. A lot of good it did him."

She paused, stopping at the edge of the obvious question, not wanting to speak it.

"I know what you're thinking. Did I believe him?"

"Yeah. Sorry."

"I think he was…walking a thin line. Those were different days. People played both sides. Cops took tribute, never saw it as a bribe. Politicians, city councilors, zoning bylaw guys—they all took money. It was the way things were done."

"Still is."

"Yeah. And even we do that sometimes, don't we? We take a gang guy down, stick him in solitary to sweat awhile, then offer him a deal if he'll give us somebody deeper inside. We work the street, we run informants we know are in the life, dealing, stealing…and we let them operate, if they give us what we need."

"We don't take money to do it, do we?"

"No. No we don't. But we do take the promotions, the credit, the pay raises. But for Clete, I think it started out that way—he figured he was working *them*. For information. For busts. And then one day, it all changed, and he had been compromised, or it could be read that way, and he was in too deep to get out. Maybe Tessio had something on him, a tape or some photos he could take to J. Edgar, or to the Kefauver people. So Clete was trapped, and he did what he had to do to survive. It was a corrupt world, Old Florida…"

"Still is. Honey, so's the whole damn country."

"Yeah. It is."

And then Pandora's phone buzzed at them. She picked it up, sighing—Dixon.

"Mace?"

"Yeah how's it going?"

"Jack and I are looking at family photographs," she said, giving Jack a sideways look.

Jack shook his head. *Don't say anything to Mace yet, okay?*

"Okay, look, I ran that plate, from the Benz?"

"Yeah? And anything?"

"Well, yes, actually. It's registered to a car dealership in Jacksonville, Nino Ferrucci's Ferraris and Other Fine Cars. Thing is Nino Ferrucci doesn't own the shop. He's just the front. The real owner is a numbered corporation, Florida level, just a bunch of numbers, but the numbers brought up a hit from the FBI office. I called Deke over there and he says that this numbered corporation is linked to the Vizzini family."

Pandora looked at Jack, held up a finger.
Interesting hit. Wait one.

"They're not active these days," Pandora said.

"No. Supposed to be totally legitimate. Cars. Real estate. Shopping malls. As if. But I thought you should know. Probably nothing to it. But… well…now you know. Okay?"

"Yes. I do. Thanks, Mace."

"Well, button down, Pandora. This storm is settling in for the night."

"We are totally buttoned."

"Yeah? Glad to hear that."

She clicked off, filled Jack in on the return on that white Benz.

They kicked it around for a while, decided it was something they should follow up on. If only for the Vizzini Family connection. Which seemed to be pushing the "mere coincidence" boundary more than a little. They were looking at a picture of Tessio Vizzini taken sixty-one years ago, and today there's a Vizzini-connected Benz parked up the block.

They were quiet for a while, thinking about the Benz. And the Vizzinis. It stuck in their heads, setting off a major cop alarm.

More as a reflex than a conscious thought, Jack reached over and picked up his weapon, handed Pandora her gun belt too, put them both down a little closer.

"Okay, this other stuff—the Benz—isn't getting us anywhere with the Bowman woman. Let's set that aside for now. Nothing's going to happen in a storm like this. And the place is a bunker."

"Yes," she said, but she moved her piece a little closer.

"So, back to it, and just for the sake of argument, what was Karen Walker saying about the Bowman woman knowing a lot about St. Augustine in the fifties? Like she had actually lived through that period?"

"She said that Bowman knew places like the Alcazar Hotel, the Reef Bar… She knew all about places that had been torn down or shut up years ago. That would probably include the Monterey Motel we're looking at right here. And there she is. Right there in the picture. Which is utterly nuts, right?"

"Yes," said Pandora, with an edge. "It is."

"So what the hell have we got here?"

Pandora went quiet for a time.

Jack saw her do it.

"Okay. You've got something on your mind."

She turned her wineglass in her hands. Outside the storm was rising to a freight-train roar and the whole house was vibrating like a bass drum. The rain was slicing in sideways and lashing the screening over the window so hard it was rattling. The sky was rumbling like a kettledrum and the underbelly of the storm was full of flashing white fire. The street was invisible, hidden by curtains of rain and the gathering darkness. And the room lights were flickering. Pandora was ignoring all of it, which took some concentration.

"When Karen was dying...you remember?" she said.

"No. Totally slipped my mind. Karen who?"

"Okay. Sarcasm. Got it. You know there was a camera running?"

Jack was tuned in to this woman pretty well. He got it in three.

"You pulled the video. Looking for the Shimmer," he said.

She smiled at him.

"Thanks for not calling the Rubber Room guys," she said.

"So, what did you find?"

She held up the iPhone.

"Would you like to see it?"

"Yes. I would."

She flicked through the apps, found Photos, clicked on Videos. Touched Play. They were getting a spider's-eye view of the hospital room, from a corner position up near the ceiling, covering the hospital bed and the people standing around, Mace and Jack standing a little closer, Karen in the middle of the video, with her head on Pandora's shoulder, Pandora sitting on the bed, comforting her. It was in high-def and color, but there was no sound. When you're talking to a subject who might be indicted based on what she says, and she's underage, and she doesn't have a lawyer, you don't want sound.

"I only took the cut with…what I saw. It's coming up. This is where you were asking her about the Shimmer and what Bowman could do with it."

"Actually, that was you."

"Whatever. Here it comes. Watch this."

Karen was leaning on Pandora's shoulder, then, in response to something that was said, she jerked back, and started shaking her head—you could see her mouth the words—*you don't know what she can do*—and then she starts to struggle—Jack goes for the knapsack, roots around it in it—comes up with the blue canister. Karen reaches for it, pauses and shakes her head—*no mine was silver*—and now the head nurse comes into the shot, moving fast and with authority.

She plucks the puffer out of Jack's hand, gets it onto Karen's mouth, supporting her back as she does so—Karen inhales once, twice—three times, and then she arches backward and starts to convulse.

"This is hard to watch," said Pandora. "But it's right here. Don't blink."

Karen was writhing on the bed, arched into a bow, her hands clutching at the sheets, her head thrown back…

"Jeez," said Jack, in a hoarse whisper.

"I know. Me too. But watch."

Karen stiffens—her face is scarlet and her mouth an open wound—teeth bared—then she stops, stops like a freeze-frame in a film. And there is a flash so bright it seems to burn out the lens. It is there—bright white—vibrating—blue around the corona—it fills the frame like a white-hot flower—and then…it's gone, and the film runs on as the crash team floods into the room—all the busy pointless things get done…then it's over. Karen is dead.

"You saw that? Jack?"

"I don't know. A reflection?"

"Off what? Mace's skull?"

"Flaw in the hard drive?"

"No. The techs checked it. There's nothing wrong with it. And they did a Gaussian read on it. That flare is real, it flamed up in a nanosecond but the source—where it started, the epicenter—was Karen Walker. Karen Walker at the moment of her death."

"Play it again. Can you slow it down?"

"I can."

And she did. Slower, faster, freeze-frame.

It was always the same. That sudden incandescent flower of blue light, flaring out at the speed of light, filling the room, burning into the lens, whiting out the image—and then gone. They watched it a few more times, as if something different was going to happen on the thirteenth repeat. Then they sat back into the couch, feeling battered, limp. And utterly at sea.

The outside world was hammering on the roof, the room lights were flickering low, like a candle flaming out. The street was full dark, lit by stroboscopic explosions of sheet lightning. There was an end-of-the-world feeling rising up in the room, and it occurred to Pandora that what she really needed right now was for Jack Redding—who was so close his heat was warming her core—to turn to her and—and the front door blew inward in a blinding flash, a deafening booming concussion—men were rushing into the room—four, now five—wearing rain slicks. Men with guns—Vizzini soldiers. And a woman came behind them—Diana Bowman—bringing the fire that Tessio had promised her.

Pandora and Jack went for their weapons—the room was lit by strobing gunfire and Pandora felt something like a sledgehammer hit her in the right hip.

She had her gun up and was firing it—carefully—but firing fast—she felt Jack at her side, a little in front of her—his face lit up by the muzzle flashes—a round zipped by her ear—she saw her bullets strike three of the Vizzini gunmen—she felt herself going down—saw Jack on his knees in front of her, firing his weapon into the pack of men—stillness and a hush was enveloping her—and then Jack was above her—bending over her—a woman—the Bowman woman—was standing over them both—the room was suddenly silent and it stank of cordite and blood and ozone.

The woman had a gun and she held it to the back of Jack's head. Her eyes flicked to the locket, lying on the coffee table.

"*My* locket."

She reached for it, and Jack grabbed her by the

wrist, pulling her down, and as she fell her weapon fired again—there was a bright blinding flash—and everything went away for Pandora Jansson, everything went hushed and silent, and she fell all the way into the silence.

selena finds a curved space in the air

*S*elena was in the Long Hall and she knew it very well, although she only remembered anything about it when she was inside it. It rose up and curved away into the shining blue distance, into a shimmering vanishing point that was always receding. There were lights in the ceiling, embedded in what looked like glass but might have been ice and she ran into and out of the pools the lights cast on the floor, which was also made of glass, but glass so clear she could see through it.

She saw what looked like the lights of a great city far down in the velvet darkness, grids and circles and squares of glittering lights in green and gold and red and blue and violet, streets and lanes and avenues, and other patterns too, leaf shaped with glowing silver veins that might have been rivers flowing in valleys between mountains, and diamonds and spheres and discs of pulsing light.

It was too dark to see anything but those ghost

lights far away down in the dark and she had no time to think about them.

Because she could feel the man following her down the hallway, a dark force, closing in on her, relentless, and it terrified her, because no one had ever followed her into the Shimmer.

But he was there, chasing her down the hallway... There were doors—gates really—tall arches set into the glassy walls lining the hallway—hundreds and hundreds of them—perhaps thousands perhaps millions—although she had never gone that far down the tunnel—each one identical—a wide Gothic arch of green stone with inlaid bands of polished steel stretching away into the blue distance—and they were all marked with signs—bars and oblongs and diamonds and circles in some silvery metal that shone with a pale moonlight glow in the haloes of light from the ceiling—signs that seemed to have a meaning that floated just beneath the surface of her understanding, and if she only had a moment to study them their meaning would arise and become clear.

But she didn't, she couldn't, because he was right there, so close behind her she could feel his radiance, his force, his heat, a steel-gray shape flying down the hallway behind her, flickering in and out of the ceiling lights, getting closer, and this had never happened before—or had it?

She had the lost locket in her closed hand—she had a faint memory of how it had gotten into that policeman's hands—and the locket radiated there, *burning her skin, and the sheer joy she should have felt because she had it back again was muted and faint. She had not expected to find it in that policeman's house, but in another part of her mind—that part that only opened up for her when she was in the Long Hall—she had always known where it would be.*

But she could savor its return later, right now she had to evade the man chasing her...so she ran faster and faster...scanning the gates looking for something familiar—a sign a shape—she didn't know what it would be, but when she saw it she would know, because that was what memory was like when she was inside the Shimmer—

So the gates arose out of the blue distance and flickered past her like the blades of a fan turning in a shaft of sunlight—shadow to light to shadow to light—and then they were gone into the shadow behind her...and she ran and ran—

And then, there it was.

The marking signs were clear, and she stopped— the gate towered above her—she pressed her hand against the stone, it was as hot as the skin on her belly—it turned into a shimmering green cloud— and she stepped into the gate...

———

...and the sun was hot on her face, and the air was full of the sound of motorboats and yachts plying the open waters of Matanzas Harbor on the other side of Bay Street, and she could feel Tessio's hands on her, smell his cigar scent on the linen of his splendid suit, feel the hairs sprouting from his ear tickle her cheek… She suppressed a shudder, and he pulled away to hold her and look at her in the shadow under the portico of the Monterey Court—

"You shiver, *Carrissima*? You are cold?"

She shook her head, noticing a heavy black Ford parked across the street, the sun lying harsh on its dusty hide. The driver's-side window had been rolled down, but the sun was on the car and she could make out nothing of who might be inside. But the car looked…official.

Tessio was still holding her, wondering now, and she didn't want him to wonder, she wanted him to desire. In her mind a faint memory of a winding tunnel…a feeling of being pursued…hovered there for a moment, and then went away, a mirage, fading into nothing, leaving only a curved space in the air. So she stopped looking at the dusty Ford sedan across the street, although she did not stop thinking about it.

That was something for later. Right now, she had Tessio to deal with, and that was enough.

"I am fine, lover," she said, kissing his neck, which she knew he loved, and pulling back.

"Let's go inside. I must have you. I must have you now!"

Tessio, breathing like a bull, smelling like a bull, heavy as a bull, trotted after her into the dark of the Monterey Court Motel lobby.

His breathing was labored and rapid and she

knew from bitter experience that the afternoon would be long, long and wearisome.

———

Out in the street the cars and trucks and buses flowed by, and the sun began to slide into the far west, and in the black Ford across Bay Street, Clete Redding snapped a final shot.

Clete was using a Nikon S for this job. It was rock-solid steel, a great lens, used 35 mm film, and the shutter was smooth as silk. No loud clattering sound as he snapped the photos. He had her right in the picture—she was kissing Tessio Vizzini very well, and, although he loved his wife, the lovely Mary Alice, whom he adored, Clete felt a pang of carnal envy just watching them get all tangled up in each other under the portico of the Monterey Court Motel.

Annamaria, Tessio Vizzini's wife, was Sicilian aristocracy, from her lush and sensual body down to her perfectly manicured toes. If she knew what was going on every Wednesday afternoon at the Monterey Court Motel she would cut Vizzini's heart out with an ice-cream scoop. And take several days to do it.

Vizzini knew this, but Vizzini had this new girl dug right in under his ribs and he was willing to risk his liver and lights to get the rest of her underneath him.

Clete leaned back, watching them as they disappeared under the shadows of the Monterey Court entrance, a final flicker of sunlight reflecting off the closing door. He set the camera down, leaned back, sighed, mopped his sweating face—it was ninety degrees out and the inside of the car was an oven—and looked into his rearview mirror, where a large man in some kind of gray uniform was looking back at him. He jerked his revolver out of his belt, turned with a snarl to stick it in the guy's face… The seat was empty.

Empty.

No.

One.

There.

*objects in the mirror
are closer than they appear*

Jack knew precisely where he was. Or at least, where he had decided to *believe* he was. Unless he was dead or dying—always a possibility—he'd seen *An Occurrence at Owl Creek Bridge* when he was just a kid but it had stayed with him—but if he wasn't dead or dying, then the view out the window told him that he was sitting in the backseat of his grandfather Clete Redding's detective car.

How he had gotten here he had no idea, but, in some weird way, he had been expecting something like this ever since he saw Diana Bowman's face in a picture that was sixty-one years old.

They were parked on Bay Street, across the road from the Monterey Court Motel—Mr. and Mrs. W. H. McLain, Proprietors—and the time was probably going to be 1430 hours on the afternoon of Saturday the twenty-fourth of August in the year 1957. Clete was shooting the surveillance photos that he and Pandora had been looking at—seconds ago?

Or sixty-one years in the future?

He did have a trace memory, fading fast, of a long curved tunnel, pools of light on a glass floor that seemed to be made of stars, and a great green gate with silver letters… but even as he thought of it, the image shimmered into a curved space in the air and was gone from him.

And he didn't care.

How this could be?

That all this should have happened, and he didn't care? Tell you in a moment…

————

Jack sat in the backseat of the Ford, accepting all of this, in a way *savoring* it, mostly because his life back in the future had been a terrible burden ever since last Christmas, a crushing weight of grief that was driving him into the ground, so much so that a grave seemed like a fine and private place, and he had spent far too many nights thinking about the .45 in his gun belt.

Thinking about that gun brought him to Pandora, whom he had loved, before Barbara, and whom he was beginning to love again, after Barbara, and he thought about her for a while, what a loving heart she was, and he was sorry that he had lied to her about the way the gun had been calling to him.

He hoped she was okay—last time he'd seen her she was shooting very well, like the Valkyrie she was—maybe she'll turn up here too—or she might be dead, killed in that gunfight—he deeply and passionately wished that this not be true, and that she was safely back in the future right now, picking through the pockets of several dead men and talking on the radio to Mace Dixon.

But then he might be dead too—and since he had no power over any of this, or even to tell if any of it was real at all—perhaps it was all a vivid dream—he let it all roll over him.

So he sat there, feeling the bake-oven heat, hearing the mutter and growl and hiss of motorboats and sailing ships and cruisers out on Matanzas Bay, hearing the far-off cry of gulls shrieking and wheeling, and the roaring of the Atlantic far away in the east, beyond Conch Island. Was it real, or just the last few seconds of his life bleeding away? Again, he didn't care.

One thought ruled him now.

It filled his mind and drove out every other consideration. And it was this: if this really was *the past*, and not the last flickering sparks from his dying brain, then the future hadn't happened yet. And Barbara and Katy, not yet born, were not yet dead. So he was going with that.

He was going with hope.

———

Clete looked into the rearview mirror. The guy was still there. Then he turned around and looked into the backseat, and the guy still wasn't there. He decided not to do this a third time because it was just going to make him feel like an idiot. He looked at the guy in his rearview, and after a moment gave him a sideways grin.

"Okay. I've had too much to drink. Right?"

Jack shook his head.

"No. You haven't. I mean, maybe, but that's not why I'm here."

"I've had a stroke? I'm dead and you're some kind of fucking butt-ugly angel?"

"Pretty sure I'm not."

"Then…what the fuck are you?"

"What do I look like?"

Clete considered him in the mirror.

"That's a uniform. You're Florida Highway Patrol. A sergeant."

"Yeah. I am."

"That a nameplate, on your tunic?"

Jack had forgotten about it.

"Yes. It is."

Clete leaned into the mirror, changed the angle. Sat back, rubbed his hands over his face.

"'Redding.' It says 'Redding.'"

"Yes. It does."

"And that's *your* name. Redding."

"Yes."

"Are we related?"

"We are."

Clete sighed, blowing his lips out, watching the cars go up and down Bay Street for a while.

"Do I want to know how?"

"I don't know if you do. I'm still trying to work out the complications myself. I'm not real sure what the hell is going on here either."

Clete spent a few minutes fooling around with

the camera and the film cases, stowed them in the passenger foot well, opened the glove compartment and pulled out a small bottle of Southern Comfort, turned to offer it to the man who still wasn't in the backseat, stopped himself, and took a short sharp pull on it. Sighed again.

"You're sure I'm not having a stroke?"

"Yeah, I think so. Try not to have one now, okay?"

"I'll try. What the fuck are you, then?"

"I'm as real as you are."

"That's a slick way of saying one of us is hallucinating."

"But we're not."

"Okay. Tell me as much as you can. I'll figure it out from there."

"Well, I have a couple of conditions."

"Rules, you mean?"

"Yeah. Before I get into this, just to check the boxes. This is Saturday, August 24, 1957. And we're in St. Augustine, Florida. It's around 2:30 in the afternoon. And you're Clete Redding, and you're a Detective First Grade with the Robbery Homicide Division of the Jacksonville Police Department."

Clete tugged out his gold shield, held it up in the mirror. Then he tapped the dashboard clock. The time was 2:35. Jack nodded.

"Okay. My name is Jack Redding. Now, brace yourself. Okay?"

"I'm braced."

"I'm your grandson. Your boy, Declan, is my father. A couple of minutes ago I was sitting in your house in Crescent Beach—"

"Yeah? Gimme the address."

"Thirty-Two Avenue A."

"Phone number?"

"904-233-6630."

"Wrong," said Clete, pouncing on it.

Jack realized Clete was talking about the phone number back in 1957.

"Right…right…it was… Jeez, Clete, that was sixty-one years ago!"

"Number." A bark, just like a drill sergeant.

Jack racked his mind…

"It was…JA something…9…something…"

"Number."

"JA for Jacksonville 9…6630! Just like it is now."

"What tattoo have I got on my right biceps?"

"You don't have a tattoo on your right biceps. Far as I know, you don't have a tattoo anywhere."

"Okay, smart guy. What was I doing on September 15 seven years ago?"

"You were in Korea. Going ashore at Inchon with the Fifth Marine Regiment."

Clete was studying him in the mirror.

"You're from sixty-one years in the future? So I'm probably dead by then. When do I die?"

"Maybe you're not dead then either?"

Clete worked out the numbers.

"Fuck that. I'd be ninety-seven. I'll never make

ninety-seven. No male in our family ever got past seventy-five. My heart'll give out long before that."

"Maybe. Anyway, I'm not going to tell you."

"Why not?"

Jack patted his pockets for a cigarette and then remembered he didn't smoke. He used to, but he quit back in 2001. Which meant that in 1957 he hadn't quit yet. But then he wasn't born yet either, so there was that. Maybe he'd buy a pack of Lucky Strikes. And then he patted his pants pocket and found a battered pack of Lucky Strikes where he was pretty sure they hadn't been a second ago.

And a flip book of matches.

On the cover was a logo for a place called the Blue Dahlia Bar. That made him smile.

A very nice touch. Whoever or whatever was running this show—the Timekeeper?—had a very wicked sense of humor. He flipped it open, but there was no Lenox phone number written inside it.

Still, Mace Dixon would have been delighted.

He pulled a cigarette out, lit it up and exhaled the smoke. It was better than he remembered.

The Blue Dahlia Bar.

That matchbook was a *signal* on someone's part—a warning maybe—but he had no idea who might be trying to warn him, or about what.

He did get the idea that reality was going to be a negotiable issue when you were time shifting. So maybe that *was* the Timekeeper's message.

Clete was still waiting for his answer. He smiled at Clete through the cloud.

"Why not? I've been thinking about that. From what I remember about time travel, if you change the past you can really fuck up the future."

Clete thought that through.

Sighed again.

"Okay. You're my grandson from sixty years in the future—"

"Sixty-one."

"Okay. Sixty-one. I take it Declan grows up and gets married and has kids. Good for him. Frankly I didn't think he had it in him. He's sort of a pantywaist. I mean, I love him and all that shit, but Mary Alice runs his ass. So when he's older I get a chance to toughen him up?"

"Dad never really toughens up, Clete. But he's a good guy, in his own way."

"Glad to hear it. I hoped he would come out okay. But you. You turned out to be a cop too?"

"Yes. Sergeant in the FHP. Just like—"

"Just like what?"

"Sorry. Can't tell you that."

"Got a kid of your own?"

That came in like a kick in the gut, and it showed on his face. Clete saw that clearly.

"Okay. Yow. Bad question. Sorry I asked."

"Yeah…well…"

"Kid died?"

Jack just nodded. It was all he could do.

"Hey… I'm…I'm so sorry. When?"

"Last Christmas Eve. Car accident. My wife too."

On the same Matanzas Inlet your wife dies on in six days.

"Jeez. I'm so sorry."

"Yeah. Me too."

A heavy silence, and all they could do was wait it out.

———

Clete looked out the window, checked the dashboard clock. A little after three. He'd been sitting here with the guy for thirty minutes. And now they were both depressed as shit.

On one level he was still convinced that this whole man-in-the-rearview-mirror thing wasn't real and that he maybe was having heatstroke or a heart attack and hallucinating the whole thing.

And on another level, he had seen a lot of strange things in his life—like the ghosts of dead men standing on blood-drenched snowdrifts in the Chosin Reservoir—and he was ready to take life as it came. This seemed pretty real, so what the hell. He was going with it.

He sighed, took another hit on the Southern Comfort, set it down and said, "Well, this sounds like a rat fuck from the get-go. Can you get out from behind that mirror?"

"I don't know. So far I haven't done much but sit around and bullshit with you."

"You're a big motherfucker, I'll admit. Maybe the rearview mirror is too small to get through. What if we go look for a bigger mirror?"

"This isn't *Alice in Wonderland*, Clete."

"Hey, I took Declan to see that movie. He loved it. Anyway, fuck this. I need a drink, and you sure as hell need a drink, and there's a big old antique mirror behind the bar at the Alcazar. Waddya say?"

"I'm in."

Clete grinned at him.

"Well, you don't have too much fucking choice, do you? What's your first name, anyway?"

"Jack."

"Jack? Declan named you *Jack*? I woulda thought Chauncey or Cornel or Lester."

"Nope. Jack."

"Okay. Jack. Let's see if we can get you pulled through the… What was it? In the movie? Alice in Whatever."

"The looking glass?"

"Yeah. The looking glass."

———

There actually was a huge mirror behind the bar at the Alcazar Hotel, and the problem of being stuck in the rearview mirror seemed to resolve itself, as Jack more or less got shifted—how or by whom he didn't want to ask—from Over There to Over Here.

The place was packed, and a kid on a stool was pounding away at a guiltless Steinway Grand, doing some serious damage to "Begin the Beguine." The bartender, a pencil-necked boy who looked about eleven, wearing a red silk vest and striped black pants and a boiled shirt with a black bow tie, the collar about two sizes too big for him, pulled up short in front of them and asked what he could bring them.

Clete appeared to know the kid pretty well, calling him by name—Freddy or something like it—it was hard to make it out over the music and the crowd chatter. The kid blushed and looked pleased to be remembered by Clete Redding.

Jack didn't think they'd have Barefoot Pinot Grigio on the list, and anyway he didn't want to risk ordering a glass of white wine with his grandfather sitting on the next barstool holding a gigantic boilermaker and watching him in a considering way, so he ordered one too.

When it came, a big glass mug of India pale ale and an oversize shot glass full of whiskey, Clete took the shot glass, dropped it into the mug of beer, tipped the frosted mug to Jack with one raised eyebrow, said, "Here's to family," set himself and drained it to the bottom in one go, his throat working and his eyes closed. Jack and Freddy, the kid behind the bar, watched this ceremony with interest.

Clete set the glass down, sighed deeply and looked at Jack expectantly. So did the bartender. Jack had never tried a boilermaker, but he had never tried time travel either, so what the hell.

He dropped the shot glass into the mug—it went down like a depth charge—and then he lifted the mug—it was as big as a toaster and weighed a ton—and he drained the thing at one go, set it down and sighed the same sigh as his grandfather had just sighed, which seemed to satisfy all three of them.

Freddy went away to get two more, and they sat there side by side on the red leather stools, looking at their reflections in the long bar mirror, and after a while spent in quiet contemplation of just how totally nuts this situation was—and two more boilermakers for each of them—Clete got around to the central point.

"Well, this afternoon has been instructive as hell, if it really happened, which I doubt, but if it did, what the fuck does it all mean?"

Jack looked in his pocket for his iPhone, pulled out a battered notebook instead, one he had never owned in his entire life.

He looked at it for a time, thinking about the Blue Dahlia matchbook cover and the Lucky Strikes in his shirt pocket and wondered—briefly—what other messages the Timekeeper had in store for him.

He flipped the notebook open—another nice touch here too because the pages were filled up with his own handwriting—and found an entry that corresponded, roughly, with what he and Pandora had found out about the woman calling herself Diana Bowman.

"You're doing surveillance on a woman who's banging Tessio Vizzini."

Clete found this professionally intriguing.

"How the fuck do you know that?"

"It's one of the things I can't tell you about. I have to let you run things your way."

Clete didn't like it, but he let it go.

"Okay. Yes. I am."

"Well, so am I."

"You're onto this DiSantis broad too?"

"I think so."

"But, this broad is thirty-four years old. There's no way she's somebody you're looking at sixty-one years from now."

"But that is *exactly* what I'm looking at."

"Same name?"

"No. She's calling herself Diana Bowman."

"Okay. And what's the beef?"

"Murder, kidnapping, robbery. She left three people to die in a storage locker, she kidnapped two young girls and got one of them shot and murdered the other while she was in Protective Custody—"

Clete snorted into his beer mug.

"Jeez, kid. How the fuck did *that* happen?"

"She put cyanide into the kid's medicine. We were stupid enough to let her take a hit of it while she was in the hospital room."

Clete gave him a look, and Jack took it.

"Yeah, yeah. I know. I know."

"You happen to have a picture of this Bowman woman?"

"I don't know. I might."

He ruffled through the notebook, and a photo fell out. It was the digital shot from the Carousel

Bar, only now it was just a color snap with rippled edges. But it was her.

Clete took the shot, held it up to the bar lights overhead.

"Jeez. That's her. That's Aurelia DiSantis. When was this shot taken?"

"Sixty-one years in the future, at the Monteleone in New Orleans."

"At the Carousel Bar, I see. So, like, a relative, a granddaughter?"

"What do you think?"

Clete studied the shot for a while.

"Fuck *relative*. That's *her*. That's Aurelia DiSantis."

"Thank you. I think so too. So far there's only two people who believe me. You're one of them, and a lady cop named Pandora Jansson is the other."

"And where's she?"

"Back in the future."

Clete took a long drink.

"Okay. So what we're saying here is that this DiSantis chick is the same chick who is calling herself Diana Bowman sixty-one years from now and who you want for assorted felony murders and robberies and all that nasty shit?"

"Exactly. It's what this woman does. She finds somebody vulnerable, isolates the target, gets control of the money, like a parasite on a host, sucks the victim dry, kills the host and moves on."

"And she's been doing this for...?"

"No idea. At least sixty years."

Clete looked at the shot.

"Fucking Spider Lady."

"Yes."

"And I've got a pretty good idea that sucking a vic dry is exactly what that DiSantis broad is doing to Tessio Vizzini."

Jack let that go by, although it was sorely tempting. Clete picked up on that.

"I meant her MO. Jeez, clean up your mind."

"Hey, I said nothing!"

"You were *thinking* it. So what you're telling me, is this woman can slip around in time, go up and down the time chute, and right now she's popped out of the chute right here in St. Augustine? And you came down after her?"

"Looks like it."

"You maybe shoulda thought this through a little better, kid. I mean, I'm all for a good police chase, but I think I woulda pulled up short when the chute opened up on *me*."

"Maybe next time I will."

"What makes you think you'll get a next time? Look around you, Jack. This is where you are."

Jack took a breath, let it out, took a hit of his boilermaker, let the reality of the Alcazar Bar roll over him.

All around them there was music—the kid on the stool was now pounding the stuffing out of Glen Miller's "In the Mood"—and the smell of cigarettes and the cheerful talk of the crowds. Now twelve years after the end of World War II, the boom times of the fifties really starting to roll, people in baggy suits and big ties, the women in flared skirts and cashmere twinsets and pearls at the neck, the bartenders in red vests and striped pants, moving up and down the bar line, smiling and mixing and smiling, the room full of smoke and perfume, and under it all the vague remnants of the sulfur reek of the pool that used to be right in the center of the casino years ago, still there, embedded in the wood paneling and the marble arches.

"Yeah," he said, reaching for his beer. "Here is where I am."

"So, what do you want to do?"

"Well, we're both cops, and we're after the same woman. So—"

"So, let's go be cops."

"Yeah. Let's. What do you have on Aurelia DiSantis?"

"What I have is she's calling herself Aurelia DiSantis, but I think it's an alias. I tossed her room here at the hotel."

"She's staying here. At the Alcazar?"

"Yes. Has a suite. Seems to have some money."

"And of course you had a warrant?"

"Don't be a putz."

"What did you find?"

"ID in her name—DiSantis, Aurelia, age thirty-four, date of birth fits—a Louisiana driver's license in that name, with an address at the Pontalba

Apartments in New Orleans, about fifteen grand in cash, mixed bills, some Mexican scrip, some old photos of an apartment interior somewhere, a snub-nosed Colt .38 with a box of shells."

"What'd you make of all that?"

"Looks legit enough, except for the Colt. But something ain't right about her and I can't quite nail it down."

"Why her in the first place?"

"Waddya mean?" Clete said, a wary look flickering in his eyes.

Jack knew he was on dangerous ground here.

"I just mean, if she's legit, then what brought her to the attention of the Jacksonville Robbery Homicide Division?"

Clete looked at him for a long time, and then down at the half-empty mug of beer between his rough-skinned hands.

"If you're really from the future, maybe I've already told you about this shit?"

Jack waited awhile before he answered.

"If I say yes, you'll know you lived long enough to tell me a lot of things."

"And did I?"

"You figure it out."

"The Rules?"

"Yes. The Rules."

Long silence.

"Okay. Here goes," Clete said, eventually. "Back in the car, you asked me if this was Saturday the twenty-fourth of August in 1957. Which means that date was important to you. It also means that, from where you were sitting, you recognized where we were. Which means that the photos I just finished taking a couple hours ago made it through sixty-one years, so you could be sitting in my beach house looking at them. Because that's the view in the shots I took, and that's the same view out the windshield. And you knew it when you saw it. You knew exactly where you were. Am I right so far?"

Jack was impressed.

"You are."

"Okay. So if you're sitting looking at these pictures way out there in the future, there was something in those pictures that you were trying to figure out, but I wasn't there to tell you about them."

"Or you were alive but you wouldn't."

Clete's head came up.

"Why the fuck wouldn't I tell you?"

"You tell me."

Clete's face went red.

"You think I wasn't doing surveillance for the PD. You think I was checking out Tessio Vizzini's new punchboard for Tessio himself."

"Clete, I work in the same kind of job you do. We have gangs and syndicates there too. And sometimes you gotta do…what you gotta do."

"Like doing sideline shit for a Mafia capo?"

"Absolutely. I'd do it too, if it gave me better information. You can't work the streets without making some risky moves. I do it all the time. If you were checking out Aurelia DiSantis for Tessio Vizzini, you were also doing it for the Jacksonville PD. Because you *are* the Jacksonville PD. You follow this?"

Clete was silent but radiating a slow burn. Jack wondered how the Timekeeper would react if his grandfather knocked him off a barstool at the Alcazar Hotel. Finally Clete seemed to work something out, and he softened up a bit.

"Kid, this is Florida in the fifties. We have the Five Families here. We have Cuba across the way. We got this asshole Castro making all sorts of trouble out in the countryside. Meyer Lansky—you know him?"

"Yes. I know all about it."

"How?"

Jack shrugged.

"It's history now. Or will be."

"Well, Lansky opened up Cuba, for now anyway, unless Castro and this Guevara guy actually take the country, and now there is some serious fucking money flowing up and down this coast, and across to Cuba, and back again, and all we can do—the PD—is try to keep the worst of things from getting the better of…"

"The best of things?"

"Yeah. Yes. And to do that…"

"You do what you gotta do."

Clete looked at his grandson then, and some kind of deep pain seemed to lighten inside him, just a little, but enough. Jack's heart went out to him, but then it always had. He loved the man.

"Lot of people, kid...lot of people...especially the fucking civilians...they *judge*... You know what I mean?"

"I do. Easy for them. They have no skin in the game."

"What?"

"They have nothing at stake. No dog in the hunt. They're in the bleachers. You're down in the arena."

"Yes. We are. Thing is, kid, inside, I'm straight. Always was straight. In Korea, it was easy to be straight. The Rules were...*clear*, you know? Us, the Corps, and them, the Dinks. But *here* on this coast, it's hard to always know what *straight* is. Tessio Vizzini is a mob guy, but if what he's doing is so bad, how come so many ordinary people are buying whatever he's selling, and how come so many city officials—state people too—are taking money to help him operate? Things get...bent. *People* get bent."

The bartender—Freddy or whatever—came back, but Clete waved him away, signaling for the bill.

"So my main worry... Jack... I wouldn't want *you* to judge. You follow? And Mary Alice, she doesn't know about any of this. She's...she's *good*, Jack...she's good all the way down. If something were to happen to me, I would never want to see her...hurt. Stained."

Jack put a hand on his grandfather's massive shoulder, left it there for just a second, feeling the heat coming off him. The crowd noise went away.

"I can tell you this, Clete. It's against the Rules, but what you're afraid of? Mary Alice ever being ashamed of you, or stained by you?"

"Yeah?"

"It never happens. It. Never. Happens."

A lot of things flickered across Clete's rough-cut face, but the main one was *relief.*

Jack didn't have the heart to tell him why.

Or maybe he had too much heart to tell him that, if everything ran the way it ran in the history books, Mary Alice Redding had six days to live.

Unless he did something about that.

Presuming he *could* do anything about it at all.

The Rules.

Freddy came with the bill, a careful look on his young face. Clete looked at the bill and saw that it was for zero dollars.

"Compliments of the gentlemen across the way, sir."

Clete and Jack looked out into the crowd. A group of lean and shiny men in too-sharp suits were sitting around in a red leather banquette, a silver bucket of champagne in the middle of the table. They were looking at Clete, smiles as wide and dangerous as sharks. They raised their glasses to him, smiled again, drained them and waved at him. They all had French-cuffed shirts with diamond links that glittered as they moved. Clete turned away abruptly, his mood darkening.

"Who're those guys?" Jack asked.

"The one with the slick black hair, that's Anthony Vizzini, Tessio's son. He's next in line for *capo* if Tessio ever dies. He's hungry for it, but Tessio isn't going anywhere for a long time. Unless Anthony finds the balls to cap him, which isn't likely. The balding guy with the scars is Sergio Carpo, the Vizzinis' main enforcer. Very bad guy. Likes to use pliers. And the big guy with the face like a beefsteak is Salvatore Bruni. He runs the Cuba drug trade for Tessio. The other two guys I don't know. Probably a coupla button men new in from Sicily. Tessio's making some moves against the Traficantes—the Five Families aren't happy about that, so I guess he's bringing in some troops in case it all goes to shit in a fucking hurry. They're all holed up in Tessio's compound down the shore, gated up and bunkered like Fort Knox."

"Going to the mattresses?"

Clete looked at him.

"What?"

Jack felt like an idiot.

"It was in a movie—*The Godfather*."

"Never heard of it."

"Never mind. They look pretty happy here."

"The Vizzinis have a forty percent share in the Alcazar. The Bonnanos and the rest own another thirty percent."

Clete turned around on the stool, picked up the

bill, held it up so the men at the table could see it, crumpled it into a ball and threw it on the ground, then he stood up, stepped on the crumpled bill, peeled a hundred off a roll—a damn big roll—from his pocket, tossed it on the bartop.

"There you go, Friday. Keep the change."

"Thank you, sir," said Friday—not *Freddy*—with a nervous glance at the five men in the booth, who were all staring at them, faces white and mouths tight.

Clete and Jack walked out of the Alcazar and into the sidelong light of late afternoon. The air was hot and thick and smelled of salt water and car fumes. It lay against the skin like a hot wet towel. The Ford was right there in the circle, just as they'd left it. Jacksonville PD parked wherever they damn well pleased, including the roundabout in front of the Alcazar Hotel.

"Where are we going now?" asked Jack, as they powered out into the crowded cross streets of old town. Clete looked across at him.

"You up to a road trip?"

"I have all the time in the world," said Jack, which made them both smile.

"Okay then. We're going to New Orleans—"

"How we going to get there? Isn't it all country roads? It'll take days."

"No. It isn't. We have actual paved highways, even way back here. Like Highway 90, which takes us all the way to New Orleans. Six hundred miles, so it's an all-nighter. We can split the driving. You got any money?"

That was a new thought to Jack. He checked his wallet, and of course there were no credit cards in it. Just his Highway Patrol ID and his badge. And no cash either. Apparently the Timekeeper didn't do cash advances.

"I had some credit cards—"

"What? Credit what? You mean like a Diners' Club card? Who're you? John Jacob Astor?"

"Never mind. Nope. I'm busted."

"Well, I'm not. We'll get you some gear on the way out. You got spare autoloaders for that Colt?"

Jack realized he hadn't thought about his weapon at all. He'd been aware of the weight of a gun at his waist, but he was so used to it he hadn't checked his belt, and there was a weapon in the holster, but not his Kimber .45. He tugged it out and turned it in the dashboard light, a blue steel Colt Python, shimmering in the glow.

Clete looked over at it.

"Yeah, the .357. Same as mine. I got ammo in the trunk, so we're good. Just got to get you some kit."

"I'll pay you back."

"Who owns my beach house back there?"

"You do," Jack lied.

"Bullshit. It's yours, right?"

"Yes. You gave it to me."

"*Left* it to you, you mean?"

"Quit it, Clete. I'm not telling you anything

about stuff like that. What about grand—what about Mary Alice and Declan? Can we just drive off and leave them?"

"Yeah. They're down the shore, other side of Matanzas. Rattlesnake Island. She had relatives down there. I sort of sent them away. Wanted them out of the line of fire."

"You expecting some?"

"Yeah. This thing between the Traficantes and the Vizzinis, it's going to get bloody. My guess is soon. In the meantime I gotta look into this DiSantis dame. And now it seems, so do you."

"This is true."

"Okay. Good. So, working on the idea that this isn't all just a bad dream fueled by too many boilermakers, what I got today, looks like she has some background in New Orleans. Figured, fuck it, let's go look. Check out her place at the Pontalba. See if anybody there knows anything about her. Okay with you? Since we're both on the same case?"

"I was thinking more along the lines of going straight at her, since she's got rooms right here at the Alcazar."

"Yeah? And do what? Cuff her and pop her back into the time chute? You got any idea how to do that?"

"No. I don't. I just meant, now we got her close, why don't we just go ask her some questions? See what she has to say?"

"Ask her questions about what? Crimes she's gonna commit sixty fucking years in the future?

She'll call the house dicks on us. No, we gotta go dig into her past, see what comes up. If we're gonna take her down, we're gonna have to build a case right here, where we are."

Jack took that in, couldn't see any other way, and he was silent for a while as Clete wound his way across the bridges that led to the highway.

The sun was sliding down over the mainland, and stars were beginning to show. The heat was leaving too, which was nice. Jack cranked the side window all the way down and let the breeze cool him off.

"The bartender, is Friday really his name?"

"Sort of. I call him Friday. After that show *Dragnet* with Jack Webb."

"Joe Friday. Yeah. Does he want to be a cop?"

"No. He's putting himself through college. And the Friday thing started off because Friday's his last name too. Well, not actually Friday. It's spelled like the Krauts do it. Freitag."

Jack looked over at Clete, Clete's face lit up ghostly green by the dashboard lights.

"Freitag?"

"Yeah. Freitag."

Jack was quiet for a while, his heart hammering against his ribs. He went carefully, as one does when crossing spring ice.

"You…happen to know his first name?"

"Yeah. Anton or Antoine or something."

"Anson, maybe?"

"Yeah. Could be."

"He's saving for college?"

"Yeah."

"For what?"

"Med School. He wants to be a doctor."

selena dreams of home

Selena stepped out of the shower, picked the heavy silk robe off the wing chair in the living room of her suite at the Alcazar, did not put it on, but trailed it behind her like a tiger's pelt as she padded barefoot across the Persian carpet—it was all reds and greens and golds, as was the suite itself.

She stopped in front of the heavy redwood cabinet that served as the bar. There was a mirror behind it, reflecting the crystal decanters and the silver champagne bucket.

And Selena herself, looking back at her.

She considered her body, well-shaped neck and head—a perfect cameo—a long-dead lover had once described her that way—he died too, as they all eventually died—the curved perfection of her alabaster body, her breasts heavy and full and rounded, the rosebud nipples, the rounded belly, the dark fragrant shadow beneath…her thighs her legs her calves…she had been gifted with a body that drew lives to her…men and women…and she loved them equally and with the same intensity…

Which was not at all.

They floated above her body or bore her weight beneath her and she felt…nothing.

Nothing.

Only the tedium of pretending.

Sighing, crying out, gasping.

All a lie.

They never reached her core.

They never would.

She waited until they were spent, droning in sleep, gone to the world, and she would sit up and look at them sleeping and think how easy it would be to cut them, how sweet it would be to end that fat snoring pig—like Tessio—with a hard-held pillow…and then she would get up and go through their luggage and files and papers…and make plans for them. She had made some plans for Tessio, but they needed work. He was going to be a challenge, but well worth it, if she handled him just right.

But tonight, she had the locket back. And that would have made her life complete, if, on her way to her suite, she hadn't looked down into the atrium where the long bar was, where all the people were gathering for afternoon cocktails.

But she had.

And there at the bar was Jack Redding, and next to him was Clete Redding. They were leaning together, talking loud over the crowd noise, close and intense, sharing two large beers.

And then a bartender arrived, with a sheet of

paper, a bill she supposed. And she watched as Clete Redding turned around on the barstool and looked hard at five men in a banquette who were toasting him with their champagne glasses. She knew them—Tessio's son, Anthony. Sergio Carpo, who had once run his rough red hands up under her skirt and defiled her with his fat tobacco-stained fingers, breathing in her ear, saying vile things, this in the lemon tree orchard next to the alligator lagoon at the bottom of Tessio's estate. And Sal Bruni, who ran the Cuba trade.

She watched as Clete Redding crumpled the bar bill up and threw it to the ground and sent a bolt of sizzling hate back to the men in the banquette.

In a way she admired him for that, even as she filed it away. She stood and watched this ugly exchange for a full five minutes, frozen in place, her lungs full of ice and panic flooding through her body. Both Reddings, Clete and Jack.

Here right now.

Hunting her.

Hunting her here in the Alcazar.

———

Selena sat down on the end of the bed, held the locket between her breasts, her hands folded almost in prayer. She closed her eyes and went away for a few moments, fighting for calm.

Would they come for her? Were they riding up in the guest elevators right now? Were they striding down the carpeted hall under the crystal chande-

liers? Were they now at the door, about to knock?
If they were, what would she do?

They were both armed, she could see that from
the atrium balcony, heavy guns at their belts. If she
tried to fight them—use the little Colt—they'd kill
her where she stood.

If she let them take her...

But *how* could they take her?

In this place, in this time, she had committed no
crimes, at least none that they would know about,
and none at all as Aurelia DiSantis.

Clete Redding was a rogue cop, a very difficult
man, but Tessio ran him, and she was under Tessio's protection here. Unless they intended to kill
her outright—and if they did Tessio's rage would
be volcanic—they would have to arrest her.

On what charges?

The younger one, Jack, had no powers here, and
Clete? Did he even believe that Jack was his grandson? Falling through time to land here? Even if
Jack had managed to persuade him of that, which
was wildly improbable, there were still only two
choices open to them: confront her here, and possibly kill her. Or arrest her and charge her with...
again, charge her with what?

They had *nothing*.

And even if they took her to a police station,
Tessio would know at once, and he would send his
lawyers, and she would be free within the hour.

And Tessio would jerk Clete Redding's chain
very hard. She had Tessio in the palm of her hand,

literally, and while her power over him lasted, he would do anything she asked.

So, for now, for this night and the next few days, she should be still, she could stay safe under the protection of Tessio Vizzini.

That would work, for now.

The single point upon which this entire framework turned, the thing that was the most acute threat to her existence, was Jack Redding, and the fact that he had somehow followed her into the Shimmer, down the Long Hall and now he was here, in 1957. *He* was the anomaly, he was the piece that wouldn't fit, he was the crack in the mirror.

Removing him would not affect the time membrane in any way that would matter to her, because he *shouldn't* be here, because he *never was* here.

But if he were to be erased now, in 1957, would that affect *her* life in the future?

She thought not. There had been very little contact between the two of them. The world he had existed in would be greatly changed, but not hers, since he had only been a part of hers for a very brief period. And how much larger would the rip be if the solution to the problem of Jack Redding's existence was the death of his grandfather, in the right here and right now?

Clete Redding's death *should* mean there would never be a Jack Redding to trouble her, either in the future, or here in this time.

However, since there actually *was* a version of Jack Redding here now, it would be the cautious and sensible thing to kill him too, just to be on the safe side.

Yes there would be ripples, reverberations, changes that would affect the future in noticeable ways. But not *her* future.

The membrane of time was too dense and too immense to be affected by the little death of one ordinary little man and the death or nonexistence of another little man. There would be a tiny rip in the membrane, but it would soon mend, and the larger universe would navigate the endless mazes of time as it always had, as it always would.

There were Rules controlling time. She had found that, while she could go back in time, she could never go *forward*, never get past the Present Time, which for her now was the moment she had broken in on Jack Redding and that lady cop at the beach house She couldn't break that barrier, see what was going to happen in 2020 or 2030. It was as if Time was creating itself with every new second, and that on the other side of *Right Now*, there was only *Nothing Yet*.

But the Past, that was different.

The Past was *always* there, and she believed that the Long Hall would go on curving into a pale blue infinity and the Shimmer would never end.

Selena went deeper into the calm, and she thought about how the deaths of Clete and Jack

Redding might be made to happen, and, in a little while, she had her answer.

————

At peace with that decision, she lay back on the satin cover of the king-size bed, held the gold locket close to her heart, and let it take her away, let it take her back.

Above all she remembered the light, that golden afternoon glow that filled her bedroom as the sun moved across Jackson Square and a jasmine-scented wind stirred the curtains.

The sunlight turned all the white things in her bedroom, her four-poster bed with its linen comforter, the dresser covered in lace, the stone fireplace, it all turned from pale white into liquid gold as she lay there listening to the music coming up from the square, a small band playing, horns and a guitar, a woman singing a song that was new that very year, the "Saint Louis Blues."

And that soft afternoon there were the familiar voices in the other rooms, soft and gentle, loving cadences, and the faint tinkle of glasses touched.

Beatrice and William, Bea and Will…and the locket Will had given Bea in 1909, on their second anniversary…how many years ago now…she was five now, five this golden afternoon—that she remembered very well because of the cake they had made earlier in the day, the white cake with five glowing candles.

So now it was 1914 and there was talk of trouble far away in the East, wherever that was, Chicago or

New York maybe, and the people in the street were gathering together in the square or strolling along under the galleries of the Pontalba Apartments, talking right underneath her windows, looking at wrinkled newspapers and arguing about someone called the Kaiser and somebody named Sarajevo and it was all too confusing for a little girl to understand.

She held the locket in her hands and sometimes she put it in her mouth and bit it… The locket comforted her, the locket was soothing and warm, and tasted of skin salt and it smelled of Bea's perfume—Bea wore it between her breasts on a chain of thin gold and when she leaned over to kiss Selena good-night it would swing out in the glow of the oil lamp on her night table and she could smell Beatrice's scent.

This was Selena's Home Dream, and she went back to this place whenever she could, but she needed the locket to take her there. Without the locket she could not open the memories. They remained elusive, dim, shadowy.

And the locket had a way of slipping away from her, of falling through rips in the fabric of time— she would have it in her hands—and then time would ripple and her memories would fade—and it would be gone from her—and it seemed that much of her existence in this web of time she was trapped in was spent in an eternal chase for that eternally receding golden locket.

It was the only key to the few memories of happiness she had ever known. It was a drug and a torment to her, and the Shimmer had condemned her to this never-ending hunt.

But she had found it again.

And now, with the locket once again in her hands, it was all rich and dense and perfectly present, and the blissful dream-memory went on for timeless days and endless nights, a never-ending sequence of golden afternoons and soft aromatic nights, with the gliding moon or the golden sun shining in through the curtains, and the music floating in from Jackson Square...

———

Selena lay on the bed in her suite at the Alcazar and felt the first tremors of the *dark thing* coming... Her chest tightened and she tried to turn away from it, to go back into the dream, but she could not, not this final time...and now came the hammering on the door and the angry voices and the sound of shattering glass and then the fearful voices, and her mother screaming, screaming, and then, suddenly, silence.

And now—as always—she could never stop this no matter how often she faced it—the black shape bursting into her room, ripping apart the gauzy fabric of her dream—the thin darting wiry black figure with the knife, a shadow against the sunlight, a silhouette only, and the blade stained with red shimmering up in a glittering arc in the sun...and then swiftly down, piercing her belly—the wild black thing shrieking at her and the knife shimmering in the golden light—pain, pain, pain—and then a great white light filling the room…and then… the Shimmer…and the Shimmer took her away… and she never got home again.

the truth about truth

A Sunday afternoon in New Orleans in August, deep down in the delta, terrain as flat and hot as a cast-iron skillet, hazy heat like a steam bath, the old city rising up and closing in around them as they rolled down Canal Street, passing the La Salle Hotel and the Jung—famous for its rooftop ballroom, the shops and bars all in full swing as they got closer to the French Quarter.

The humid air was heavy with the greasy smoke from wood fires and the choking fumes of the cars and trucks rattling along beside them. Dark green streetcars, as heavy as Tiger tanks, packed with people, clanked and screeched down the rusty tracks, and from over the low roofs of the Old Quarter they heard the steam whistle blast from a riverboat pulling away from the landing and heading out onto the Mississippi. Now and then they picked up a burst of French horns and jazzy piano coming from the open windows of a passing bar, and the sidewalks were crowded, black and white and every shade in between.

There was a hum in the air itself, a high-pitched vibration, and under that a deeper rhythmic pounding that Jack finally realized was just the background thrum of New Orleans in the fifties.

He rolled the window down as far as it would go, shifting in the old leather bench seat, sweat dripping off him, his uniform shirt drenched. He looked at Clete, behind the wheel. He seemed to be handling this sauna of a city better than he was.

"I know I'm not supposed to tell you stuff about the future, Clete, but someday there's going to be a thing for your car called *air-conditioning*, and it'll keep your car cool and nobody will have to die from this fricking heat."

Clete looked over at him, grinned around his cigarette. "Already got that on Cadillacs and Buicks and Oldsmobiles. Man, you do look like a boiled crawdaddy."

"I feel like one."

"Yeah well no offense but you smell like a dead bat. I'm gonna put us in a couple of rooms at the Monteleone. Place is air-conditioned. Mostly. You can have a shower, change your clothes, get that uniform cleaned."

"What about my sidearm? I can't wear a patrol belt with civilian clothing."

"I've got spare shoulder rigs in the truck."

"Are we going to meet your guy with the NOPD?"

"Court of the Two Sisters, just along Royal from the hotel. She'll be there at five."

"She?"

The Court of the Two Sisters turned out to be a wisteria-shaded courtyard filled with tables and lit by lanterns, a secluded garden that you reached by going through two ornate wrought-iron gates that, according to Clete, were a gift from Queen Isabella of Spain.

"How'd you know that?"

"Mary Alice. This is her favorite place in New Orleans. It was started by a couple of Creole sisters back in the 1850s. Supposed to be haunted. There she is."

Clete was looking in the far corner of the courtyard where a young woman in a pale green sundress was sitting at a round table covered in pinkish linen, set out under a spreading canopy of flowery wisteria vines.

Her head was down and she was reading something on the table in front of her, possibly a file of some kind. She was very blonde and her hair glimmered like fire in the sunlight that filtered through the vines and lay in scattered pools on the cobblestone floors. Lanterns hung from the wisteria vines and the table, like all the others, was set with candles.

It was a lovely place, cool and quiet even in the steam heat of August. Barbara would have loved it, and Jack was wondering what, if anything, he could do about Barbara and Katy from here in 1957—*shoot the bartender at the Alcazar* was the only idea that had come to him—when the woman lifted her head, saw them, smiled and stood up as they reached the table. And, of course, the woman was Pandora Jansson.

Or at least her identical twin in another life. Jack managed not to stop dead in his tracks—thinking *Anson Freitag and now Pandora*—but he slowed so abruptly that Clete had to step around him to get to the table, giving Jack a look as he passed him. The woman—Pandora—was smiling at Clete as she shook his hand, obviously a meeting of good friends.

"Annabelle, thanks for coming. Jack, this is Annabelle Fontaine. Annabelle, this is Jack—"

A momentary hesitation, which she noted.

"Kearney," Clete finished, giving Jack his wife's maiden name.

Annabelle smiled at Jack and he saw a momentary flicker of an unidentifiable emotion in her eyes and the lines around them—although strong looking and tanned—just like Pandora—she wasn't as young as he had first thought, now that he was seeing her clearly. Maybe in her midthirties, just like Pandora. The puzzled look was still there, although veiled now, as she gave his hand a strong masculine shake and said, "Kearney? Are you related to Clete's wife?"

She had the rolling cadences of the Deep South, and her voice was low and throaty, a whiskey baritone. Jack felt the sensual heat coming off her, almost a visible erotic radiation, like an aura, and his blood was rising up to her.

"Yes, in a roundabout way," said Jack, controlling his voice because his throat was a little thick. Clete, taking a seat at the table, was watching them with interest, a little smile on his lips. Annabelle released his hand and took her seat, lifting the hem of her sundress a bit as she sat, and sunlight shimmered across her knees and a brief flash of strong white thighs.

Bare-legged, no stockings.

Christ, thought Jack, as he pulled in his chair, trying not to stare at her, *I'm fucking doomed*.

Apparently she had noted his accent.

"You're not from around here?" she asked.

Clete stepped in.

"Jack's with the Florida Highway Patrol, the Criminal Investigation Division. He's based in Jacksonville too. We're sort of…associates."

"I know why Cletus is here, but what brings *you* to New Orleans?" she asked, looking at him with a disturbing intensity.

Clete put a hand up and said, "No, first some food and something to drink. We've driven all night and most of the day, and if I don't get something to eat I'm going to fall over and die."

Which they did, and a lot, platters of seafood and salad, crayfish in a spicy Cajun sauce, French bread with olive oil and oregano and, eventually, three bottles of Dom Pérignon, which Jack had never had before because it was insanely expensive, but here in this time period it was $25 a bottle.

They kept it light all through the first courses,

Jack letting Annabelle and Clete do most of the talking since his grip on the current events of 1957 was pretty sketchy. He gathered that Annabelle had retired from Naval Intelligence at the end of the war and—after an apparently disastrous love affair with a Marine officer—had found herself in New Orleans, where an old friend from the Navy had persuaded her to come onto the NOPD in their Intelligence Division.

She had accepted the offer, and was now a detective in the plainclothes section of the 8th Division, which covered the French Quarter.

And no, she wasn't married or currently engaged, questions Jack didn't ask but he managed to infer from the table talk.

When the third bottle was sitting upside down in the silver bucket, the sun had set and the cool of the evening was sifting down through the wisteria canopy. Annabelle called for coffee all around, and she ordered a chocolate parfait for herself, which she ate with what seemed to Jack to be a wonderfully erotic appreciation.

After dessert the mood at the table became much more focused.

Jack realized then that they did everything differently in New Orleans in the fifties; they did it all *slowly*, and they *savored* it as it went drifting past. As far as he was concerned, right now at any rate, looking at Annabelle Fontaine, if he had to stay here, he'd be fine with that.

Clete took a sip of his coffee, sighed, offered

cigarettes to Annabelle and Jack, both of whom accepted, lit Annabelle's cigarette and flipped the Zippo to Jack.

"So, Annabelle, here's the thing, why Jack is here. He's looking at the same woman, this Aurelia DiSantis."

She turned to Jack, eyebrow raised.

"And what has she done that has brought you into it?"

"Basically, I think she's a serial killer."

Both Clete and Annabelle gave him a puzzled look.

"What's a serial killer?" she asked, and Jack realized the term hadn't been invented yet.

"Sorry, I mean, I think she's making her living going from victim to victim, getting close, getting access to money, jewels, bank accounts, and then she kills the victim and takes the money."

"So, a *serial* killer, yes? And where has she been doing this serial killing?"

"Jacksonville. Amelia Island. St. Augustine. My own case with her involves kidnapping and the murder of two people at Amelia Island, and the poisoning death of a third, a young woman."

"And you think this is the same woman that Cletus is investigating?"

Jack looked at Clete, who pulled two photographs out of his suit jacket and laid them side by side on the table. Annabelle picked them up, studied them by the candlelight.

One was the surveillance shot Clete had taken at

the Monterey Court, and the other one was Jack's photo of Diana Bowman at the Carousel Bar in the Monteleone.

"You're right. That's the same woman."

"We think so."

"And what name do you know her by?"

"Diana Bowman."

Annabelle shook her head as if confused, uncertain, looked down at the file folder she'd been reading when they arrived, picked it up and took out several sheets of paper.

"Cletus asked me to see what I could learn about this person. Apparently he's asking for...a friend."

She said this with a sly smile.

Clete said nothing, and so did Jack. Annabelle took that in, noted it and went on.

"Okay. So, I went into the Parish Registries and other city records looking for an Aurelia DiSantis, born on the date that Cletus got from her Louisiana driver's license. You won't be surprised to hear that there was no such person born on that date, or on any date within five years either way. Nor was she ever issued a Louisiana driver's license, so what she has must be a forgery. Which was useful, since there are only three places you can get a convincing forgery of a Louisiana driver's license. I went to all three places, one in Metairie, one in Slidell and the third in Angola Prison."

"Angola?" said Jack.

She sighed.

"I'm afraid so. The facility has all the equipment needed, and the prison has all the forgers you could ever hope for."

"Angola Prison deals in forgeries?"

Clete laughed.

"Jack, you think Florida is corrupt. We've got *nothing* on Louisiana."

"And I am afraid that the NOPD is the most corrupt police force in Louisiana," said Annabelle, with a sideways smile. "Which is saying a great deal. But, in a way, things are much easier when almost everyone is corrupt."

"How?"

"You can get things done, if you are willing to pay, and Cletus's…ahh…*friend*…was very willing to pay for what we would call…special consideration."

"Meaning you bribed the hell out of a whole bunch of people?"

She smiled again, but now it was not so kindly.

"Precisely. And who I bribed is none of your affair, is it? Any more than it is my affair to ask Clete who his wealthy *friend* really is, or why I am being told that you are a Kearney when you are so obviously related to Cletus by blood. You could be his grandson, if he ever lives long enough to have one, which I doubt. But I do not ask, do I?"

Although deeply shaken by the comment—*why grandson instead of son or even brother?*—Jack smiled back. "Hey. No offense."

"Then don't be offensive," she said, her voice a low throaty purr.

"And what did you get?" said Clete, leaning into the tension. Annabelle held Jack's look for a heartbeat longer, long enough to make her point, and then she turned to Clete.

"It is not necessary to actually go to Angola to arrange for the forgery. That would have been foolish under any circumstances. Especially for a woman. There is a place here in town where the Angola forgeries may be arranged. I will not tell you where that place is since it is in an NOPD-controlled building. The woman who commissioned the forgery did not leave her name, but she paid so much money for it that the person who met with her..."

"So a woman?" asked Jack.

"Yes, and yes, she answers the description of the woman you are both interested in. So, the person thought it worthwhile to have her followed when she left the building...just in case she might have been an agent of some higher level of law enforcement."

"Like the FBI or Treasury?" said Clete.

"Exactly."

"And..."

"And the woman wandered through the streets of the French Quarter for a very long time, moving erratically, stepping into shops and then back out again quickly, changing directions, and once even entering a bar and leaving by the back door."

"Shaking a tail," said Jack.

"Yes. But not successfully. She was an amateur.

Finally, after much walking about, she arrived at what appeared to be her residence, where she used a key to enter an apartment on the upper floor."

"And where was this apartment?"

"The Pontalba, on St. Peter Street, next to Jackson Square. Apartment nine. The woman remained until the next morning, when she reappeared, wearing different clothing, looking quite refreshed, and went for coffee and beignets at the Café du Monde. Where she sat for two hours, reading an F. Scott Fitzgerald novel. *The Great Gatsby*."

"So she was out of her apartment for two hours?"

"Yes."

"During which time your…person…had apartment number nine at the Pontalba searched."

"Yes. It is the natural course of such things."

"And what was found?"

Her confusion returned here, and she was quiet for a while. They waited. From the street came the sound of a jazz quartet, and the crowds were building up as the evening came on. The courtyard was full of customers and the chatter and clatter of the place was growing louder.

"Several items that indicated that the person living in the apartment was named Selena D'Arcy, and that her family had lived in this apartment since the early 1900s. The original names on the lease—dated the seventh of November, 1903—were Beatrice and William D'Arcy."

D'Arcy, thought Jack, remembering their talk

with Gerald Walker in his hospital room. The name that Diana Bowman had been looking for.

D'Arcy, not *Dorsey*.

D'Arcy.

And the locket's inscription.

To Bea from Will Xmas 1909.

But Annabelle was still talking.

"According to the records—at least the records as they were last week…"

Here she paused, gave a strange look, as if to say, *Remember that point.*

"The—the apartment has been vacant since September 8, 1914. Rent all paid up, decade after decade, but unoccupied."

"But that's wrong, isn't it?" said Jack. "The records were wrong? Had to be."

She shook her head.

"It's much more complicated than that. Let me tell you in my own way. No interruptions, okay?"

"Okay."

"So, the apartment itself looked as if it had remained untouched since 1914. It was neat and well maintained, very clean and well-ordered, but there was nothing in it that looked newer than the early 1900s. And the clothes in the closets were all decades out of date. The person searching the apartment was…unsettled…by the way it looked. The person described it as a well-preserved tomb, a kind of mausoleum. The person also observed that all of the mirrors in the apartment had been covered with linen cloth."

Clete heard that.

"That's a Creole superstition, isn't it?"

She nodded.

"Yes. They believe that the spirits of the dying will confuse the mirror for the gates of eternity, and so will pass into the mirror instead of going through to eternity."

"And their souls will remain trapped in the mirror?" said Jack, who had heard of this superstition years ago.

"Yes. That is their belief."

"Okay. Got all this," said Clete. "But something's bothering you, Annabelle. I can see it in your eyes. What is it?"

She looked down at the file, but not because she was reading it. She was looking for time.

After a while, she looked up.

"Well, yes, there is something very strange here. Will you listen, and try not to say anything?"

"I'll try," said Clete.

"Try harder," she said, softening it with a hand on his wrist. "Well, in this place, apartment nine of the Pontalba, according to the police reports, something very bad happened on the afternoon of September 7, 1914. The people down in Jackson Square hear screaming, and the sound of breaking glass, and then the kind of silence that comes after something terrible has been finished. So the neighbors arrive, they knock at the door, and there is no answer. So they break it down."

Silence, finally, from Jack and Clete, and Annabelle paused, took some coffee. The jazz band had moved off down Royal Street, and the evening had gradually become night.

"In the parlor, two dead people, Beatrice and William, both stabbed many times, stabbed with a big knife, and by someone very strong. Beatrice is on the divan, very much mutilated, torn as if by wolves, and the husband, William, it looks as if he died first, in the hall, and they think maybe he was the one to open the apartment door, because the first wound is in his belly, as might happen if you were to open the door—you stand there, one hand on the doorknob, you are exposed, open, and so the knife goes in. And he is down, in the hall, and the killer slices him up, the throat, the belly…the eyes are gone, so the report says, stabbed out, gouged, and then the killer goes for Beatrice, catches her on the divan, and so she dies too."

Jack and Clete said nothing, but Jack thought, *This woman feels this, as if she had been there to watch. Pandora had that gift too.*

A sigh, and then…

"So there is also a little girl, a five-year-old, we are told, since there is a birthday cake on the parlor table, with five candles, all blown out, and three slices taken from it, and the plates with silver forks set down. The little girl is in the second bedroom, a lovely room, all white—or at least it was—with windows that open onto Jackson Square. And she has been killed also, stabbed many times, in her bed, twisted into the sheets. You can see this? I do not have to go on?"

She was speaking in a whisper now, living it. Jack and Clete waited. She shook herself, lifted her head, came back into the present.

"So we have the three dead—Beatrice, William and the little girl. The little girl, according to her birth certificate, is Selena D'Arcy. She died on the seventh day of September in 1914. It was her fifth birthday."

A long silence.

Finally, Jack had to ask.

"Did they catch the killer?"

Annabelle looked at her file.

"The D'Arcys also had a ward, apparently a relative of Will D'Arcy's. Her name was Philomena. Last name not recorded. Her age is uncertain, because the record is confused. I will return to that in a moment."

She sighed, went inward, took some coffee, organizing her thoughts.

Neither man interrupted her.

"Well, Philomena, last name unknown, age unknown, was confined for a time to a mental hospital. She was violent, and dangerous, and was taken away by the authorities after she had begun to set fires, and they think she also killed some animals, cats and stray dogs. Birds when she could trap them. The authorities had to do something, since the D'Arcys could not control her. She was committed to East Louisiana State Hospital, in the town of Jackson, in East Feliciana Parish. On the third of September of that year she escaped by hiding herself inside an ice delivery wagon. She was believed to have made her way to New Orleans, and it was also believed that she broke into apartment nine of the Pontalba on September 7, and it is believed that she killed every person in it, Beatrice and William and Selena, who was five at the time. As I have said."

She sighed, picked up her cup and took a sip.

"What did they do with the ward? Philomena?"

"What did they do? They did nothing."

"Why?"

"She was never caught. She was never seen again."

"So who is living in apartment nine right now?"

Annabelle shrugged, a very French gesture, but it was also very much a Pandora Jansson expression.

"According to the records, at least as they were last week, no one is in the apartment. I am coming to that. I have a theory. But you're not going to like it."

She took some more coffee, lit another cigarette.

"Well, as I have said, apartment nine at the Pontalba has been under the control of the D'Arcy family for many years. So the records tell me. But there is something very wrong with the records. For several years after the killings of September 7, 1914, the apartment was listed as sealed and unoccupied. Yet the rent continues to be paid, not regularly, but consistently over the years, by drafts from various banks, handled by one law firm after another. And this goes on for a very long time, *decades*, from after the Great War, through the Depression, through the Second World War. So mysterious, yes, but not unheard of, especially for New Orleans."

"So what is it that caught your eye?" asked Jack, caught up in the story and her voice as she told it. She smiled at him, a secret element in it meant only for him. Or so he hoped. She looked down at her notes, and then sighed again, a cop confronting something not easily explained, and harder still to convey.

"Well, now we come to it. I searched the records very thoroughly—Cletus's friend was paying a great deal of money—and I came across something I can't explain. Understand that I went through these records over a period of several days. I had to return to the Parish Registry because you cannot take the books out of the building. Last week, the record was quite clear. Apartment nine had been vacant from September 8, 1914, to October 2, 1943. You understand me?"

They did.

"So yesterday I go back to confirm, and the records have *changed*."

"They've *been* changed, you mean?" said Clete. She shook her head.

"No. That's impossible. The record pages are in bound books, a series of huge ledgers, kept over many years, very old, the pages are yellowed with age, brittle, the script of many clerks, all writing in ancient green ink, all written by hand. *Different* hands. It would be *impossible* to alter them without it being detected."

"But…?"

"But the registries have *changed*. Physically *changed*! This is *impossible*. But it is also *true*. Now the records in the Parish Registry show that apartment nine of the Pontalba has been occupied continually from October 2, 1943, to the present day. This is impossible. But it is also true. The records have *changed*. They changed—as far as I can see—perhaps two days ago."

"Apartment nine is occupied. By whom?"

She shrugged, letting her frustration show.

"By a woman named Selena D'Arcy. According to her birth certificate, she was born in Plaquemine Parish on the seventh of September in 1909."

"So she'd be…forty-eight now?"

"Yes."

"But Selena D'Arcy was *killed*? Stabbed to death. At the age of five, on September 7 in 1914."

She smiled, closed the file folder, pushed it across to Clete, patted it with her hand.

"That was then, my friend. This is now."

———

They gathered to go, since there was nothing left to say. Clete went to pay the bill, and Annabelle caught Jack's arm, a gentle touch, and she leaned in close to him.

"You are at the Monteleone."

Not a question.

"Yes."

"Your room?"

"Room 319."

"Tonight, I will come to you."

"Yes, please."

"Do you know why?"

"I think so."

"Good," she said and kissed his cheek, and then she turned and walked away down Royal. She didn't look back, but then she didn't have to.

the death and life and death
of mary alice

How to break the Reddings, how to distract them, destroy them if possible, this was Selena's goal. She felt the solution might lie in an oblique approach. If they had other and more pressing concerns, such as a war with the Vizzini Family, she might slip between their minds. But she needed a key, and she knew of only one.

Clete Redding's wife, Mary Alice.

She remembered that in the original time stream, Mary Alice had died in a single-car crash. An *accident*, as far as she remembered—Tessio had denied any involvement in it, saying that the Vizzinis did not make war on wives and children— but the accident did have fatal consequences for the Vizzini family.

But that was only because the Vizzini family had been taken by surprise, so many vital men killed before they could react.

She could do something about that.

She could warn Tessio this time, and if she did,

she was certain that Clete Redding would end up dead shortly afterward. Which would solve her problem with the Redding family once and for all.

But in *this* time stream, that decisive crash hadn't happened yet. Could she leave it to chance, wait and see if her arrival back here wouldn't have a cascade effect on the time stream, that Mary Alice would still die in a single car crash on Friday, the thirtieth of August?

No. She could not. She had no choice. She had to make certain of it. She had to arrange it herself. And, to be safe, it had to happen at the same spot where, sixty years later, Jack Redding's wife and child would die, in a head-on crash with a Mercedes-Benz driven by Anson Freitag.

Because Selena was what she was, and not what she thought she was, it never occurred to her that the only reason Mary Alice was going to die at the same spot where Jack's family would die sixty years later was because Selena, at this precise moment in 1957, decided to make that happen.

This turned out to be a bad decision.

———

She called down to the front desk of the Alcazar, and a few minutes later the bellman brought up a copy of the telephone directory for St. Augustine, Florida.

She still remembered the address of the beach house Redding lived in—it hadn't been lost in her flight down the Long Hall—it was 32 Avenue A in Crescent Beach. She leafed through to the listings for Redding…and found four, but none of them had the first name listed as Cletus, or even began with a *C*, and not one of them showed an address of 32 Avenue A in Crescent Beach.

She sat down on the couch, wrapped up in her silk robe, sipped a glass of Chianti and thought about it. Redding was a police officer. It would stand to reason that he wouldn't want his home phone and address listed in the phone directory for any vengeful criminal to look up.

So what would he do?

Put it in his wife's name?

She sat back, closed her eyes, thought about that obituary she had read when she first realized that Clete Redding was Jack Redding's grandfather. She had looked it up on Will Coleman's computer. She remembered that his wife's first name was Mary Alice, because it had been mentioned in the obituary. But was her maiden name listed?

They usually were, weren't they? She was sure it had been…but she couldn't bring it back. This fragmented memory stream was a side effect of the Shimmer, and it was maddening. Would she have to go through every page of the St. Augustine Telephone Directory looking for 32 Avenue A, Crescent Beach? Over seven thousand listings, at a rough guess?

And then hope that—*if* he had used his wife's maiden name—she would recognize it when she saw it? Is that what she would have to do?

Yes, she would have to do that.

So she did.

Kearney, M. 32 Ave A, Crescent Beach JA9-6630

She looked at the number for a while, thinking about how to handle the call and what to say. After a while she dialed it, waited, waited…let it ring…and she was about to hang up when the call was picked up.

"Hello?"

A woman's voice, a Spanish accent.

"Hello, may I speak to Mary Alice Kearney, please?"

"Sorry she not here. I take a message?"

"Oh…do you expect her back soon?"

"No. She gone to see her cousin family in Rattlesnake Island. Not come back for a while."

"Oh dear… I was hoping to reach her."

"Is an emergency? Something happen to Mister Cletus?"

Selena got the idea that she was talking to a maid. And that Clete Redding wasn't home either.

"No, no. He's fine. I'm calling from Personnel, actually. We're trying to update Detective Redding's life insurance policy and we needed to—"

"You working very late."

"Yes, yes…records have to be accurate. Time isn't waiting. Thing is, we need to have Mrs. Redding's permission to amend the policy to include enhanced health benefits—"

"Okay, she will send a letter, okay?"

"Well, thing is, my filings all have to be in by noon tomorrow? It's our Year End, and all I really need is her verbal permission. Would you know the phone number? Where she is now?"

"Yes...*momentito, por favor*...she leave on a note here...*a dónde, madre mia, a dónde*..."

Selena waited, listening to the sound of the woman's breath in the mouthpiece, and papers being shuffled, and then she came back.

"Yes, here, Mister and Mrs. Frank Forrest, *numero*—the number—is Jacksonville 9-7522."

"Oh, lovely, thank you so much."

———

"Hello?"

"Yes, hello...am I speaking to Mrs. Forrest?"

"Yes. Who is this?"

"I'm sorry to call so late. My name is Alice Stein. I'm calling from the United States Postal Distribution Center in Jacksonville, and we have a registered letter for a Mr. Frank Forrest, but we're showing an address in Flagler Beach, and that address doesn't show a Mister Frank Forrest resident there. Do we have the right address?"

"What is the letter?"

Selena took a moment, shuffled some newspaper pages, came back.

"It looks like it's from the IRS."

"Oh dear."

"So we have the wrong address?"

"Oh, I think so. Yes. You do. We're at 77 Florala Parkway, on Rattlesnake Island."

"My, that's an exotic name. Where is that?"

"We're right on the coast, just south of Matanzas Inlet."

"Oh my. Sounds lovely, Mrs. Forrest."

"It is, it's very pretty here. Can you tell me what the letter is about, perhaps?"

"Sorry I can't. But, since you ask, and don't tell anyone I said this, we are seeing a lot of them, and they all look to be some sort of survey."

She sounded relieved when she answered.

"Oh, well then…so you'll send it on?"

"Right away. Thank you so much. Sorry to have called so late. You have a great evening now."

"We will. And you, as well."

"I'll try. Bye-bye."

"Bye."

———

She sat back for a while, thinking this through. Mary Alice Kearney was already very close to Matanzas Inlet. And Clete Redding wasn't with her. Was this significant? Where was he, and why was his wife staying with relatives? Did it have to do with the time stream, or was it the mob war that was brewing between the Vizzinis and the Traficantes?

Or was it just a coincidence?

No, it wasn't a coincidence.

It was a ripple in the time stream, perhaps the

same ripple that had carried Mary Alice to a natural death the last time around. But this wasn't enough to change Selena's mind. There was too much at risk to be indecisive.

Another element to think about. Where would Clete and Jack Redding be right now? They certainly weren't in the Alcazar Hotel. And the only person at his beach house seemed to be the maid.

Who would know where they were?

Tessio, or one of his people. They always knew where people were, especially cops they were bribing, or cops who were likely to be trouble, and Clete Redding was both of those things. She picked up the house phone, dialed a private number.

"Yes…Is Tony around?…Tell him Aurelia…No, I can hold…"

And she did, for about a minute.

Selena looked at herself in the mirror as she waited, but not for long, because there was *something* about mirrors, something she remembered from her childhood. Mirrors were dangerous and it was good to keep them covered, especially when death was coming around. And death was coming around tonight.

"Yes, hi, Tony…No, no I don't need Tessio right now…Just a favor…It's about Clete Redding… Yes…I heard…actually, I saw some of it…I was up in the balcony…not as long as Tessio is alive, Little Anthony…He protects Clete and Clete protects the Vizzinis…I can't get caught up in that, Tony…No I don't want to hear it…what I need now…No I can have *that* whenever I want…Do any of your people know where Clete Redding is?…He did?…New Orleans? When?…Okay…At the Monteleone…He's there now? And the other one?…Yes, the big one, looks like a cowboy?…Both at the Monteleone?… Good, thank you, Tony…No, I'm alone…Thanks that's very kind of you…but not tonight…"

Selena wanted to sound as if she were breaking off, but she very much wanted him on the line. And he wasn't going anywhere but into a blind rage.

"Yes, I know… I know you want to pay Redding back for that thing at the bar, Tony, but you can't go up against him without your father's permission…yes?"

His voice was a strangled snarl, his pride even more wounded now that he knew that she had seen the whole humiliating confrontation. If *she* had seen it, so had everyone else in the hotel, and now his manhood was at stake.

"Yes, yes, I know…Actually, he's only got one weak spot, Tony, that's his wife, Mary Alice…Actually I do…She's down the shore below Matanzas Inlet…Rattlesnake Island…I don't know why… Maybe he sent her away in case this stupid war between you and the Traficantes actually starts… Yes with relatives, the Forrests I think is the name, Frank Forrest or something…Why are you asking?"

She knew why he was asking. It was what she wanted all along.

"No. No! Don't you go near her, Tony…Your father won't allow vendetta against wives and kids… Don't be stupid, Tony. Don't do anything stupid…"

She listened for a while longer as Tony wound himself up, vendetta and honor and all that manly dago crap, smiling to herself as he got closer to his redline—Tony was an undisciplined hothead and if he ever got control of the Vizzini operation the family would be wiped out in a year—then she said, "Look, I'm not hearing this. I'm not listening to this childish crap. If you have a problem with Clete, then go after Clete, not his poor wife…Yes hurting her would mark him up badly…Maybe you don't have the balls to go after Clete directly…Oh, you'll do him next, will you? No, this is horseshit, I'm hanging up…Now…No I don't want you to come to my room…Goodbye, Tony!"

She put the receiver down harder than she had to, looked at herself in the mirror, smiled again, thinking that had gone just about perfectly, then she looked away again, because mirrors were dangerous.

So, Clete and Jack Redding were in New Orleans. There was only one reason why they would have gone to New Orleans, and sooner or later they would find out about her apartment at the Pontalba, and what her real name was, and everything that had happened there, including what that monstrous thing called Philomena had done, and that was something she could not allow to happen.

She got up and poured herself the last of the Chianti and looked out the window onto the central square. A bunch of kids were pretending to ride the old Spanish cannon in the middle of the park, and over by the old fort fireworks were lighting up the underside of a bank of clouds.

Music was coming from somewhere, a woman with a rough but haunting voice and a strong French accent, singing "Je Suis Seule Ce Soir" with a slow sad piano keeping her company.

I am alone tonight.

Yes, Selena was certainly alone.

She turned away and picked up the phone.

"Hello, this is Miss DiSantis…Yes, I'm fine thank you…No, not yet…But I do have request. I'm going to need a car tomorrow. Can you do that?… Yes. Good. Then done. I will be out front at noon. Have it at the gates…No, I will not need a driver."

Walking back to the Monteleone, weaving through the chattering crowds, passing open bars and jazz clubs where the music flared out at them like blue flames, the steamy heat of the delta night and the scents and sounds of the Old Quarter all around them, Jack and Clete moved in a companionable silence.

Clete was a little ahead of Jack, a big broad bull of a man, threading his way through the crowds, moving and shifting, light and nimble, a man in the prime of his life, and Jack felt a strong rush of love for the man, and with it came the guilt, the panic, the fact that he had no idea what he was supposed to do, or not do, about Anson Freitag and Mary Alice Redding.

They passed a newsstand where the paper— the *Times-Picayune*—was shouting in bold black print above the fold about something President Eisenhower was doing, and then below the fold something more about the new *Richard Diamond* series, and then on the sidebar something about a new toy by Wham-O called a Frisbee and a column on Abdel Nasser—and all he could think about was "what do I say?"

They got to the hotel, and it wasn't until they were riding up to their rooms that he decided to say this: "Look, Clete, I can't say much—"

"Well, you been thinking it all along Royal, so what the hell is it?"

"You can tell?"

Clete shook his head, a bull shaking off the picadors.

"Yes of course. And you have something to tell me. About Mary Alice."

Jack was silent.

Clete shook his head.

"No shutting up, kid. You know *something*. What is it?"

The elevator rose up, grinding and rattling. The air got colder. The music from the Carousel Bar grew faint. Clete was looking at Jack.

"Clete…"

"Look, ever since you got here, whenever I mention Mary Alice, you get a look on your face like a guy who just backed over his dog. You got something to say about her, and I want to hear it. So, for fuck's sake, Jack. Tell me what it is."

Jack sighed, hunted for the words.

"Don't try to honeysuckle it, kid. What the fuck is it?"

"Okay. All right. On Friday, the thirtieth…"

"Yes?"

"Don't let Mary Alice drive."

Clete took that in.

"Okay. She doesn't drive. Drive when?"

"On Friday. On the thirtieth of August."

Clete looked at his grandson.

"Something happens then?"

"Yes."

"Something bad?"

"Yes."

"What is it? It happens in a car? Like an accident or something?"

"Yes."

"Jeez, kid. This is like talking to the Magic 8-Ball! Reply hazy. Ask again later."

Clete turned on him, backed him into a corner.

"Jack, so help me fucking God if you know something about Mary Alice you had better goddamn tell me now because if she dies and you could have stopped it…"

He stepped back, releasing Jack's space, his face changing into sorrow.

"She *can't die*, Jack. If you know something, *anything*, you have to tell me. Fuck the Rules. FUCK the Rules. Tell me. If you don't tell me and she dies, I swear I will…"

"What? Kill me?"

Clete backed away, seemed to shrink.

"No. Of course not. No, no, but, Jack, she's the world to me. The world. What do you know? Tell me. What do you know?"

The elevator came to their floor, ground to a rusty halt. The doors opened with an asthmatic wheeze, ending in a grating clank. They stepped out into the hall, walked toward their rooms.

"I don't really *know* anything. It's all just a guess. But I think it would be a good idea to keep her out of a car from now until next Saturday. Don't let her drive."

Clete took that in.

And then he said something surprising.

"If you tell me this, and I act on it, what does it do to the future?"

"How do you mean that?"

"You lost your wife and kid."

"Yes. I did."

"But not yet, right? It happens in the future, right? Hasn't happened yet? Right now, in this time, your wife isn't born, your kid isn't born. So if you save Mary Alice…"

"Yeah?"

"Do you pay a price?"

Jack wasn't sure, but he didn't want Clete to think about that.

"No. I don't think so. Not yet."

"Why? What can you do about it here? Do you know how your wife dies?"

"Yes. I do."

"And is there something you can do about that here, in this time?"

"Yes. There is."

"What is it?"

Jack was quiet for a time.

"I know who kills her."

"Who?"

"Friday. The kid at the bar in the Alcazar Hotel."

"How does he kill her?"

"He grows up, gets to be a famous doctor, re-tires in his eighties, and on one Christmas Eve sixty fucking years from now, he loses control of his Benz and hits my wife and kid head-on in the middle of the Matanzas Bridge—"

"There's no bridge over Matanzas Inlet—"

"There will be. And he hits her head-on and kills them both."

Clete stood back, dropped his hands, went in-ward and was silent for a while. From down the hall came the sound of a song, something very French, a woman singing about her being alone this evening. "Fuck, kid. What will you do?"

"I don't know. I know if I kill the kid now a whole lot of people whom he might have saved will die."

"So the thing you're worrying about is how many lives are your wife and kid worth? If you kill Friday and he never gets to be this famous doctor?"

"Yeah."

"And the same thing goes for Mary Alice?"

"Clete. I don't know. And if I do, so be it."

Clete took that in.

They were at his door.

"Okay. I get that. I can't do any other. I have to

save her if I can. No matter what happens in the future. The cost to you. You understand that?"

"Yes. I do. And you're right."

"I am? You say that I am?"

"Yes, Clete. I say you are right."

A long pause, while Clete looked into him and considered him.

"Yes, you mean it. Thank you. I will call Mary Alice tonight. She's safe until Friday. She's at the Forrests' down at Rattlesnake Island. Declan is down there too. I'll tell her to stay there."

"And not get in a car."

"Yes. I'll call her right now."

———

And he did.

But the line was busy.

So he lay down on the bed, in his suit, tired and troubled, closed his eyes and tried to calm his fevered mind.

He thought about Jack, and the strange events that had brought him to this place. He thought about Mary Alice, and how much he loved her.

He sat up, tried the number again.

This time it rang and rang and no one answered. He looked at the clock. It was almost midnight. The Forrests were nice people, but old and frail. He remembered that they sometimes turned the ringers down when they went to bed. And they went to bed damn early. He pressed the cradle hook, dialed again, got the same thing. They had definitely packed it in for the night.

He lay there, feeling the Dom Pérignon and the heavy meal, closed his eyes and listened to the music out on Royal Street…someone singing, "I went down to St. James Infirmary," in a rasping pain-filled voice…and the scent of jasmine drifted in through his open windows…

A riverboat wheezed out a long foghorn farewell as it churned its way out into the Mississippi…and the night came down slow and deep and easy as it does in the delta…

…and the music floated in on the night wind off Lake Pontchartrain, and his eyes closed…opened…and closed…

And then, being a cop, five minutes later, he snapped awake, worried sick. If he couldn't reach the Forrests, he could sure as hell have the Forrests reached. He sat up, got on the phones, dialed the duty desk back in Jacksonville.

"Yeah this is Detective Clete Redding, I'm with Jacksonville Robbery Homicide…Yeah, Shield Number 2355…Yeah well call Beau Short at the HQ—here's his home number go wake him up…"

A silence…somebody got through to someone.

"Yes, we got that, what would you like us to do, Detective Redding?"

"I have an address under threat. It's 77 Florala Parkway…Yes, Rattlesnake Island, one mile south of Matanzas Inlet… I'd like a unit there…No, not a County car. I want one of *ours*. This is a cop family matter…Yes, right now. As soon as possible…

Yes…I'm good for the overtime okay…I'm Detective Clete Redding, Shield Number 2355—I'm with Robbery Homicide in Jacksonville…Yes thank you…I need a car on that driveway at 77 Florala Parkway…Frank and Helen Forrest…Yes…Yes as soon as you can get one there…No *right now*…Why the fuck not?"

He listened, with rapidly diminishing patience, to a lot of horseshit bureaucratic chatter, and then he cut back in:

"So fucking find one!…Roll one out of motor pool! Reassign a traffic car!…Okay, okay I get it. I *fucking* get it."

He took a deep breath, getting his temper under control.

"Okay yes, yes, if tomorrow is the best you can do, which is *fucking horseshit*, by the way, then do that…Call the County sheriff guys then, and get them to get out to that address right now, get them to cover that address until you can get one of our own cars out there in the morning."

He listened as the duty officer said he'd get right on to Flagler County and see that they got a sheriff's car out there ASAP.

"Okay, good, thanks, and remember, when the County car gets there, *nobody* gets in…nobody gets out. Okay?…Yes. Badge 2355…Okay…Good. Make sure this happens. Make sure a Flagler County car gets there tonight, within the hour. Because it's important, yes?…Yes…Life-and-death. Thank you."

———

At a quarter past midnight, the knock Jack had been waiting for came, a gentle three-by-three, and he had the door open before it ended. Annabelle was there, in the same pale green sundress, but with a lace shawl to cover her, because the evening was cooling.

Jack stepped away, opening the room to her, and she came in, bringing the scent of bergamot with her. She stopped in the middle of the room—a very nice room, in blues and reds, with a Juliet balcony, framed by satin curtains in blue and gold, open to the square…the sound of "St. James Infirmary" drifting in on the evening wind… Jack stayed back, let her take in the room.

She turned to him, dropped the shawl and came to him, put a finger on his lips, looked up at him—she was Pandora at that moment and it made him dizzy as he took her in—opened herself to him with a delicate but searching kiss…her tongue flickering like pink fire… She moved into him and he lifted her… There was a bed, and they found it and there they opened each other, as lovers do.

———

On his back, watching the lights play on the ceiling, Jack turned to Annabelle, touched her naked belly, kissed her nipples, one and then the other, and then back again, as she rose up to his lips, and then he pulled her in close, as if she were the last flight out of Lisbon.

"So…"

"No," she said. "Not yet."

Jack lifted up, reached for what was left of the champagne, held a glass before her. He had also ordered two chocolate parfaits, apparently her favorite dessert, which she had shared with him in several unique ways, and which she enjoyed with the same erotic intensity that she had shown at The Court of the Two Sisters.

She sat up, lifting the sheet to cover her breasts, as women will when they intend to be heard instead of desired, took the warm glass and sipped it, her eyes lowered, thinking what to say.

Jack, who was not a boy, knew when to be quiet, and he waited for what was coming.

———

"I need to know about the records," she said, after a long silence.

"And you think I know something about the records?"

She raised up, the sheet dropping away—her breasts were full and shell pink and teardrop round and her nipples were small and pink and tight, perfect rosebud nipples—he looked at them—how could he not?—and she tapped his cheek, a ritual rebuke, gentle, loving, but it got his attention.

"You are not Cletus Redding's relative."

"Well, yes, I am."

"You are deceiving. You use language to be oblique. Yes, you are a relative, but not in any way that word is usually understood. I'm not here to play those word games. Why did the records change? You know they did. And you know that it is impossible that they changed. So tell me, please, how this impossible thing happened, because I am very unhappy with what I fear I know, and I would be very grateful if you could tell me a lie I could believe so I could go back to sleep, thinking the world is what I always thought it was."

"And it isn't?"

"The record books *changed*. The ink was years old, the paper ancient, the books bound in linen thread. There is no way in this world that those record books could have changed. But they did. From three days ago to now, they *changed*. This is impossible, but it is also true. So, I think you know the answer to this."

Jack looked away, came back, and in that gesture, gave it away. She saw it and took it.

"Yes. You look away. But you are not a gifted liar. So tell me…what is *happening* here."

Jack sighed, leaned back into the pillow, looked at her, thinking, *Who are you?*

"I'm not lying to you—"

"Not yet. But you are trying to find a way."

"Why would I be doing that?"

"Why did you let me come to your room?"

"Because…I wanted you to come to my room."

She gave him a sideways smile.

"After one evening at the Two Sisters? A dinner and champagne. No, I don't believe you. I am pretty, but I am no Valkyrie."

That word shook him.

Why would she use it?

She was still giving him that sideways smile.

"So, I would love an answer to my question."

"The records. How they could change?"

"Yes. Please."

Jack was silent for a while, partly because he wasn't really sure of a good answer. She seemed to get this, and softened a little.

"Okay, you can't find a way to answer this yet. But I think you will, if I leave you alone with it for a while. I think I know what it is even now."

She turned into him, resting her cheek on his chest, laying a hand lightly on his belly, putting her leg across his hips, moving into him, her full rounded tummy on his hip, her pussy warm and scented, pressing against him, her breath a whisper on his neck.

"May I ask you another question, then?"

"You have already asked a lot of very difficult questions."

"Yes," she said. "But this one is different."

He kissed her forehead, and she lifted her head up for a kiss on the lips. They shared that, and then she put her head back on his chest, and said, half asleep, half in a dream, softly into his skin.

"Have you ever known a woman named Pandora?"

———

"Yes. I have."

"So have I. She has been coming to me in dreams. She looks like me, but she is not me."

"And what has she been telling you?"

She lay down on her belly, drew the cover over her head, leaving nothing but her perfect bottom to admire. From under the covers, she said, "You are not from around here, are you?"

"I am here now."

She threw the covers off, got onto her knees, came ferociously into him.

"I am in trouble here, real trouble, and if you are truly a good man, then you will help me. I am asking for you to tell me the truth. What is *happening* here? What is happening to me? Who is Pandora and why is she coming to me in my dreams? When did the records change? HOW did the records change? WHY did the records change?"

Jack looked at her and searched his soul for a good reason to be lying to her and failed to find it. *When a woman is naked in your bed, and she is asking you for the truth, and if you have some illusions about being a good man, attention must be paid. Are you a good man? Then be a good man.*

"You're right. I'm not from around here."

She lifted up, sensing a break in the iceberg.

"So, then, from where?"

———

Jack took a deep long weary breath, and then he told her everything. And she listened, as only a woman naked in your bed can listen, and she asked only a few clarifying questions, until he got to the end of his story, which was where they were right now, here in room number 319 at the Monteleone.

She took it all in, as if memorizing it.

Her mood got colder.

"No. I do not believe you. This is not possible."

"Then how did the records change?"

She put her head back under the covers.

"Why can't you tell me a story I can believe?"

He pulled her up to him, held her close.

"I am telling you a story you are going to have to believe, because it's the truth."

A long silence. He could feel her thoughts coursing through her skin, an underground river. She sighed and looked at him, the hurt in her eyes because she felt he was lying to her for reasons she was about to understand.

"So. You say you are from another time? And you got here by chasing this woman down a long glass hallway lined with green stone gates, and the gate that opened for you was the one that led you here, to this time and place?"

"Yes."

"How can this be?"

"I have no idea."

She looked into him for a long time. The hurt in her eyes slowly dissipated as she studied him.

"You know… I think you truly believe what you are saying."

"Yes. I do. Can you?"

She was quiet for a long time.

"Can you persuade me to believe you?"

"I'm trying right now."

"So who is Pandora? This person who looks like me and comes to me in my dreams."

"Her name was Pandora Jansson. She was a friend of mine."

"When?"

"In another time."

"In the future, then?"

"Yes."

"So why is she talking to me in my dreams?"

"What is she saying? In your dreams?"

"That you can't kill this boy?"

"What boy?"

"I don't know the name. Wait. Yes I do. His name is Anson. He is a bartender at the Alcazar Hotel."

That shook him and she saw it.

"How do you know about the bartender at the Alcazar Hotel?"

"As I said. Because Pandora tells me about him. This dead woman who talks to me in my dreams."

"The dead woman?"

"Yes. The dead woman."

"Why do you think she's dead? The Pandora I know—"

"The Pandora you love!"

He stopped, took that in.

"The Pandora I love—"

"Is dead."

"She isn't dead. She is not dead. Why do you say she is dead?"

"The night you left where you were, the night

you came to here, to this time, there was a storm? Yes?"

"Yes."

"So in my dream, Pandora tells me this story. You are sitting together on a sofa, a bench, something like that, in a white place with windows that look out onto an ocean and there is a storm coming. It is a big black storm, full of fury and wind, like a hurricane, yes? And there is this motorcycle, it is green and has sparkles, and Pandora sees this white car, no, a truck, and she thinks that this truck, this white truck, is important…but you don't. And because you don't, some men come and she is killed."

"She told you this? In a dream?"

"No…not like that. She has no memory of dying. Only of being shot, and then you go away."

"But she didn't say she was dead?"

"No. But if she isn't dead, she is close to it. Wherever she is."

Jack was trying to refuse to believe that what he was most afraid of had actually happened that night, and that Pandora had been killed. Annabelle saw him making this effort and her heart went out to him.

"So this is true, then? What Pandora is telling me? This thing actually happened? I can see in your face that you think it *could have* happened."

He sighed, looked at her, and everything that had happened to him since he and Julie Karras has spotted the black Suburban southbound on

A1A rolled over him and drove him down. As she watched he seemed to fade away, and for a moment she thought he was actually going to disappear. But he didn't. It was just an illusion. She reached out and touched him, just to make sure.

"Actually, Annabelle, right now, in this time, none of this had happened yet. Pandora won't even be born for another thirty years."

He tried for a smile, failing miserably. Annabelle considered him, her expression neutral.

"So I'm being visited by the ghost of a dead woman who isn't even born yet."

Not a question. A statement.

Acceptance? Perhaps.

"Yes. You are."

"And why is she asking me to warn you about a bartender?"

"Because that young bartender wants to be a doctor when he grows up. And he does exactly that, and he has a long and admirable career as a surgeon working in Jacksonville and very late one Christmas Eve sixty years from now, when he is eighty-three years old, for no reason we can discover, he crosses the median on a bridge over Matanzas Inlet on the east coast of Florida and he kills my wife, Barbara, and my daughter, Katy."

"Is that why you are here. To kill this boy before he can kill your wife and child?"

"No. I never meant to be here at all. I got pulled into this time stream because I was chasing the woman you know as Aurelia DiSantis."

"The one you call Diana Bowman?"

"Yes."

"And you both—you and Clete—think she's the same woman… What did you call her? A serial…?"

"A serial killer, someone who kills over and over again."

"And you now think that this woman's real name is Selena D'Arcy, the woman who lives at the Pontalba? Where the three people were killed?"

"Yes. And that's what you saw, in the records."

"About the records, the ones that changed?"

"Yes."

"They changed a few days ago. Did they change when you got here?"

"I think so. I think they changed because the woman Clete and I are hunting came back here, and when she came back, *everything* changed."

"Including the records?"

"Yes."

"This woman…Selena D'Arcy…she is also this Diana Bowman, who is still alive sixty years from now?"

"Yes. That's what we think."

"And she can slip through time?"

"Yes."

"And now she is back here?"

"Yes."

"And you have followed her?"

"I was pulled back, I think. I didn't intend to follow. I was caught up…"

"In what?"

"In the Shimmer."

"What is the Shimmer?"

"It's something that happens when people die. I think something opens up when they die, and this woman knows how to ride that force."

"Ride the Shimmer, back in time?"

"Yes. I think so."

"And now you are here. Hunting her. But you also have the death of your wife and daughter. And now you know where the man who will kill her sixty years from now is working? As a bartender at the Alcazar Hotel, in St. Augustine?"

"Yes."

"So you believe that if you kill this boy, this bartender, who wishes someday to be a doctor, then sixty years from now he will not kill your wife and child?"

"Yes. Yeah, that's about it."

"So there is this question."

"Yes?"

"This is what Pandora has been saying to me, in my dreams. If he dies now, this boy, how many people will *not* be saved by him?"

He had already considered this.

It was the main question, the one Clete had asked, as well. How many lives were his wife and child worth?

"Actually, I think I might try to kill him later—"

She smiled at him.

"Closer to the death moment?"

"Yes. That's what I was thinking."

"But you tell me you have no control over this… traveling thing. Through time?"

He admitted this.

"So then how will you manage to arrive at exactly the right time? Before your wife and child are dead, but after this boy has saved all the lives he can save?"

Jack had no answer for this.

"So what if you just made sure your wife isn't on this bridge on Christmas Eve?"

"Same problem. I have no control over this thing. I may not even be able to go back at all."

"Well," she said, "I have mixed emotions about that," and she kissed him softly, and then not so softly. The champagne was gone.

She released him, sighing, said something pithy in a Cajun dialect, got on the phone and ordered up another bottle of Dom, came back to him.

"So…"

"Yes?"

"So… I believe you. I believe all of it."

"Because of the way the records changed?"

"That, yes, but also because of what Pandora is telling me. I hadn't even met you when she started talking to me. Yet I knew about the bartender at the Alcazar. And the records *have* changed. There is no other explanation for any of this. It *has* to be true. It's *impossible*, but it is also true."

"That's what you said this evening, and earlier, at The Court of the Two Sisters."

"There is one thing we are not talking about, and we should."

"Yes. Where is Philomena? Where did she come from, what was her connection to Will D'Arcy and why did she kill them all?"

"Yes. And where is she now?"

Jack considered her for a while.

"I think we both know where Philomena is now."

"Do we?"

"If Selena D'Arcy was killed at the age of five—"

"Yes. She was. The records were very clear on that. I read all the reports. She's buried with her mother and father—with Bea and Will—in a cemetery in Plaquemine Parish Church."

"Then who is there left to be Selena?"

Annabelle got that in a heartbeat.

"The one who was never found. Philomena?"

"Yes."

There was a knock at the door.

Jack pulled on a bathrobe and answered the door, a bellman with a silver ice bucket full of ice and champagne and two fresh crystal glasses, the shallow bowl-shaped ones they used before flutes became popular.

He tipped the boy and closed the door and came

back into the bedroom, eased the cork out of the bottle and poured two glasses while Annabelle watched him.

He came back to bed, leaned into the pillows, sighing. "So, you believe me?"

"Yes. I do. We need to find out more about Philomena. Go to the hospital and look at their records. And then we need to confront Selena— or Philomena—whoever she really is."

"Yes. In the morning. We'll drive there."

"Yes."

She paused, took a breath.

"But I have two questions? Before you make love with me again."

"Yes?"

"The first is, do I look like Pandora?"

"Yes. You could be her twin."

"So I am Pandora in another life?"

"Yes. I think so."

"And you loved her?"

"Yes. I did."

"So you loved *me*, then? When I was Pandora?"

"Yes."

"And now you love me, here in this time?"

"Yes. I do."

"Because of who you *think* I am? Or who I will be sixty-one years from now?"

"Because of who you are right now."

She kissed him, a slow lingering kiss, pulled away a few inches, looking into his eyes.

"That is a very good answer."

And because it was a very good answer, they didn't go anywhere in the morning. They stayed in bed, more or less, not counting some time spent in the shower and a couple of interludes on the sofa in the parlor, all day and into the night.

Clete, who was nothing if not discreet, left them to themselves.

With Jack clearly occupied elsewhere, Clete spent the next couple of days wandering the streets of New Orleans. He went to the Hall of Records, where he confirmed that the Tenancy Logs for the Pontalba were exactly as Annabelle had described them.

He called Mary Alice at the Forrests', had a lovely talk, and she reassured him that there was a patrol car out front, that it had arrived there late Sunday night, and that she was certainly not going for a drive until she heard from him again. He told her he loved her, and she told him that she loved him very much, and they said goodbye.

Adrift, lonely, vaguely envious of Jack and his Annabelle, he thought about Aurelia DiSantis and Jack the Time Traveler, and what his own future might be like. Tuesday evening he ended up at The Court of the Two Sisters again, where he drank quite a bit, and then he drank some more at the Carousel Bar at the Monteleone, and then he went—unsteadily—to bed.

Clete Redding slept the sleep of the dead, still in his suit, splayed out on his back on top of the spread, his face slack and his chest rising and falling with a slow tidal rhythm.

A square of sunlight was shimmering across the floor and making its way up the side of the bed when the phone rang, a shrill insistent clattering buzz.

It jerked him up from a deep blue sleep, like a gaffed fish being plucked out of the water. He sat up, his head spinning, confused, and now full of alarm as he remembered Mary Alice and the danger Jack said she was in.

But no, he'd handled that, he'd sent a County car. And he had spoken to her. And she was going to be okay until the thirtieth anyway. And Declan was safe too. Safe with Frank and Helen Forrest. Both of them were safe.

And today was only Wednesday, the twenty-eighth of August.

The phone stopped ringing just as he reached for it, and he sat up on the side of the bed, holding his head in his hands, trying to shake himself awake.

Call the front desk, find out who just called, probably Jack.

He was reaching for it when the phone rang again, sending an electric jolt through his nerves. He snatched up the receiver, fumbling it a bit, got it to his ear and said, in a growling snarl, "Yeah, Redding here, what?"

"Clete? Did I wake you?"

"No. Not at all. I had to get up to answer the phone anyway."

"Clete, this is Beau Short."

Clete sat up straighter, stared into the middle distance. Beau Short was the CO of his Detective Unit. And a good friend.

"Yeah, Beau, what's up?"

"You alone, Clete?"

Clete laughed, because a lot of guys on the job believed in the Five Hundred Mile Rule. If you're more than five hundred miles away from your wife, it's not adultery.

"Yeah, of course. I love my wife. This about my call the other night?"

"Can you just sit tight for a bit?"

"Sure, of course. Why?"

"Stay on the line, will you?"

Now his belly started a slow roll.

"Why? What's going on, Beau?"

And then there was a double knock at the door.

"Hey, Beau, hold on. There's someone at the door, okay—hold on?"

"I will."

Clete went to the door, opened it. There were two New Orleans Police Department harness cops filling up the doorway, one black, one white. They both had their hats in their hands and they both looked a bit scalded.

"Detective Redding?"

"Yeah, what is it?"

"Can we step in, sir?"

It was said gently, softly, politely.

Too softly.

"Yeah, sure, come in, hold on, I got a guy on the line here."

The two cops came into the room, stood in the middle of it, looking deeply uncomfortable.

"Beau, look, I got—"

"You have two New Orleans PD guys in your room, right?"

"Yeah. I do. But why?"

He looked at the cops, waved them to a couple of chairs. "Sit, guys, will you?"

They sat. He went back to Beau.

"Why do I have two cops in my room?"

"Clete… I didn't want you to be alone."

Clete went silent. He felt that he was on the brink of a whole new reality. That his old one was about to change. And he had the thought that if, right now, he didn't ask the next question, if he just said goodbye and put the phone down, then everything would be all right. Nothing would change.

"Beau?"

"Yeah, Clete."

"Is it Mary Alice?"

There was a long silence. Too long.

"Yeah, Clete. It is."

"She hurt? Is Declan okay?"

"There was an accident—"

"A car accident?"

"She was out driving—"

"With Declan?"

"No. Alone. Or not. We're not—"

"How? Fucking how? I sent a County car on Sunday night! They were told, nobody in, nobody out!"

"They were there. At the Forrest house. Two civilian cars in the driveway. And they were there for two days. So last night, the house was all dark, so they just parked it and settled in for the night. Babysitting. Two hours later, the house got a slow pass, a black Caddy—it looked hinky—they rolled after it, lights and siren, and the Caddy took off. They pulled it over a mile down the road. It was two Vizzini guys."

"Who?"

"Tessio's kid, Anthony, and Sergio Carpo."

"What the fuck were they doing down there?"

"They said they were just out for a shore drive."

"In the middle of the fucking night? Right where my wife happened to be staying? Bullshit. You still got them in custody?"

"Clete, there was nothing to hold them on. The Vizzini guys, I mean. No law against a drive down the shore. They released the Caddy, deputies went back to 77 Florala. There was only one car in the driveway. Not Mary Alice's Oldsmobile. They went looking for it."

"*What about Mary Alice*, Beau?"

The two NOPD cops looked at each other. They

heard the rising tone in Clete's voice and they came over to stand a little closer to Clete, hats still in their hands, but braced for anything.

"Clete… I'm so sorry."

"What happened?"

"They found her two miles up. She lost control of her car, went off the highway, up by Matanzas Inlet."

"She's okay? Right?"

"No, Clete. She's not okay."

———

They took two cars back to St. Augustine, because Clete wouldn't—or couldn't—be in the same car as Jack, and he insisted on driving alone, and nothing anyone said was going to change his mind, so he drove off in his motor pool squad, and Jack followed behind, a mile or so back, in Annabelle Fontaine's cobalt blue Lincoln Continental.

Annabelle was at the wheel, Jack in the passenger side of the long white-leather bench seat, staring out at the highway, watching Clete's unmarked squad car pulling rapidly away into the blue distance.

They were now out in delta country again, heading east on Highway 90, two-lane blacktop all the way to the Atlantic, under a clear blue sky, a golden light on the land, and other than the music on the car radio—Johnny Mercer singing "The Midnight Sun"—nothing was being said. Nothing had been said for the last fifty miles.

———

They were both in a state of shock, both of them mentally still back in the suite at the Monteleone this morning, replaying the scene, both of them sitting at the low round table in the front room, sipping black coffee and eating chocolate croissants, Annabelle in Jack's oversize white terry-cloth bathrobe, Jack in his suit pants, shirtless, shoeless, the early morning sunlight filling the room. His Highway Patrol uniform, starched and crisp and fresh, was hanging on a hook behind the front door.

When Clete kicked the door open, the uniform flew across the hallway, and then Clete was in the room, in the same rumpled blue suit he had been wearing the day before.

He had his .357 out and he came straight at Jack, who was on his feet by now, and behind Clete he saw two uniformed NOPD cops, who showed every sign of chasing after Clete.

Clete got about two feet from Jack, stuck the .357 in Jack's face, his finger white on the trigger and Clete had time to say, "Can you go back, can you fucking go back and fix this?" in a strangled growl, before the two patrol cops took him down in a tangle, shoved him face-first into the rug, bent his arms back and wrested the revolver out of his hand, one cop kneeling on the back of Clete's neck.

The other cop pulled out a pair of cuffs, jerked

Clete's arms behind his back and clamped the cuffs on Clete's wrist.

Clete turned his head sideways, lifted up and looked at Jack and then at Annabelle, both of whom were standing now, staring back at him, stunned into silence.

"Can you go back? Can you fix this?" Clete asked, in a ruined voice, and then he put his head back down, and Jack realized that the deep rasping sound he was making was Clete Redding crying.

The cop who had put his knee on Clete's neck, a fridge-sized black man, got slowly to his feet, breathing hard. He looked at Jack, took in the room and the woman, and noticed the Highway Patrol uniform crumpled in a heap by the wall.

"Sorry," said the cop. "He got away from us."

"What is it?" said Jack. "What has he done?"

The cop shook his head, his eyes soft.

"Nothing. We're here to help the poor guy. Jacksonville PD called, asked us to show up here, see that he didn't do anything crazy when he got the news."

"What news?"

The cop hesitated.

"Mind if I ask you to identify yourself, sir?"

Annabelle stepped in.

"I'm a detective with 8 District—"

"Yes, you're Detective Fontaine. Everybody knows you, ma'am. But who's this gentleman?"

"My name is Jack Redding. I'm a sergeant with the Florida Highway Patrol."

"You a relative of Detective Redding, then?"

"Yes. I am."

He nodded, considering Jack, deciding.

"Well, I'm sorry to tell you, Sergeant, but Detective Redding's wife got killed last night."

Jack sat down in the chair, suddenly chilled through, a steel band clamping around his chest. He felt limp, boneless. He looked down at Clete, who was lying motionless on the carpet, still making that terrible rasping sound. Annabelle, silent, was standing beside him, her hand on his shoulder.

Annabelle took a deep breath, tightened her hand on Jack's shoulder, and asked, "How did it happen?"

The cop ran his fingers through his hair, still breathing hard from the takedown.

"You'd have to get the whole story from Jacksonville, Detective Fontaine. But what we got told was the lady, Mrs. Redding, was out driving along the coast there, middle of the night, northbound on Highway One, near a place called Matanzas Inlet—"

Annabelle felt the shudder run right through Jack's body when he heard the name.

"When something goes wrong, and she swerves into the bay, and that's about the size of it. Except, now they're saying there's more to it, doesn't look so simple. Like I say, you gotta check with Jacksonville."

Annabelle looked down at Clete.

"Thank you, Officer. Can you help Detective Redding to his feet?"

They thought about it, and then managed to get Clete upright. His control was back. His face was pale white and he was stony silent.

He looked at Annabelle.

"Ask these guys to uncuff me."

Annabelle nodded to the cops, and the smaller one, the silent white cop, did that, easing the cuffs off. Clete rubbed his wrists, looked at both of them, Jack and Annabelle, took in that situation, smiled grimly, went back to Jack.

"Jack, do you think you can undo this?"

Jack was still sitting, looking sick.

He shook his head slowly, lifted his hands, palms up.

"I don't know."

"So that's a maybe?"

Jack said nothing.

"You got any idea what the fuck happened? Today's the twenty-eighth of August. We had until the Friday. The thirtieth. That's what you said."

"Yes. It is."

"Looks like you were fucking wrong, doesn't it?"

"Yes. I was wrong."

"So, like I said, can you fix this?"

The two cops were watching this back-and-forth and looking puzzled as hell. Annabelle knew what Clete was asking for, and she knew it probably wasn't possible. Clete kept his attention fixed on

Jack, a stony accusative glare. He was waiting for
an answer. Jack shook himself, like a wet dog, got
to his feet, faced Clete squarely.

"I don't know. I can try. I did what I could. Did
you send a car? To cover the house?"

"Yes. I did."

"And did they?"

"Yes. For two nights. But something went seriously fucking wrong, didn't it?"

"Yes. But what?"

Clete dropped his eyes, rubbed his wrists again.

"No fucking idea. But I'm going to find out."

He turned, held out his hand for his Colt, got it
back, brushed past the two patrol cops and left the
room. The black cop looked at Annabelle Fontaine.

"Should we let him go, ma'am?"

"Yes," she said, after a moment. "Let him go."

"The Midnight Sun" came to its majestic close,
Annabelle sighed, shut the radio off and there was
only the wind rush and the drumming of their tires
on the uneven blacktop. Clete's Ford was almost
out of sight, and the rest of the road was empty.
Annabelle glanced over at Jack.

"You okay?"

"No."

"Neither am I. There's a flask of cognac in the
glove compartment. And I'm going to need a cigarette."

She rolled the window down, and the scent of
rich red earth and saw grass filled the car. Jack

opened the glove box, found a silver flask with a little silver cup as a screw cap.

Annabelle was lighting a cigarette from the dashboard lighter, and she handed it to Jack, so she could light another. The smoke filled the car, briefly clouding the windshield, until the slip-stream drew it out. Jack poured out a capful and offered it to Annabelle, who drank it all in one shot and handed the cap back to him.

"What do you think he'll do?" she asked.

"Clete?"

"Yes."

"What do *you* think?"

"Find out who did this and kill them all."

"You talked to him, just as we were leaving the hotel. What did he say?"

"He said he'd been on the phone to a man named Beau Short. His CO at Robbery Homicide. Short told him that last night a black Caddy had cruised the house where his wife was staying, and the sher-iff's car went after them because they looked sus-picious. They pulled them over a mile down the road. There were two guys in the car, Anthony Vizzini and Sergio Carpo—"

"There you go," said Jack. "There's your Satur-day Night Massacre."

"What do you mean?"

"I'll explain later. Go on."

"Okay, please do. Anyway, when the deputies got back to the Forrest house, Mary Alice's car was gone. They went looking, found tracks running down the slope and into Matanzas Inlet. Got the divers out, and they found the car in twenty feet of water. Mary Alice was at the wheel. And Short said there was an antemortem bruise on her right temple. She'd been hit hard, possibly with a gun butt. She was unconscious when she went into the water."

"Not a bruise she got when the car hit Matanzas Inlet?"

"No. She was hit maybe ten, fifteen minutes before that, judging from the spreading of the bruise mark. You don't bruise after you're dead."

Jack shook his head.

"Yeah? That's not been my experience."

Annabelle smiled, a rueful twist, said nothing, both of them concentrating on the diminishing gray dot that was Clete Redding's squad car.

"He's moving pretty fast, isn't he?" said Annabelle.

"Yeah. He's like a human cruise missile."

Annabelle needed that explained to her, and when Jack finished she said, "Yes, that's exactly what he is right now. What I'm wondering is, who's he going to target?"

"The Vizzini Family."

"The whole family?"

"Yes. He'll go right in after them. He'll hit their compound and shred everyone he comes across."

"That doesn't sound like a guess."

"It isn't. It's happened before. They called it

the Saturday Night Massacre. Now it's happening again."

"What will you do? Should you warn the Vizzinis?"

"No. Fuck the Vizzinis. Excuse me."

"Excused. Did you know that his wife was going to die?"

"Yes. I warned him about it. That's why he sent the sheriff's car. But she was supposed to die—I mean, the last time around, she died on the thirtieth of August."

"This Friday?"

"Yeah. That's what was in the history books."

"But she didn't. She died last night, or today."

"Yes. On the twenty-eighth. Three days early."

"But how could that happen?"

"I don't know. Maybe when Selena and I came back here, we changed how things happened. The timing, the order, something like that. In the end it doesn't matter, does it? She's dead, and Clete will try to kill every Vizzini he can reach."

"They'll kill him."

"They'll try."

"Are you going to let him go in there alone?"

"No. Probably not."

"Then you'll get killed too."

"Maybe not."

"And if you get killed and Clete gets killed, who goes after Selena D'Arcy?"

"You will."

"Yes. I will."

He looked over at her, saw Pandora right there, and Annabelle too, like a double image, one riding on top of the other, and as he watched they kept switching back and forth. He loved them both and he had no idea what he was supposed to do about either of them. Annabelle sighed.

"I can hear you thinking."

"Yeah? What am I thinking?"

"You're in a serious tangle, and you don't know what to do about any of it."

He was quiet for a while. The road went into a long graceful curve and they passed a road sign.

BILOXI
30 miles

"How many miles between Biloxi and St. Augustine?" he asked.

"Around five hundred."

"Speed he's going, he'll get there by sundown."

"Will he go straight to the Vizzini compound?"

"No. He'll see to Mary Alice. He'll go wherever she is first. To say goodbye."

They were both quiet for a while, thinking about what that would be like for Clete.

"It bothers me," said Annabelle.

"What bothers you?"

"That she died three days early. It means something. It's like the way the records changed."

"They changed because Selena came back here, and changed the *history* of the place."

"Yes. And she *caused* that change, didn't she?"

"I think so. Maybe not on purpose. But yes."

"Do you think that's not the only thing she caused? Maybe she caused Mary Alice to die three days earlier than the last time she died."

"You mean, she went out last night and killed Mary Alice herself?"

"I'm thinking it. Yes."

"You know, I've always wondered why Barbara and Katy died at the exact same spot where Mary Alice died. In Matanzas Inlet."

"Yes. It's like somebody *made* it happen that way. And who's the only person who could make things happen in two different times?"

"Selena."

"Yes. Selena. Or Philomena, if that's who she really is."

"But if she had a *reason* for doing it, what was the reason?"

"The last time Mary Alice died, Clete went after the Vizzinis. He finished them as a power. Wiped out most of their talent. Killed Anthony, killed a whole lot of their people."

"But he survived, didn't he? Why did *he* live?"

"Far as I know, because the Vizzinis didn't know he was coming at them, and by the time they reacted, most of them were dead."

"Nobody warned them?"

"Nobody *knew*. And he came at them after Mary Alice died."

She was quiet for a long time. The sun was sliding into the west, purple stains spreading across the fields.

"But now somebody *does* know he's coming. Selena knows."

"And if she warns Tessio…"

"This time, Clete dies. And if he dies…"

"So do I. And Selena would think she was safe."

"Until I find her. And what else *would* happen?"

"I never meet Barbara. Katy isn't born."

"Yes. And…? What else *doesn't* happen?"

The thought pierced him like an icicle.

"Barbara doesn't die."

time lockets

Selena was back in her hotel suite in the Alcazar, having breakfast, trying to think about how she would handle Tessio today when they met at the Monterey Court, as they did every Wednesday.

But she was really thinking about what she had done last night, and she was not happy. She felt something had gone terribly wrong, although it had all worked exactly as she hoped it would, because she was a meticulous planner and it had been her experience that, if you planned carefully, and considered every possible twist, and if you were always ready to adapt to changing events, most of the time it would all work out satisfactorily. And, on the face of it, it had gone exactly the way she had hoped it would go.

She had goaded Little Anthony into a run at Clete's wife, and he might have been successful, and her problem was solved that way. Or, as it turned out, Clete might have put a police detail around her, and if so, she was going to have to improvise.

And Clete *had* put a watch on the house, so when the Vizzinis' car went cruising by on the second night, the County gun dogs had followed after it like greyhounds chasing a mechanical rabbit.

And she was surprised, and delighted, when the Forrests had come out to watch the chase. She waited in the darkness at the edge of the road as the three of them stood on the porch, the police lights and sirens fading into the distance.

After a while, when everything was quiet again, the old couple wandered off to bed, and the single woman, a delicate blonde flower, Mary Alice Redding, stood out on the porch, taking in the sound of the ocean roaring out there in the velvet night and breathing in the salty tang of the onshore breeze.

Selena, improvising, had materialized out of the darkness at the bottom of the drive, coming into the glow of the porch light, smiling, simply a neighbor brought out by all the excitement, just like everyone else.

A few friendly words at the bottom of the drive, a comfortable connection established, and then the woman was taken. Into her own car, a massive Oldsmobile, at gunpoint, Mary Alice at the wheel.

Two miles up the road, to the place where Highway One curved around the headland of Matanzas Inlet, Mary Alice in tears, but brave, a true cop wife, asking questions that Selena didn't bother to answer, since the gun at the woman's right temple was explanation enough.

Pulled over at the edge of Matanzas Inlet, a vicious blow to Mary Alice's head, making sure she was unconscious, waiting awhile to see that no one was coming. And then Selena put the car into Drive, and it eased its ponderous way down the steep bank and into the water, where it floated, bubbling and bobbing for a while, sinking slowly, until, by the engine's forward weight, it heeled up, trunk rising, like the *Titanic* tilting its massive stern, and the tank-sized car took the woman down.

Selena had watched it go until the last of the bubbles floated away under a gauzy veil of starlight, and Matanzas Inlet grew quiet again, as if nothing at all bad had ever happened here, although in Spanish its name meant Massacre Bay.

Then the long walk back to her car, parked in a stand of palms a mile down the road, thinking, as she walked through the salty cool of the shoreline road, that it had all been so easy, that perhaps it was supposed to happen that way in the first place.

Although she knew that couldn't be true, because, in the original event, Selena had actually not been involved.

It had been exactly what it had looked like, a terrible accident, just as Tessio had told her when she had visited him in his seaside compound before the Shimmer brought her back here.

So this time, she had *made* it happen, and yes it was three days early, but she was sure that the outcome would be much the same. Clete would attack the Vizzinis, but this time, the Vizzinis would be waiting for him.

And he'd die. And all would be well.

She reached the car, opened the driver's door—

And then this happened.

———

As she slipped into her car she was suddenly overwhelmed by a tidal shift in her reality. She seemed to fall down into a spinning eternity of time, always repeating the same series of events— the gun the car the drive the blow, and into the water, the gun the car the drive the blow, and into the water, the gun the car the drive the blow, and into the water—over and over and over again, an endless roundabout circle with no escape, no exit, no way out, for the rest of eternity.

It only ended when she found the locket on its chain around her neck. She clutched it so hard she broke the chain, held the locket to her breasts, closed her eyes, willing the locket to take her back to that soft white room at the Pontalba, the one fixed time point in her long chaotic life...and the locket helped...she felt the spinning slow down, the cycle became irregular, the vortex dissipated, and then only gradually, but the time loop slowed, faded and, finally, eventually, released her.

———

She sat there for a long time, clutching her locket, sick with shock and fear—this had *never* happened to her before—and she only snapped out of it when a sheriff's car sped past, lights on, racing north toward Matanzas Inlet, going by so fast they never saw her car parked deep in a stand of palms.

She gathered herself together, took a deep breath, sighing, deeply shaken to her core, put the rental car in gear and headed south, staying far away from Matanzas Inlet, taking an inland route back to St. Augustine.

On the way down the coast she thought about what had just happened, and she wondered if the fact that she had deliberately altered a real event—causing it three days early, and not allowing Mary Alice to die in a natural accident—had somehow created a dangerous ripple in the time stream.

But, as usually happened with Selena, the farther away she got from Matanzas Inlet, the weaker her memory of that looping time lock became, until finally, as she came back up the mainland and turned right toward the coast and saw the lights of St. Augustine up ahead, and the Alcazar Hotel waiting, it faded away into nothing.

By the time she laid her weary head back onto her pillow in her hotel suite, it was utterly gone from her, and all that was in her mind, as she drifted away, was to remind herself that she was seeing Tessio Vizzini tomorrow—no, later today, at the Monterey Court—and she would have to handle that meeting carefully.

And so she slept, secure in the feeling that, although the evening had been challenging, she had risen to it, achieved her goals, and that all was now perfectly right in Selena D'Arcy's world.

Tessio was late. He had left a message at the desk of the Monterey Court. He had a story but she didn't believe it. His message was that his wife had required him to go shopping. Annamaria Vizzini was an imperious Sicilian black-haired blue-eyed beauty who ran Tessio up and down the staircases of her whimsical moods like a hotel bellhop.

But in the matter of their meetings at the Monterey, this had never happened before. She didn't believe the message. Something else was going on. So Selena was on her guard.

An hour late, he called the room.

"*Carissima*, I will be—"

"Already are late. *Troppo tarde*, Tessio."

"Annamaria—"

"Annamaria what?"

"She required to go shopping—"

"Fine. I will go shopping too."

"For what?"

"For a more timely lover."

"Aurelia, *per piacere*—"

"We have much to talk about. You heard about Clete Redding's wife?"

"Yes. Of course. She's dead. Little Anthony and Sergio Carpo were near the house—"

"And you have heard that Clete—"

"Aurelia, this is a phone. People listen."

"But you need to know—"

"And I will. When we meet."

"When will that be?"

"I don't know. I have to talk to Anthony. And then consider what to do."

"Did Little Anthony have anything to do with this death?"

Tessio's voice grew colder.

"*Cara mia*, I have told you. This is not the place for talk. When we meet—"

"But did he?"

"I will put him to this question, and we will see what he has to say. And Sergio was with him, and Sergio doesn't lie to me. So I must deal with this. I will see you soon, and we will—"

"When will that be?"

A labored sigh.

"Not today, *cara*."

"Not today?"

"No. I am sorry. *Mi dispiace.* You know how I wish to see you. This death, it has made things difficult for our family. I am not free to move about—"

"Tessio, I have things to tell you. About this death. Important things."

More chill. And more cold steel.

"Aurelia, I love you, but I do not see how you can know things that I do not. I do not have time for women's talk. This is a serious thing, this death of Mary Alice, and I must find out if this *infamita* is on our hands, on the hands of my son, and then I must meet with Clete, and resolve this."

"Meet with Clete? Why?"

"If Little Anthony did this thing, I will let Clete kill him. Honor requires this. We do not make war on the wives, on the children. But I do not believe this was something Little Anthony could do. For one thing, Sergio was with him, and Sergio wouldn't allow it. That is why he agreed to go with him in the first place. Little Anthony is a fool, but Sergio is not. I will meet with Clete and convince him that it was not our doing. I say again. We do not make war on wives and children. And then— with Clete's help—we will find the people who did this, and they will go into the alligator pool."

"Tessio—"

"*Ciao, bella.* We will talk soon. I am busy now."

"With something more important than me?"

"No not like that. But I must find out how this woman died, and then deal with what I find."

"Tessio—"

But he was gone.

————

And she had a lot to think about. If Tessio put Little Anthony to the question, and he was very good at that—the alligators down by the lagoon were a convincing argument—then Little Anthony and Sergio Carpo would probably convince Tessio that they had not been the agents of the death of Mary Alice Redding.

Which was a very dangerous thing to happen. Because if Tessio wished to look deeply into the matter, he would soon find out that she had taken a rental car out of the Alcazar yesterday, and that she could not account for her actions…

If he turned his unkind attention to her, if he ever came to believe that she had been responsible for the death of Mary Alice Redding, she would be in an impossible position. He said he was in love with her, and with another man you'd say, *Well, he will protect me no matter what.* But not with Tessio Vizzini. He had the sentimental heart of a pit viper.

She thought of running.

Yes. It had come to that.

She was going to have to run.

But to where?

No. Wrong question.

Not to *where.*

To *when.*

though hell should bar the way

Clete got to Immaculate Heart Hospital in Jacksonville just after sundown, shut the car down, shoved his way through a phalanx of well-meaning friends who tried to make the meeting easier. This wasn't possible, but he appreciated them for trying.

He found the Forrests, Frank and Helen, in a little chapel off the lobby. Declan was with them, a tousle-haired blond kid with large brown eyes that were much too old for him.

Declan got up and ran to him, and he picked him up and held him tight, feeling the kid's breath on his neck, smelling the grassy scent of a child. Declan was crying, but silently, and it tore his heart apart to feel it.

Only blood can fix this, he was thinking.

Only blood.

They sat together in the chapel for a long time, Frank and Helen and Declan and Clete. Frank and Helen told him about the sheriff's car and the way it had gone off with lights and siren after the big black Caddy, how Frank and Helen and Mary Alice had come out onto the porch to watch the chase, how Mary Alice had stayed behind, and that was the last time they saw her.

Declan sat silently through this, staring at his hands, and then he looked at Clete, his face tight.

"She's dead, Dad. Mom is dead."

"I know, son. I know."

"And you killed her."

That rocked him. Helen moved in to say something, but Clete stopped her.

"How did I kill her, Declan?"

"With your stupid job, your stupid cop job. Those Italian people you're friends with, the ones who give you money, who paid for our house on the beach, and for Mom's new car, the one she died in—now they don't like you anymore, and that's why you sent us down to be with Uncle Frank and Aunt Helen. And now Mom's dead, and you're not."

"Do you wish I was dead?"

Declan flared up at him.

"Yes. I do. I wish you had died and not Mom. You're the one with all the bad people who give you money. They should have killed you. Not Mom."

"Declan," said Helen, her voice sharp and shocked, but Clete held up a hand.

"Declan...I am so sorry about this."

"So what? Mom's still dead."

"And I'm not?"

"Not yet. But that's okay. You will be soon."

Clete tried to hold him, but Declan pushed him

away, hate in his eyes, and he turned to Helen, and she took him in her arms. She looked at Clete, shock and sorrow and just a touch of blame.

"Clete, he's just upset. He didn't mean it."

"No? I think he did. Maybe he's right."

"No, Clete, he's not. He's young… Give him time."

A long silence.

"Helen, I have something to do."

"I know. You go do it. We'll keep Declan with us until you can…take care of things."

He looked at her, saw that she knew what he was going to do. He touched Declan's shoulder, but the boy just burrowed deeper into Helen's arms.

He stood up then, looked at them, in the pew, in the soft amber light of the little chapel, with the scent of sandalwood and candle wax and dead flowers, and then he turned and walked away.

He didn't look back.

———

He found the morgue attendant, got the tray number out of him and walked him down the rows of stainless-steel lockers until they got to Row Five Tray Two.

He stood before Row Five Tray Two for a good five minutes, thinking, *This is what it comes down to, all of our married life, all of those moments, at the beach, in bed, being apart, being together, and now we are here, in this final moment, and I will never have another moment where we are to-*

gether, other than this, our last moment together, the one where I am alive and you are dead.

The attendant waited until he said yes, and then pulled out the tray. There was a sheet, and a figure beneath, mounded in the shroud.

The attendant waited until Clete was ready, and then he lifted it and pulled it back, stepped away, and Clete looked at Mary Alice, his golden girl, for the last time in this living world.

He stood there for a timeless time, the cold light of the morgue pouring down over him as he froze solid inside.

After a while, he let out a long deep shuddering sigh, kissed her on the lips, folded the sheet back over her body, turned and walked away. The attendant, a biblical man, watched him go, and thought, *Comes a pale horse...*

feral is as feral does

Jack and Annabelle got to the morgue a couple of hours after Clete had been and gone, no one knew where.

So they looked for Clete at his beach house and then at the Jacksonville offices of Robbery Homicide, didn't find him anywhere, and no one had any idea where the hell he was, or, if they did, they weren't saying, and then they were met, unwillingly, in a top-floor hallway, by Beau Short.

Beau Short was Clete's boss, a straight razor of a man with close-cut blue-white hair and pale green eyes made even more piercing by a deep mahogany tan. He was wearing a well-cut navy-blue pin-striped suit and his shoes were buffed to a jewellike gleam.

"In my office," he said, not implying tea and scones. They went, of course.

Behind his aircraft-carrier desk, he took in Jack's rumpled blue suit, his .357 and his unfamiliar Highway Patrol badge, and sat back in his swivel chair, his manner hostile and wary.

"I'm not getting how the hell you fit into this, Sergeant."

"I can vouch for him," said Annabelle. "The main thing, what we're worried about here, is Clete Redding, Lieutenant—"

"Call me Beau."

"Thank you. Beau. What we're worried about—"

"Is where in hell is Clete Redding right now and what is he planning to do? That about right?"

"Yes. That's right."

"Mind if I ask you a couple of questions first?"

"If you think we have time for that."

He inclined his head, gave her a sideways smile.

"I do, so bear with me. First of all, I've known Clete Redding for over twenty years. Both linebackers in high school football, and then the Corps and then in Korea, and then we came onto the Jacksonville PD as harness bulls. And he has never once, in all that time, told me that he had a— What are you, a cousin or something, Jack? Because you sure as hell are a Redding."

"Kind of a cousin."

"Yeah, well, he's never mentioned that he had a 'kind of a cousin' working Highway Patrol. Not once. Kind of weird, you think?"

"Yeah. It is," said Jack.

"Got anything useful to say about it?"

Annabelle broke in.

"With respect, Lieutenant—"

"Beau."

"Beau, do you know where Clete is right now?"

"Haven't a clue, and I've got good people out looking for him. He's not answering his radio, I've sent a car to the beach house—they saw your car there, very nice big blue Lincoln Continental by the way—and he's not there. As you know. About three hours ago, he blew into Immaculate Heart, shoved his way through a lot of his cop friends, had a few words with the Forrest family, hugged his kid."

He stopped there, for a moment, because Frank Forrest had called to fill him in on what Declan had said to his father, and Clete's reaction to it. He said nothing about that to Jack and Annabelle, but went on in a cold hard voice.

"Then he went down to the basement, to the morgue, and stood looking at Mary Alice for maybe fifteen minutes, didn't say a word to the attendant, and then he left, looking like rolling thunder, and now we have—excuse me, Annabelle—no *fucking* clue where the *fuck* he is."

He drew in a long breath, a man at the edge.

"But…but I do have *you*, Sergeant Redding, and you do look like a Redding and you do look like a real cop, but nobody over at Highway Patrol HQ has ever heard of you—"

He stopped, got himself under control.

"But know what? I don't give a fuck about that right now. Maybe you're the fucking CIA or maybe you're another one of those three-letter swear words I really don't give a fuck about either. How about one of you—either one, pick a card—just sits up straight and tells me what the fuck is going on here?"

And he sat back, templed his fingers and, aside from a slight tremor in his right knee, smiled and indicated that he was prepared to wait until Columbus Day for an answer.

Annabelle and Jack looked at each other for a moment, and then Annabelle turned back to Beau Short.

"You checked me out too, yes?"

"Sure did. Very impressive. Naval Intel and now one of the best plainclothes cops in 8 Division, and you're even suspected of being sort of kind of occasionally, intermittently semihonest."

Annabelle smiled, not sweetly.

"For a New Orleans cop."

"Yeah, well, what can I say?"

"But that's not my point."

"Fine. What *is* your point?"

"Somebody killed Mary Alice Redding. Clete thinks it was probably done by Anthony Vizzini."

"Or somebody working for him. We'll know soon enough. Word is Tessio Vizzini is, right now as we speak, hanging the kid by his nuts over a pool full of gators. He calls it 'putting a guy to the question.' Most guys tell him the truth."

"What do you think?"

"I think Little Anthony is as dumb as a box of mice and as low-down mean and stupid as a re- tarded stoat. I also think Little Anthony couldn't recognize the Up button in a freight elevator. So, no, there's no way he killed Mary Alice Redding."

"What does Clete think?"

"Right now, *thinking* is not what Clete is doing. Clete believes that, one way or another, the Vizzinis hit his wife. He thinks the drive-by with Tony and Sergio Carpo was a distraction, and those butt-stupid County boys went for it like kittens after a string of Christmas tinsel."

He sighed, rubbed his face.

"Tell you what I'm afraid of. I think Clete is out there in the dark right now, making plans, and when he's through getting ready, he'll go through the Vizzini compound like Sherman through Georgia. Unless we can find him and stop him. So now you tell me, what do you think?"

"We think we know who killed his wife, and it wasn't any member of the Vizzini family."

Long pause.

"Okay. Not a Vizzini. Then who?"

"A woman named Aurelia DiSantis."

"We know her. She's Tessio's punch—his mistress. They meet at the Monterey Court. One of our guys has the shots."

"Clete Redding."

"Yeah. Yes. Clete. He's been on a surveillance op with the Vizzinis. So why do you like this DiSantis woman for the death of his wife?"

"DiSantis is more than she looks," said Annabelle.

"Which means?"

She looked at Jack, who stepped in.

"She's a serial killer—"

"A *what*?"

"A repeat offender. She finds vulnerable people—women, men, whatever—and she digs her way into their lives—"

"A parasite wasp?"

"Yes. Exactly. A parasite wasp. She works her way into their lives, and she sucks out everything they have, and then she kills them."

"Does Clete know about this? He's been looking into her background, I know."

"For you?"

He flared up at that.

"For who the fuck else? And what does that mean?"

Jack didn't back off.

"Hey. She's Tessio Vizzini's mistress."

"Yeah, I know. I've seen the Monterey Court shots. She's got her stinger sunk deep in that mook. Look, I know where you're going with this. Clete walks a narrow line. Annabelle, you're from New Orleans—you know what it's like. One hand washes the other. Favors get done, info gets delivered, order is maintained. If Clete's been letting Tessio know what he's found out about this DiSantis woman, I don't care. I've been getting everything he's got, and that's all I give a good goddamn about."

"Has he talked to you at all, about this woman, since he got back from New Orleans?"

"Hell no. He went through here like a howitzer shell. Why? Did he come up with something new?"

"He didn't," said Annabelle. "I did."

"Like what?"

"Like her name isn't Aurelia DiSantis, it's Selena D'Arcy, date of birth September 7, 1909—"

"No way. That'd make her…forty-eight?"

"That's her real age."

"But she doesn't look anywhere near that. Gotta be wrong."

Annabelle was thinking about Philomena now, about how the child Selena had died and about how much they could say and not open up dangerous ground.

"It's right there in the Plaquemine Parish records. Date of birth, current address. She lives in number nine at the Pontalba Apartments, next to Jackson Square, and, according to the records, she's had the place since 1943."

"I know the Pontalba. The rent is a fortune. How's she affording this?"

Jack stepped in.

"Like you said, she's a parasite wasp and she's been one for a lot longer than Clete thought. Years longer. And now she's doing it to Tessio Vizzini."

"So, yeah, well, good for her. Fuck Tessio Vizzini. He deserves whatever he gets."

"But does Clete?"

"How is this DiSantis woman a threat to Clete?"

This was a hard question to answer, because a complete answer would have ended up with Beau

Short smiling very sweetly at them, saying "Excuse me for a moment" and then stepping out into the hall and calling for some muscle guys to toss them into a psych ward.

"She's trying to deflect Clete from her case. And Jack here is on the same case, but he has her under a different name, a Selena D'Arcy. But now we know she's the same woman Clete is investigating. And she's trying to distract all of us by killing Mary Alice and laying it on the Vizzinis."

He took this in, assessing them as he did so.

"And how is that supposed to help her?"

"She sets Clete onto the Vizzinis, and then she tells Tessio that Clete's on his way, and they kill him. Problem solved."

"Okay. I see that. Where is this woman now?"

Annabelle and Jack glanced at each other.

Annabelle answered first.

"We think she's in a suite at the Alcazar Hotel in St. Augustine."

"Yeah? When? Like right now?"

"Yes. We think so."

"And you think she might have what we in the parlance of professional police departments like to call 'material knowledge of the case in question'?"

"Absolutely."

"Hold on."

He picked up the phone, dialed a number.

"Yeah, do you have a woman registered there, name of Aurelia DiSantis…You can't say? Or you

don't know?…Okay…I get that. Look, I'm Lieutenant Beauregard Short, Jacksonville PD, and I'm
officially asking if you have a woman by that name
registered at your *fucking* hotel?"

Silence, the wall clock ticking, muffled voices
in the outer hallway.

"Yeah, okay…Suite 1408…You happen to know
if she's in right now?…Keys are in the box?…Yeah,
thanks…No, I don't want you to put me through to
her…Can I have your name?…Okay, look, Marco,
don't be calling her after I hang up, got that? If
you do, that's interfering with a police matter,
comprende? We understand each other?…Good.
Thanks."

He put the phone down.

"She's there right now. Room 1408."

He sat up, pushed his chair forward, opened a
drawer and pulled out a shoulder rig with a large
Smith & Wesson tucked into the holster.

"Well then," he said, standing up and grinning
wickedly at them while he stripped off his suit coat
and tugged the rig over his shoulders and got his
jacket back on, all in one seamless flow:

"Let's us three go have a talk with her."

———

The Alcazar Hotel ballroom was at full bore,
redlined, the atrium lounge packed with couples
and triples of every combination, all dressed to the
hairline, dancing to the thirty-piece swing band on
the podium, the brass section putting out a high-
velocity swing number, the music pulsing through

the smoky air and bouncing off the walls as the three of them walked around the upper balcony looking down into the ballroom floor.

It was a glittering crystal bowl full of cigarette smoke and candlelights and bright chatter and good-looking wealthy people and over it all the driving percussive power of Benny Goodman's "Sing Sing Sing."

The long bar was packed five deep and Jack saw Anson Freitag behind it, in his red vest, along with five other bar kids, moving quickly, pouring drinks and taking cash tips and smiling at all the people they knew—Freitag was a healthy young man in the prime of his life—happy and vital and destined for a brilliant future with so many innocent lives hanging in the balance.

———

Jack knew right then that there was no way he was going to shoot the kid down in cold blood—Barbara would never forgive him for that.

He would have to find another way, if he was ever given the chance. In his heart he was beginning to fear that there was no way he was going to be able to save them.

It was up to whoever made the Rules.

———

He turned away, sighing, a heavy sadness on him, and he found the Vizzini table down there, in the middle of the crowded ballroom, and it was empty, chairs tipped inward, roped off with a red velvet cord, obviously being held for the family.

But tonight, no family, and, according to Clete, there were always Vizzinis at that table every night.

Interesting.

———

The elevator bank was at the far end of the gallery, a mahogany wall with gleaming brass fittings, four elevators, all with buffed brass doors. A group of people in evening dress were milling around, laughing, martini glasses in hand, and they parted for the three of them the way tropical fish will make room for a trio of sharks.

A deep brassy bong, and the doors to number three whispered open. They got in, followed by none of the tropical fish.

The doors hissed closed, wrapping them in a ponderous stillness. Beau Short pressed the button for 14, an engraved Art Deco medallion made by Tiffany's. The elevator rose up in the same hushed and ponderous silence.

———

In Room 1408, Selena was packing her bags. She intended to be gone—no checkout thank you—in thirty minutes. Marco, the assistant concierge, who always called if anyone had asked about her, had not called this evening. But when she had phoned down to have a rental car brought around, he had sounded wary, distant, not his usual sunny and exceedingly well-tipped self.

Alarms went off down in her limbic system. She checked the Colt, made sure it was loaded, and now it lay on the coverlet beside her overnight bag. She was leaving the suitcases. There was nothing in the closets and drawers she couldn't easily replace.

The locket was… Where was the locket?

She stopped, thinking hard.

Where was her locket?

She touched her throat, but the chain was gone. And then she remembered, she had broken the chain last night, in the rental car, when that terrible pinwheel vortex had happened to her… The broken chain was in her purse…but where was the locket?

Where is the locket?

She was frantically pawing through her things, her heart pounding, her mouth dry—*Where is the locket?*—and there was a hard knock at the door.

Three solid raps that sounded like it could only be the police, followed by a harsh male voice, saying, "Miss DiSantis? Jacksonville PD. Open up."

The words froze her right down to the ground.

Her heart stopped.

Three more brutal knuckle raps, followed by the same voice.

"Open up, please. We need to talk to you."

Trapped.

Life in a concrete box.

No. In Florida, in 1957, death by electric chair.

She picked up the little Colt, held it to her temple, put her index finger against the trigger, held that pose for a moment and then the anger rose up inside her, a red blossom, and she took the revolver away from her temple.

No. Not me. Not yet.

Selena bared her teeth in a feral snarl, aimed the revolver at the broad wooden panels of the hotel door and fired five rounds through it as fast as she could squeeze the trigger. The rounds punched through the boards, leaving little round circles of golden light.

She heard a man grunt, as if hit with a fist, and then, after a stunned pause, five heavy cracks, and five bullets coming back through the door, a quick murderous volley, five, now six shots, coming in fast, one after the other. One plucked at her hair and the other stung her earlobe as they hummed past her, like killer bumblebees.

———

And then came the Shimmer...

The suite walls wavered and flared like a candle flame in a strong wind, and the walls suddenly gave way to a long glassy upward-curving hallway lined with deep green marble gates, a blinding blue-white light rose up from the carpet, and now the carpet was gone and there was a sea of glimmering lights beneath her feet, and she was standing on a clear glass floor, and there was a sound like a great wave crashing through a reef, and the Shimmer was all around her, a luminous rushing river, and she stepped into it, and into the Long Hall, and it took her away.

———

Beau Short took two bullets in his throat, and they had torn him wide-open. Annabelle knew he was a dead man, but not quite yet, and he was coughing up pink foam and a hot jet of arterial blood was spraying against the walls.

She was kneeling beside him, his blood sheeting her dress, trying to press her fingers into his carotid artery, trying to pinch it shut, not finding it, a slippery snakelike tube squirming in blood and tissue.

Her fingers kept slipping away, and the blood wouldn't stop and she felt him going…going…and then he was gone.

He was dead.

And now something else was happening.

She looked up at Jack, still holding his Colt, aiming it at the door, which was now shredded and splintered, but Jack was being pulled into and surrounded and consumed by a blinding white luminous mist, he was disappearing into it, fading, now almost transparent.

She reached for him, crying out—he caught her hand—she held on tight, a death grip—she felt a gravitational pull of immense force, a blinding white light erased the world, and the Shimmer took them both. The Shimmer took them all.

———

Selena was in the Long Hall and she knew it very well, although she only remembered anything about it when she was inside it. It rose up and curved away into the shining blue distance, into a shimmering vanishing point that was always receding. There were lights in the ceiling, embedded in what looked like glass but might have been ice and she ran into and out of the pools the lights cast on the floor, which was also made of glass, but glass so clear she could see through it.

She saw what looked like the lights of a great city far down in the velvet darkness, grids and circles and squares of glittering lights in green and gold and red and blue and violet, streets and lanes and avenues, and other patterns too, leaf shaped with glowing silver veins that might have been rivers flowing in valleys between mountains, and diamonds and spheres and discs of pulsing light.

There were doors—arches set into the glassy walls lining the hallway—hundreds and hundreds of them—perhaps thousands perhaps millions—although she had never gone that far down the tunnel—each one identical—a wide Gothic arch of green stone with inlaid bands of polished steel stretching away into the blue distance—and they were all marked with signs—bars and oblongs and diamonds and circles in some silvery metal that shone with a pale moonlight glow in the haloes of light from the ceiling—signs that seemed to have a meaning that floated just beneath the surface of her understanding, and, if she only had a moment to study them, their meaning would arise and become clear to her... As she ran she scanned the gates looking for something familiar—a sign, a shape—she didn't know what it would be...and the gates arose out of the blue distance and flickered past her like the blades of a fan turning in a shaft of sunlight—shadow to light to shadow to light—and then they were gone into the shadow behind her...and she ran and ran... And then, there it was.

When he left the morgue, Clete had gone to ground at the Monterey Court, under the name Mickey Hargitay, a name Tessio knew. Clete was hoping that Tessio would look for that name, and would send some people to take him out because they'd be easier to kill at the Monterey Court than inside the Vizzini compound.

And Tessio did call.

He asked for a meet.

Clete thought about it, figured it was a trap, but he said yes because getting into the compound would have been the hardest part of what he planned to do. He didn't care about getting out.

Didn't want to get out.

So he said yes.

Clete gunned up—his .357 with a pocket full of auto-loaders, a little hammerless Smith in his hip pocket, and a cut-down M2 Carbine on a shoulder rig hidden under his suit jacket.

It was a full-auto machine and had a thirty-round magazine. He drove to the Vizzini compound with death in his heart, for him and for everyone he could take with him.

The stone-walled compound had two wrought-iron gates as massive as the gates to hell. Two button men stood behind the gates as Clete pulled up to the gates, his Colt Python at his side, the cut-down M2 digging into his ribs.

The left-side guard, a recent arrival from Abruzzo, stepped through a small door in the gate, bent down and put a hard white flash in Clete's face, held it there long enough for insolence and then stepped away, waving to the other man—the gate-keeper—to hit the button.

The gate creaked and ground its ponderous way along a buried track. The Abruzzi, still a boy, but hard enough, smiled at Clete as he pulled through.

"You are expected," he said, and the other guard showed his teeth, store-bought in Napoli and blue-white like tombstones.

Clete drove up the long curving drive and parked inside the walled compound, in the midst of a cluster of shiny blue-black Cadillacs and Lincolns and Packards and Oldsmobiles.

There another Abruzzi guard, with a cut-down *lupara* hooked over his left arm, lifted a hand and with a cold smile invited Clete to walk down the long sloping lawn to where the alligator lagoon shimmered in the moonlight, framed by a stand of saw palmettos.

Eight men, at Clete's rough count, stood around

the edge of the lagoon, four of them armed with shotguns. As he got closer, Clete could see Tessio Vizzini standing in the foreground of the group, watching him come down the long lawn.

He had a machete in his left hand, the tip pointed low and by his side, and in his other hand a glass of what looked like red wine.

Sergio Carpo and Sal Bruni stood near, and the rest of Tessio's soldiers, six of them, stood around in scattered groups, and all of them tracked him as Clete came into the wavering glow of the torches.

Behind Tessio, Little Anthony sat in a wooden beach chair, naked, trussed up like a roasted pig, coated in sweat, his face streaked with tears.

In the darkness beyond the compound lights the lagoon waters were ruffled and uneasy, and the red glitter of the torches were reflected in the slitted eyes of the gators waiting in the shallows.

As Clete came up to him, Tessio stepped forward and met him halfway.

"I know why you are here, Clete. Your beautiful wife is dead. But we did not do this thing. On my heart, on my honor as a Vizzini, we did not."

Clete looked past Tessio, to where Tony Vizzini slumped in the lawn chair. Tony's eyes were wide and Clete could see that he had fouled himself.

"I have put him to the question. He admits that he was at the house. On Florala. He drove by it. With Carpo. In the middle of the night."

"How did he know where my wife was, and why did he go there?"

"Because Aurelia DiSantis sent him there."

"Why did she do that?"

"She saw what you and your cousin did to Tony and his people at the Alcazar. She made trouble. She taunted him with it, and then she told him where your wife was. Yes he is a stupid boy, and yes he went down there, but Sergio was with him, and Sergio would never have let him hurt your wife."

He stepped in close, looked into Clete's haggard face, saw the loss, how deep the wound was. And although he had a lizard heart, he felt it.

"My old friend, we do not make war on the wives and children. You know this. You have come here to die, and to kill as many of us as you can as you die. With your pistol and that little rifle you have under your coat. And we understand this, and if we had done this *infamita*, we would have shot you down by the front gates."

He stepped closer, put a heavy calloused hand on Clete's shoulder.

"But here you are, alive, and I tell you, we did not do this thing. And if we could bring your wife back, my friend, by putting a bullet into my son's head, we would do it. Here, take this."

He reached into his belt, pulled out a heavy Smith & Wesson revolver, cocked it and handed it to Clete.

"Here is my only son, my Little Anthony. If you do not believe me, go put a bullet in his head."

Clete had to smile at that.

"If I do, your people will shoot me dead before his brains hit the grass."

Tessio laughed.

"Yes. Of course. But Mary Alice will be avenged, and then your pain will end too. All at once. This is a kindness I offer you, Clete. Go kill him, if you do not believe me. Kill my son. Then die and be at peace."

Clete took the revolver from Tessio's hand, checked that it was loaded and walked down the slope to the edge of the alligator lagoon.

He could hear the gators, churning and moving in the black water, hungry, impatient, smelling the blood and anger in the air.

The night was humid and salty and the air was hazy. Flies buzzed around Tony. He looked up as Clete came to stand in front of him.

Clete could smell him from five feet away, and the flies were clustering thick on his skin.

"You went down the shore to kill my wife?"

"You insulted me. In front of my friends."

"So then you decide to kill my wife?"

"No. I was looking for you."

"No. You knew I was in New Orleans."

A dim-witted flicker in Tony's eyes, and he cut away. His tongue ran over his lips.

"I was angry. Look at me. I have paid."

"This will burn inside you. You will want to get your balls back. You'll come for me some day, shoot me in the back. Or come for my son."

No one spoke.

Clete considered the boy for a while longer, and then, sighing, turned away, letting the revolver come down at his side. The anger was gone. Let it go. Don't keep it in your future. He started back up the long grassy slope.

A gator hissed in the outer dark, and then thrashed his tail, a white explosion of water that caught the torchlight and sent it glittering back, ruby-red sparks in the white waves.

Tony watched him walk away, a sneer forming on his bruised lips.

"That's right, fat boy, paid boy. You Mick prick. Walk away. Fuck you, paid boy. Some day, I will kill your fucking paid-boy ass."

"Tony!" said Tessio, a warning tone. "Enough. Shut the fuck up."

Clete stopped, his shoulders slumping. He glanced at Tessio, then he turned around and walked back to Tony, lifted the revolver, pointed it at Tony's head.

"Clete, no," said Tessio. "He's just a stupid kid!"

Clete stood in front of Tony, thinking what to say. Finally, after a long silence, he said, "You know what, Tony, I believe you."

He shot him in the head, and Tony, his skull a blown-out ruin and his brains spattering across the lawn, flew backward in the chair, legs flying.

Clete turned around and shot Sergio Carpo in the chest, because Sergio Carpo was an excellent gun hand, then he pivoted and shot Sal Bruni too, for the same reason—didn't wait to see either man fall—the other six, panicked, were fumbling for their guns—Clete dropped Tessio's revolver, tugged the M2 out from under his coat, stood rock still as the six men facing him started a hurried and ragged fire—he felt big rounds hissing past him, felt a blow in his hip that almost knocked him down—saw the muzzle flare of their guns—and then he opened up on them, full-auto, shooting carefully, aiming at their silhouettes, adjusting for the muzzle climb—he had done this kind of thing for a living in Korea—another body blow in his left side—another round scored a shallow furrow in his neck—he wasn't dead yet…he stood his ground and raked the standing men with fire—and they all went down—back and down—and now the magazine was empty and the bolt was locked back.

Silence, except for the echoes of gunfire coming back across the bay.

Clete stood there, weaving, fighting the shock of his wounds, standing on a grassy slope littered with dead and dying men. The gunfight had lasted about twenty seconds.

Tessio was on his feet, waiting.

Clete reached down, feeling the pain now, his wounds beginning to wake, picked up Tessio's revolver, walked slowly up to where Tessio was standing, the gun in his left hand, the M2 in his right, until he was five feet away.

"My men," said Tessio. "Why not me?"

"We have an understanding."

He flipped out the cylinder in Tessio's revolver, dumped out the remaining three rounds, handed it to Tessio.

"Why? Why do this?"

Clete studied him, a long silence.

"Mary Alice."

Selena was back in her sunlit room at the Pontalba. It was the afternoon of her fifth birthday. There had been cake and cognac and kisses from Mother, and now she was lying in her soft white bed, wrapped in her soft white sheets, drifting away on the sound of her parents' voices, talking softly and with love in the parlor.

The brassy tones of "Saint Louis Blues" drifted in through the curtains, a band of players in Jackson Square, carried to her on a scented wind off the Mississippi.

In the middle distance, a riverboat sounded its deep bass note, shaking the air and driving pelicans into the sky. She turned into the sheets, feeling them wrapped around her, tightening.

Too tight.

And too warm, and too wet.

She lifted her hands, and they were red, slick with blood. She pushed the sheets off, writhed herself out of the bed, and now the room that was softly sweetly white was pink and wet and bloody.

She looked down at herself, at Selena in her bed, and saw a bloody mess of ripped flesh and soaked sheets and a dead little girl.

And she stood over her, looking down at her, and in her hand was a knife. She turned to the mirror covered in a linen towel, tore the towel way and looked into it.

A haggard black shape, a woman, her matted hair in a tangle, in a shapeless black shift, covered in blood, holding a bloody knife, panting, staring back at her, eyes wild, mouth open, breathing hard.

"Who are you?" Selena asked the figure in the mirror.

"I am Philomena D'Arcy. Who are you?"

"I am Selena D'Arcy."

"No, you are not. Selena D'Arcy is dead in the bed behind you. We just killed her."

"We?"

"Yes. You and I."

"Who are we?"

"We are Philomena D'Arcy. Will is our brother."

"Where is Will?"

"In the parlor. We have killed him."

"Killed Will?"

"Yes, and that bitch he lives with."

"Why?"

"Because they left us in that place. That prison. Because Will would no longer lie with us."

"Lie with us?"

The figure in the mirror arched and twisted.

"We used to lie with each other. Like brother

and sister often do. And then he tired of us. He chose that other woman. He put us away. In that place. He shut us away. He left us."

"No. He left you. I am not you."

"Yes, you are."

"No. I am Selena."

"Look behind you. That is Selena D'Arcy. She is their love child. We hate her, and we have just killed her. We are in this mirror. You are me, and we are Philomena D'Arcy."

"No."

"Yes."

"No."

A long silence.

"I am not you."

"Yes we are. We have always been Philomena. We came here to kill Bea and Will for leaving us in that awful place."

"But I know I am Selena! I have been Selena all my life!"

"Selena just died here at the age of five. We killed her."

"Then why do I know I am Selena?"

"When Selena died the Shimmer came, and we took it, and it changed us. We decided to become Selena because being ourselves is terrible."

"Then why are you telling me this?"

"Because we can change it. We can go back again and change everything."

"How?"

"Find our locket."

"Yes. We need our locket."

"I know," said the haggard witch in the mirror.

"Do we know where it is?"

"Yes. It's where we last held it."

"In the car? By Matanzas Inlet? The night we drowned Mary Alice?"

"Yes. We were holding it. We broke the chain. Go back to before we break the chain."

Go there.

Find it.

Bring it back.

———

Jack and Annabelle found a different gate. It opened onto that last night at the beach house, and the storm coming in. They were in the white room, Barbara's white room at the beach house, and there were three dead men in the hall.

Pandora Jansson was lying on the ground, her chest bloody, dying, but she was still breathing, and her eyes were open. Jack knelt down beside her. She looked up at him, her voice a whisper.

"Jack. Go. Go get her."

"No. We have to get you to a hospital."

Annabelle stepped in, pushed him aside.

"No. She's right. Go. Find Selena. I will take care of Pandora."

"What will you do?"

"When you come back, we will both be here."

"How?"

"Just go."

Pandora looked up at Annabelle, her lips bloody.

"Who are you?"

"You know me. You've been talking to me for days."

"Annabelle?"

"Yes."

"So, now I'm dead?"

"No. You are not. Not yet."

—————

The rental car. Matanzas Inlet. The last place Selena had held the locket. She hunted through the time gates until she found what she thought was the right one. She opened it, stepped through, and she was at Matanzas Inlet.

But it was cold, and not the right time of the year. There was a mist on the water, and a thick fog on the bridge, and she thought, *There is no bridge at Matanzas Inlet in 1957*, and she stepped out onto the middle of the bridge, wandering, wondering, looking for the rental car, looking for a way back to her locket. And she realized then that she had made a terrible error. The place was right, but the time was all wrong. She had come in through the wrong gate. It was Christmas Eve, the Christmas Eve Jack's wife and daughter died.

She heard a wind-rush sound, heavy tires on the road. She turned to her right, and saw, from the south, coming fast, a big black car, a Mercedes-Benz, coming north across the bridge, the bridge that shouldn't be there, and now, from the north, out of the fog, coming fast, a bulky rounded shape, another car.

She stepped into the middle of the road, trying to cross, trying to get out of the way of those two cars...and they must have seen her, a figure in the middle of the bridge that wasn't there, a vague shape in the path...she heard the shriek of brakes and the sound of tires squealing on wet pavement.

The big black Benz swerved left to miss her, and the other car swerved left to miss her...and so, inevitably, they met in the middle, a violent clash of metal on metal, and the big black Benz drove the smaller car across the median and through the lane and into the guard rail, where they locked in grinding steel and hot blue sparks—the tangled wrecks hit the rail, bounced once and then broke through, and there they hovered on the brink...she heard a child screaming...a moment of balanced forces... a moment frozen in time...and then the shriek of bending steel...and they went over the edge...they hit the surface of Matanzas Inlet yards apart... floated for a moment, the Benz going first, and then the black truck...bubbles rising, an oil slick, and the lights of the black truck visible under the water for a short while...and then dark water, and a shimmering veil of starlight, and then silence.

She stood there in the middle of the bridge, shivering in the cold wind off the ocean, the fog swirling around her, watching the ripples subside, seeing bubbles of air rising up from the deep, and she saw a faint blue glow far down in the water, the black truck down there, the lights still on, not yet shorted out, and she thought, whoever was in that truck would be dying, dying right now, and, hope rising in her heart, she stood on the bridge and watched. For the Shimmer.

She walked over to the edge and looked down, and yes, there was the Shimmer, the water was changing, dissolving into a veil of blue light, a glowing mist that came up out of the deep and flowed around her, and she felt herself dissolving into it...

———

The Long Hall opened up... And Jack Redding was standing inside it, looking at her, barring the way.

She flared at him. "You have to get out of the way!"

"You've just killed my wife and child."

"I didn't—"

"You were the figure in the middle of the road. Barbara told me about you. You killed my wife and child."

"How could I have killed your wife and child? They died last Christmas. I read about it. It happened months ago."

"No. It happened here and now. Tonight."

"How can that be?"

"You don't know what you do, when you travel, do you? What you make happen when you travel."

"What do I do?"

"You make a new world each time you do it. A

*world that is just a little bit different from the one
you left. It looks the same, but it isn't."*

*She looked past him, at the Long Hall behind
him. It stretched away into a hazy infinity, a hall of
mirrors with a floor made of stars, and the green
gates receding into the blue distance, each one
a door into another time. She had to get by him
and find the right gate. Find her locket. But he
wouldn't move.*

"What do you want from me?"

"We're going back."

"Back where?"

"Back to that bridge, you and I."

"We can't."

*"We will," he said, and then the Long Hall
faded...*

———

...and they were back on the Matanzas Bridge.
They stood there together, and there was no crash,
no broken barrier, no black truck deep in the water,
no Mercedes-Benz lying on its roof fifty feet away
on the ocean floor.

"What are you doing?"

"Making another world," he said, and they both
heard the wind-rush sound of tires on the pavement, and they felt the surface of the bridge begin
to vibrate. The glow of headlights shone through
the fog, and now they could hear engines: two cars,
one coming from the north, and one from the south.

"It's them," she said. "The cars are coming. The
accident. It's going to happen again."

Jack took in a deep breath, looked up at the faint veil of stars shining through the mist.

"You feel that?" he said.

"Feel what?"

"You don't feel it?"

Selena stepped back and away, and she realized that there was something happening, something familiar, although it had only happened to her once before. But it had happened right here, at Matanzas Inlet, sixty years ago, when she had killed Clete Redding's wife. The vortex that had held her, the force broken only by the locket, the locket she didn't have. Her heart hammered in her chest, and her mouth was suddenly dry.

The headlights were coming closer, the bridge was vibrating. Jack looked to the north, and saw the black Jeep materialize out of the mist. And from the south, the big black Benz, moving much too fast. He turned and stepped into the middle of the road, facing the oncoming black SUV. He walked away from Selena and into the path of the black truck. Behind him he heard the Benz, now less than a hundred yards away. He stopped in the middle of the lane, facing the Jeep, lifted his bright gold badge case into the air and waited.

He heard Selena calling his name, and the sound of the ocean booming and roaring out in the darkness beyond the seawall, and then the Jeep was on him, and he saw the headlights dip and waver as the driver hit the brakes, hit them hard. The truck slipped and swerved as the driver fought the wheel, the tires fighting for traction.

And then it came to a stop, less than twenty feet away from him, and then the big black Benz went flashing by in the northbound lane, a blast from the horn as the car hurtled past, pushing a wall of wind, and then it was gone, into the dark, a glimmer of taillights, fading into the mist.

Jack walked forward, came to the driver's side of the Jeep. The woman at the wheel was Barbara, and she rolled down the window, and looked at him.

"What's the problem, Officer?"

Jack looked at his wife, and then into the backseat, where Katy sat staring back at him, eyes wide, holding a stuffed bear that Jack had given her on her last birthday. Warm air flowed from the car interior, and with it came the sound of Christmas music, Judy Garland singing "Have Yourself a Merry Little Christmas," and it nearly broke his heart. Barbara had no idea who he was.

Barbara was looking at him oddly. "I almost hit you," she said. "Is there an accident?"

Jack shook his head, pulling himself together. "No, just a pedestrian in the roadway there." He turned and looked back. Selena was still standing there.

The Long Hall was gone, and they were alone on the bridge. Jack turned back to Barbara, who was studying him carefully.

"Is she okay, Officer? That woman?"

"Yes. She's just a little shaken up."

Barbara looked at him. "Do we know each other?"

"Do we?"

"You look familiar."

"Do I? I guess I have that kind of face."

"Okay...well, thanks for stopping us. Is she going to be okay? That woman?"

"Yes. I'll take care of her."

"Well then." And she put the car back in gear, stepped on the brake. "Where's your patrol car?"

"Just down the road."

"Well...okay then." The truck started to roll, but slowly. She stopped it and said, "So, Merry Christmas, Officer."

"Yes," he said. "Merry Christmas to you. And your little girl."

And she drove away.

———

Selena was standing in the middle of the median, watching him walk toward her, very aware of the pistol at his belt.

"That was your wife?"

"Yes."

"She didn't know you."

"No. Different worlds. In this one, she doesn't know me. We make a new world every time we travel. You've been doing it for years."

"What happens now?"

"I go back to my house."

"And what do I do?"

"You stay here."

"I stay here? You're not going to arrest me?"

"No. I don't think I'm going to have to do that."
He looked up at the stars again, and then back to
Selena. "You feel that?"

The air was filled with a humming sound,
and the fog seemed to be turning slowly, turning
around them. The mist took on a glow, and the vibration grew into a deep bass rumble that seemed
to come from everywhere around them.

"What's happening?" she said.

"I have no idea. But I think you do."

She stepped away from him, and turned to face
into the darkness, and out of the mist came the
glow of headlights, and she turned to say something to Jack, but he was gone, and she was in the
middle of the road, and out of the night came an
Oldsmobile, a big ancient tank, and at the wheel
was Mary Alice Redding, and sitting beside her
was Selena, looking back at Selena, standing in
the middle of the road, looking back at herself,
and then the car was on her, and the vortex closed
around her, and she stood there in the roadway
waiting for the impact—

———

*She stepped away from him, and turned to face
into the darkness, and out of the mist came the
glow of headlights, and she turned to say something to Jack, but he was gone, and she was in the
middle of the road, and out of the night came an
Oldsmobile, a big ancient tank, and at the wheel*

was Mary Alice Redding, and sitting beside her was Selena, looking back at Selena, standing in the middle of the road, and then the car was on her, and the vortex closed around her, and she stood there in the roadway waiting for the impact—

She stepped away from him, and turned to face into the darkness, and out of the mist came the glow of headlights, and she turned to say something to Jack, but he was gone, and she was in the middle of the road, and out of the night came an Oldsmobile, a big ancient tank, and at the wheel was Mary Alice Redding, and sitting beside her was Selena, looking back at Selena, standing in the middle of the road, and then the car was on her, and the vortex closed around her, and she stood there in the roadway waiting for the impact—

She stepped away from him, and turned to face into the darkness, and out of the mist came the glow of headlights, and she turned to say something to Jack, but he was gone, and she was in the middle of the road, and out of the night came an Oldsmobile, a big ancient tank, and at the wheel was Mary Alice Redding, and sitting beside her was Selena, looking back at Selena, standing in the middle of the road, and then the car was on her, and the vortex closed around her, and she stood there in the roadway waiting for the impact—

She stepped away from him, and turned to face into the darkness, and out of the mist came the glow of headlights, and she turned to say something to Jack, but he was gone, and she was in the *middle of the road, and out of the night came an Oldsmobile, a big ancient tank, and at the wheel was Mary Alice Redding, and sitting beside her was Selena, looking back at Selena, standing in the middle of the road, and then the car was on her, and the vortex closed around her, and she stood there in the roadway waiting for the impact—*

She stepped away from him, and turned to face into the darkness, and out of the mist came the glow of headlights, and she turned to say something to Jack, but he was gone, and she was in the middle of the road, and out of the night came an Oldsmobile, a big ancient tank, and at the wheel was Mary Alice Redding, and sitting beside her was Selena, looking back at Selena, standing in the middle of the road, and then the car was on her, and the vortex closed around her, and she stood there in the roadway waiting for the impact—

Early morning, the first day of September. Clete was in a single bedroom in the Post Op Care ward at Immaculate Heart, getting his gunshot wounds dressed by a pretty young nurse and staring out the window, where the sun was shining on the stand of royal palms that lined the long entrance drive to the hospital.

Mary Alice was gone, and Declan hadn't come to see him yet, although Helen and Frank Forrest had been in the day before. There was a stone on his heart and he knew it would always be there.

He was suspended with pay while the investigation into what had happened at the Vizzini compound worked its way through the system. The death of Beau Short and the disappearance of Annabelle Fontaine after the shootout in Room 1408 of the Alcazar was wrapped up in that too.

There was still no sign of Aurelia DiSantis, the woman who had shot and killed Beau Short. Clete suspected they would never find her.

At least not in this time zone.

He knew, or hoped he knew, where Jack had gone to, and he was pretty sure that, wherever he was, he had done—or would do—something pretty final to that creature.

He also suspected that, wherever he was, Annabelle Fontaine was with him. Or maybe he had managed to get his wife and kids back. One way or another, it was out of his hands. The nurse finished with the bandages, pulled the coverlet up around his chest and asked him if there was anything she could get for him.

"I could use a boilermaker," he said, and she smiled down at him, the sunlight making an aura around her, so that she looked like a visiting angel.

"I'll get you an orange juice. By the way, while you were asleep, there was a police officer here. He left something for you on your side table."

She picked it up and handed it to him. It was a large brown envelope with something inside it.

"Thanks," he said.

And she said, "You're welcome, Clete," and slipped silently out of the room.

Clete opened the envelope. There was a brief note:

Clete...Crime Scene guys found this on the floor of the hotel room where Beau Short got shot. Since you're still the detective of record on the Aurelia DiSantis thing, we figured you'd want to have it.

No idea what it means. Get better soon,

and between you and me, what you gave the Vizzini Family was long overdue.

All the best, and get back out here soon. We need you.

Mike Bukovac

Clete tipped the envelope up, and a gold locket fell out onto the coverlet.

He picked it up, turned it in the light, held it close and read the inscription.

"'To Bea from Will...Xmas 1909.'"

He had no idea what it meant either, but he suspected there was a story in it somewhere. He decided to put it in his file on the DiSantis case.

Maybe someday it would turn out to be important. You never knew about these things. He closed his eyes, wished the best for Jack, wherever he was, and drifted into sleep with the locket in the palm of his right hand.

the beach house

When Jack got back to the beach house, Pandora was sitting quietly on the couch.

The dead men had never happened, the raid had never happened, and Pandora was not dead.

Pandora smiled at him.

"So. Jack. You're finally back."

"So I am."

"What were you doing?"

"Looking for Selena D'Arcy."

"Did you find her?"

"Yes."

"Where is she?"

"On the bridge at Matanzas Inlet."

"Was it Christmas Eve?"

"Yes."

"Were you able to stop the accident?"

"Yes."

Pandora's face grew solemn, seeing the loss that was about to come upon her. Jack would have his wife and child back, and she would lose him forever.

"So Barbara is alive? And Katy?"

"Yes. They are."

"Oh, Jack…how wonderful? Where is she?"

Jack was quiet for a while. And then he told her that Barbara hadn't recognized him, that she was alive, but the world had changed.

"How? How can it change?"

"I think, when we travel, we make a different world. This one is just a little different from the one we left."

"But Barbara is still your wife?"

"No. She's someone's wife. Just not mine."

A long silence.

"But, Jack, if it's true, that's terrible."

"Yes. It is."

"You can't let that stand. You have to do something."

"I know."

"So what can you do?"

"Nothing."

"Why not?"

He was silent for a very long time. She let him be silent.

"When I was back there…"

"Back where?"

"Back in…back in your time."

"Yes."

"There were things I couldn't control. My badge, my gun…even how I dressed. It was as if there was…someone…making the Rules."

"The Rules?"

"Yes. The Rules about what could and couldn't happen in time."

She took that in. "A Rule Maker?"

"Yes. That's what it felt like."

"You don't really think there's someone in *charge* of…all of this, do you?"

He smiled. "No. But maybe there *used* to be. Like we were an ant farm or something, and that power set up the ant farm Rules, and then it lost interest, and it wandered away, other worlds, better worlds, to attend to, but the Rules still applied back here, like the glass walls on an ant farm box."

"So, not to put too fine a point on it, you have just reduced the entire sweep of our ideas of justice and truth and the value of the human soul from Hammurabi to Plato to Thomas Aquinas down to an ant farm analogy. Yes?"

He smiled and looked at her. "Looks like it."

"Which means?"

"Which means that if Selena was going to be stopped, a price had to be paid."

"And Barbara and Katy were the price?"

A very long silence, so long that they both realized they were not breathing at all.

"Yes. I think so. They're still alive. They just don't belong to me anymore."

"But are you going to be able to live with that?"

"I *have* been living with that, one way or another, for months. She was dead, but now she's not, and that is the way it will always be. So I have two choices."

"Which are?"

"Find a way to be happy in the face of all that."

"Or?"

"There is no other choice. I live with it."

There was no answer for that, and Pandora didn't try to find one. Sometimes a loving silence is the only useful thing you can offer.

They sat there together for a very long time. The wind died away and there was moonlight on the water. The palm shadows lay on the window. Morning was on the doorstep, but not yet knocking.

Jack turned to her, smiled at her. "Did you meet Annabelle? Or did you meet Pandora?"

"Both. We got along beautifully."

"Where did she go?"

"Nowhere. She's right here."

Another silence, but now of a different kind.

Pandora moved into him, put her arm across his chest, moved in much closer, breathing him in.

"So. In this world, do you love *her*, or do you love *me*?"

"Well, which one are you? Are you Pandora, or are you Annabelle?"

"Ask me what my favorite dessert is?"

"I know that one. Chocolate parfait?"

She kissed him, a long lingering kiss. "That was a very good answer."

departures

Two weeks later, the season changing, Jack and Pandora and Julie Karras flew up to Florissant to attend the burial of the Walker family, in a pretty glade of cottonwoods beside a little river.

Gerald Walker was there, surrounded by friends and family. Four caskets lay in a shaft of sidelong sun, gleaming oak, suspended over the open graves.

Walker saw them, standing at a distance, unwilling to intrude, but feeling that something was owed. He came up the long grassy slope, walking with a cane, still thin, but filling out. His face was etched in grief, and it would stay that way.

"You came," he said. "Thank you."

He looked at Julie Karras, also a little thinner and a pale white scar on her temple. She stepped forward, ready to take whatever he had to say. But he just offered his hand, and smiled, a sad smile, but kindly.

"You're the police officer my daughters attacked. Officer Karras?"

"Yes. I can't tell you how sorry—"

"I know. I'm glad you're here. I want to apologize for what my daughters did. I want you to know I have no anger in my heart. I'm glad you're alive, Officer Karras."

Julie Karras, touched, found she had nothing to say.

Walker released her hand, looked at Jack and Pandora. "I hear you got her."

"Yes. We did."

"Good. Where is she now? She gonna get the chair, or what?"

Pandora looked at Jack, and then came back to Gerald Walker. "No, not the chair."

"Then what?"

"Time, Mr. Walker. She got time."

* * * * *

The Rules of Engagement with Time

Einstein and Gödel disagreed about the nature of Time, but they both agreed that Newton's idea—that Time moved in a straightforward direction throughout the universe—was wrong, at least on a quantum level. So writing about Time is fair game, and many good people have tried their hand at it, with varying degrees of success. And now I have, and along the way I learned some Rules of Engagement.

1. *Be consistent.* There will be contradictions and paradoxes and lots of very smart people will be judging how well you deal with them. So deal with them. Have it clear in your mind what is happening, what has just happened and what *will* happen because of the first two.

2. *Play fair.* There is only one way to get your reader to go all the way to the end without throwing your book at the wall. Have an idea how Time works in your story, and *stick to it.* Convince the reader that *it might actually work* and your reader

will go along with you, if only out of curiosity. Which is wonderful.

3. *Your idea about how Time works had better be a good one.* In *The Shimmer*, I deal with the various Time Travel Paradoxes by stealing from a much better mind, and it belonged to Hugh Everett.

He believed—on the quantum level—that each event in Time that could have gone either way actually went *both* ways, and when it did, a second parallel universe was created, one that was *very slightly* different from the previous one.

If you take Everett's view, you dodge the usual paradoxes about how screwing up the past will screw up your own future, because what you are doing is creating a new world that is very much like your previous one, but *not quite*. So that is the time travel idea in *The Shimmer*.

Jack and Clete and Selena and Annabelle and Pandora aren't changing the future they left, they're changing the one they're headed for.

Which, by the way, is what we're all doing, whether we realize it or not.

Carsten Stroud
New Year's Day 2018
Destin, Florida